STREET RAP

Also by Shaun Sinclair

Blood Ties

The Crescent Crew Series

Street Rap

King Reece

Published by Kensington Publishing Corp.

STREET RAP

SHAUN SINCLAIR

KENSINGTON PUBLISHING CORP.
www.kensingtonbooks.com

DAFINA BOOKS are published by

Kensington Publishing Corp.
119 West 40th Street
New York, NY 10018

All Kensington Titles, Imprints, and Distributed Lines are available at special quantity discounts for bulk purchases for sales promotions, premiums, fund-raising, and educational or institutional use. Special book excerpts or customized printings can also be created to fit specific needs. For details, write or phone the office of the Kensington special sales manager: Kensington Publishing Corp., 119 West 40th Street, New York, NY 10018, attn: Special Sales Department, Phone: 1-800-221-2647.

Dafina and the Dafina logo Reg. U.S. Pat. & TM Off.

ISBN-13: 978-1-4967-2104-4
ISBN-10: 1-4967-2104-7
First Kensington Trade Edition: October 2018
First Kensington Mass Market Edition: January 2020

ISBN-13: 978-1-4967-2103-7 (ebook)
ISBN-10: 1-4967-2103-9 (ebook)

10 9 8 7 6 5 4 3 2 1

Printed in the United States of America

This book is dedicated to my brother, Anthony Sinclair. Your love of hip-hop was passed down to me. Your love of the streets was embraced by me. This book is a marriage of the two. Rest easy, Big Bro!

Acknowledgments

As always, all praises due to the Most High, Most Merciful, the Creator of all things in existence, Grand Architect of the Universe. I am continuously humbled at the blessing to be able to write the things I envision in my mind, and bring them to life as words that inspire, entertain, and enlighten my people. If not for this craft, I would probably go crazy with all the characters living in my head. Thankfully, I have been given a platform to stay sane.

Thanks to my family for supporting me throughout my literary journey. You have always been and continue to be my biggest supporters. To my mom, Brenda, you are the strongest woman I know. You have taken everything that life has thrown at you and used it to stand even higher on your pedestal as a queen. To my Big Sis, Mishell, I always say that I owe you because if you had not taken the time to type this very book, then I probably would have never picked up another pen again. My Big Bro Roy, you remain one of the most thorough dudes I know. To my lil' Big Sis, Sheryl, you've always had my back, always supporting me and never judging me, no matter what. For that I am eternally grateful. To my brother Anthony, aka Ant Live, although you have transcended to chill with the ancestors, I know that you are still proud of me. I know that every time I do something cool, every time I do something amazing, it is you and your example I am following. To my Pops, Johnny Gore, I'm honored to follow in the footsteps of *Black Gangster*. *Alhamdulillah!* To my sons, Shaun and Supreme, you remain my biggest motivation, because part of being a good father is leading by example. I hope I do you proud. To Amanda, Lord knows we don't always see eye-to-eye, but regardless, we always put our differences aside for the sake of our child. You have never tried to prevent me from being a father to *Daddy*, and for that I am eternally grateful. To Qima, you have always had my back and supported my dreams. We loved each other the best way we knew how, and for that I am eternally grateful. We have always loved each other, and we always will. Love is love. To Gwen and Ted, Trey, Gayle, Shajuania, Shinika. You know what? I'm going to just say the whole Sinclair clan because all of you, in your own way, helped me out on this journey.

To the block . . . Atlantic Beach stand up!!! Words cannot express the amount of gratitude I have for you guys. All of you have shown me so much love and support, and that encourages me to go that much harder. My lil bro, Joey Sinclair, Omar, Tody, Asiatic, Squirrel, A.B., Tip, Steph, Tootie, Keisha, Teresa, Tommy Gunn (R.I.H.), Snipes, Mama Mima, just to name a few.

Thanks to my Metro family, Neek, Rahlo, Milly, Chamondra, Ronnie, Woosie, Quon, and Yoshi. Special thanks to my big brother from another, Mr. Darvyn "Saadiq" Higgins, and his beautiful wife, Angela.

To my ATL family, Tameeka and Rodney, Muhammed, Amin, Tisa, and many others. Special massive big up to Em Edge, my homie, my partner, and the talented designer of all my book covers, and game-changing book trailers. Special thanks to Kisha Green. You keep me popping in the cyber world and we did a great thing with Digital Foreplay. Much more to come!

Special thanks to all the authors keeping this thing going, particularly some of those I rock with real hard. Shaunta Kenerly, John Bowens, Jo Dee Sanders and Kenitra Jordan (R.I.H.), Yolanda Arrington, Honesti, Tamika Newhouse, Ni'cola Mitchell, Nene Capri, and a special salute to the legend himself, Mr. Al-Saadiq Banks. This is one of the most authentic, knowledgeable, humble brothers I've had the privilege of knowing. Still the same from Day One!

Thanks to all the brothers in the belly of the beast. L.B., Allworld Eddie Mack, Jaba, Marc Majeed, Wack, Hanif Adisa, and any brother I've had the pleasure of meeting along the way. Every time I put the pen to the paper, I have you in mind. I am you, you are me. Keep your head up.

Last, but certainly not least, I want to thank the readers. Without you, there would be no me. I know that dollars are important in this economy, so the fact that you take a chance on me is humbling. I feel appreciated and I don't take your time for granted. When I sit down at my laptop, my goal is to craft a classic tale, something that you can give to your kids and their kids, something that will ring true to the era in which we live. Hit me up on Twitter, or IG. @IamShaunSinclair and let me know if I achieved my goal. Peace!

Prologue

The courtroom was packed with spectators as everyone awaited the defendant's arrival. All of the leading TV news crews were present, as this was sure to be the top story of the day. The prosecutor repeatedly checked his watch while glancing cutting looks at the judge.

The defendant's attorney was present as well, and obviously perturbed at the slight tardiness of his client. He had just spoken with him that morning, and his client had assured him he would be on time. He did not like to start a trial on a bad note, and being late on the first day showed a blatant disregard for the judicial system.

Judge Epps looked over his half-moon spectacles to address the defense attorney. "Mr. Shabazz, if you'd like to take a brief recess to contact your client, feel free. However if he does not show by ten o'clock, we must go on." Judge Epps raised his hands in surrender, then added, "The wheels of justice move on, regardless of tardiness."

Almost as if on cue, the outer doors of the courtroom burst open, and in walked the defendant, accompanied by a modest entourage.

Mr. Shabazz stood, shot his cuffs, smoothed the lapels

on his Italian suit, and greeted his client with a nervous chuckle. "Heh heh, you had me worried there for a second," he whispered.

"No need to worry," his client returned. "Everything's under control. Had a problem finding a parking space. Something's going on real big somewhere in this courthouse. Could you believe there's news people staked outside?"

Mr. Shabazz had dealt with a lot of notorious criminals in his day, as he was one of the best defense attorneys around. However, he had never come in contact with a client such as this one. So young, yet so thorough. So smart, yet so . . . gangsta.

Judge Epps tapped his gavel to gather court in session, immediately silencing the cacophony of sounds that had slowly crescendoed from the time the defendant had entered the courtroom. Judge Epps motioned for the prosecution to begin opening statements.

Federal Prosecutor Long stood to address the court. He pulled his crimson tie as if adjusting it and polished the lenses in his Cartier spectacles with his silk handkerchief. He went through the whole rigmarole to appear very important. He knew the attorney general was present in the crowd, and he wanted to do his best to impress his boss. He began speaking in an authoritative tone.

"Ladies and gentleman of the jury, I come to you today for justice. Justice for society. Justice for the victims—some nameless, as well as the victims named in this indictment. I even come to you for justice for the defendant, if the facts permit. However, the facts will show that for the past two years, the defendant has wreaked havoc upon the streets of the Carolinas. Just to make myself clear, when I say defendant, I am referring to the man sitting right there with the smug look on his face. Mr. . . . ."

The defendant sat and listened to the federal prosecutor with all of the surety he could muster. For unbeknownst to the federal prosecutor, judge, and even his own attorney, he had a ringer in the jury. He could guarantee he would walk. It was just a matter of time.

Meanwhile, in the same courtroom, juror number six sweated profusely. He paid vague attention to the federal prosecutor. His thoughts were more on the note he had received upon coming to court today. He had already placed a call and verified the contents of the note. It simply read: *"Your daughter's tied up in a basement."*

Juror number six told no one about the note, save family. He knew precisely what the note meant. He had been paying attention to the news coverage the trial was receiving. He knew exactly who had taken his daughter, and he knew exactly what it would take to get her back. And only in movies were people stupid enough to go against the grain.

Part 1

Crew Business . . .

Chapter 1

The black Tahoe crept onto the rooftop of the parking garage overlooking downtown Fayetteville and stopped. The driver lumbered his hefty frame out of the truck and stood to his full six-foot-seven-inch height. He flipped the collar up on his heavy mink coat, readjusted the sawed-off shotgun tucked beneath his arm, and scanned his surroundings for danger. Satisfied that the area was clear, he tapped on the passenger window of the truck. The tinted window eased down halfway, and a cloud of smoke was released into the air.

"It's clear," the giant reported.

"Good. Now go post up over there so you can see the street, make sure no funny biz popping off," the man in the truck instructed.

The giant hesitated a moment. "You sure about this? I mean, I don't trust these dudes like that," he said.

The man smiled. "You worry too much, Samson. Nobody would dare violate this thing of ours again. Look around you, it's just us and them. This is crew business, and this shit has gone on long enough. Tonight, it ends, one way or another."

The window glided up, and the giant assumed his position near the edge of the parking garage.

Behind the dark glass of the Tahoe, two men sat in the back seat sharing a blunt while a brooding hip-hop track thumped through the speakers. The men casually passed the blunt and enjoyed the music as if they were at a party, and not on the precipice of a drug war for control of the city's lucrative narcotics trade. Although partners, each of the men was a boss in his own right. Their leadership styles were different—one was fire, the other was ice—but it was the balance that made their team so strong.

In the back seat of the Tahoe sat Qwess and Reece, leaders of the notorious Crescent Crew.

"Yo, that beat is bananas, son!" Reece remarked to Qwess. "You did that?"

Qwess nodded. "You knowwww it," he sang.

"Word. You already wrote to it?"

"I'm writing to it right now," he replied. He pointed to his temple. "Right here."

"I hear ya, Jay-Z," Reece joked. "So, anyway, how you want to handle this when these niggas get here?"

Qwess nodded. "Let me talk some sense into them, let them know they violated."

"Son, they know they violated."

"Still, let me handle it, because you know how you can be."

Reece scowled. "How I can be? Fuck is that supposed to mean?"

"You know how you can be," Qwess insisted.

"What? Efficient?"

"If you want to call it that."

Headlights bent around the corner and a dark gray H2 Hummer came into view. The Hummer drove to the edge of the garage and stopped inches in front of Samson. He spun around to face the truck. The giant, clad in a full-length mink, resembled King Kong in the glow of the xenon headlamps.

Inside the truck, Qwess craned his head over the seat to confirm their guests. "That's them," he noted as he passed Reece the blunt. He climbed from the back of the truck and tossed his partner a smirk. "Stay here, I got it."

Qwess joined Samson while men poured out of the Hummer. When the men stood before Qwess, someone very important was absent.

Qwess raised his palm. "Whoa, whoa, someone's missing from this little shindig," he observed, scanning the faces. "Where is Black Vic?"

One of the minions stepped forward. He wore a bald head and a scowl. "Black Vic couldn't be here tonight. He sends his regards." The man thumbed his chest with authority. "He sent me in his place."

Qwess frowned. "He sent you in his place? Are you kidding me? We asked for a meeting with the boss of your crew, and he sends you?"

The man nodded. "Yep."

Qwess shook his head. "Yo, get Black Vic on the phone and tell him to get his ass down here now."

The minion chuckled. "I see you got things confused, dawg. You run shit over there, not over here. Now are we talking or what?"

Samson took a step forward. The other three men took two steps back. Qwess gently placed a hand on Samson's arm. The giant stood down.

"I need to talk to the man in charge," Qwess insisted. "Because we only going to have this conversation one time."

"Word?"

"Word!"

Suddenly, the back door to the Tahoe was flung open, and all eyes shifted in that direction. Reece stepped out into the night and flung his dreads wildly. Time seemed to slow down as he diddy-bopped over to them, his Cuban link and heavy medallion swinging around his neck. He pulled back the lapels on his jacket and placed his hands on his waist, revealing his Gucci belt and his two .45s.

"Yo, where Victor at?" Reece asked.

Qwess scoffed. "He ain't here. He sent *these* niggas."

Reece looked at each man, slowly nodding his head. "So Victor doesn't respect us enough to show his face and address his violation? He took two kis from my little man, beat him down. My li'l homie from Skibo hit him with consignment, and he decided to keep shit. Now, we trying to resolve this shit 'cause war is bad for business—for everybody, and he wanna say, 'fuck us'?"

"Black Vic said that you said 'fuck us' when you wouldn't show us no flex on the prices," the minion countered.

"Oh, yeah? That what he said?" Reece asked. He shook his head and mocked, "*He said, she said, we said . . .* See, that's that bitch shit. That's why Victor should've came himself. But he sent you to speak for him, right?"

The bald-headed minion puffed out his bird chest. "That's right."

"Okay." Reece nodded his head and looked around the rooftop of the garage. "Well, tell Victor this!"

SMACK!

Without warning, Reece lit the minion's jaws up with an open palm slap. Samson lunged forward and wrapped his huge mittens around the neck of one of the other minions, who wore a skully pulled low over his eyes. Qwess drew his pistol and aimed it at the other minion in a hoodie, while the soldier in the passenger seat of the Tahoe popped out of the roof holding an AK-47.

"Y'all thought it was sweet?" Reece taunted. He

smacked the bald-headed minion again, and he crumpled to the floor semiconscious. "I got a message for Victor's ass, though."

Reece dragged the man over to the Hummer and pitched his body to the ground in front of the pulley attached to the front of the truck. He reached inside the Hummer to release the lever for the pulley, then returned to the front of the Hummer. While the spectators watched in horror, Reece pulled bundles of metal rope from the pulley and wrapped it around the man's neck. Qwess came over to help, and when they were done, the two of them hoisted the man up onto the railing.

"Wait, man! Please don't do this!" the minion pleaded. He was fully conscious now, and scrapping for his life. Qwess cracked him in the jaw and knocked the fight right out of him.

Reece fixed him with a cold gaze. "*We* not doing this to you, homie. Your man, Victor, is," he explained. "His ass should've showed up. Now, of course, this means war."

Reece and Qwess flipped the man over the railing. His body sailed through the air, and the pulley whirred to life, guiding his descent. His banshee-like wail echoed through the quiet night as he desperately tugged at the rope around his neck. Then suddenly, the pulley ran out of rope and caught, snapping his neck like a chicken. Both Qwess and Reece spared a look over the edge and saw his lifeless body dangling against the side of the building.

Reece turned to face the others. Slowly, he slid his thumb across his naked throat, and the AK-47 sparked three times. All head shots.

This was crew business.

Chapter 2

The following morning Qwess walked into Crescent Sounds, the studio he had erected when he really started getting money. After making his rounds through the building he learned he was all alone, which was how he preferred it. He left the lights low, walked into the vocal booth, and inhaled the scent of the place. This was his sanctuary, his home away from home, the place where everything in his world made sense.

Qwess stepped before the mic, closed his eyes, and visualized himself on stage commanding the crowd. In his mind, they showered him with love as he spit a vicious rhyme about the streets. His vision was so vivid he could've sworn he heard the roar of the crowd ringing inside his ears. He bobbed his head to the imaginary beat, the brooding track he and Reece had been listening to just before they tossed a man over the edge of a rooftop at two in the morning. He felt light, free. He felt as if he were on top of the world. Unconsciously, he started rapping aloud . . .

"Niggas bleed when they romp with the Crescent Crew, heard tales 'bout the kinda evil shit we do/ like stay true and put it down for the culture, a savage act up we give 'em wings like vultures . . ." he spat, referring to the incident from last night.

This was his shtick, the thing that set him apart from everyone else. The rep of his crew preceded him, so when Qwess spat some gangsta shit, the streets embraced him because they knew he was authentic. However, while most rappers were desperate to run toward street cred, Qwess was actually trying to run away from his.

Qwess opened his eyes, and his attention fell on the television hanging on the wall outside the booth. The midday news was on, broadcasting live from downtown about a gruesome murder that had been committed during the wee hours of the morning. Qwess rushed from the booth and turned the volume up.

"Authorities are still trying to piece together the details of a gruesome scene they discovered this morning. Apparently, a man was thrown from the rooftop of this hotel behind me. Now what happened next isn't clear. Apparently, some type of mechanical device was wrapped around his neck from his SUV *before* he was thrown over the roof. The tension from the rope caused the man to become decapitated . . ." Qwess silenced the TV. He had heard enough. He watched the remainder of the report on mute.

The door to the studio opened, and in walked Reece, swagged out and beaming from ear to ear. "Peace, my brother! Beautiful day, huh?" Reece asked.

Qwess pointed to the TV. "You see this shit?"

Reece watched a few seconds of the news, then spread his arms expansively. "Yeah, it's beautiful, isn't it? I bet Victor got the message now."

Qwess shook his head. "Bro, we don't need this right now. I got some big things on the table right now, things that can set us all straight."

"You talking about this music shit again?" Reece asked. "Bro, I respect what you got going on with that, but, man, they don't let guys like us in that industry. The industry is full of move fakers."

Qwess shook his head in exasperation. "They respect units, man! Numbers. We've been doing numbers like crazy out here in these streets."

Reece reached deep into his pockets and pulled out a huge wad of cash. "These type of numbers?" he asked. "I got a Louie bag in the trunk of the Masi with about ninety bands in it, too. Half of that is yours. Are they showing you that type of respect with the numbers?"

Qwess walked over to the mixing board and cued up a track. "This is the ticket right here, Reece. This music shit *is* the new dope game. You know they just gave them niggas down in New Orleans a thirty-million-dollar distribution deal? Where else can you see that type of money legally?" Qwess posed. "Now I got love for the crew. We built this shit from the ground up, but like I told you before, I'm out. That shit last night can never happen again. I only agreed to come along because me and Black Vic got history. Thought I could talk to him."

"Well, you see how that worked out," Reece sniped.

"Yeah, because you didn't stay in the truck!" Qwess pointed out.

Reece walked up to Qwess and got right in his chest. "Look, the day I let a muthafucka disrespect me, you, or this crew we built is the day I'd rather die," Reece vowed. "Now you ain't the only one out here making moves. I got some shit lined up that can put us in a real good position also, and that's what matters most. A'ight? Crew business, all the time. Remember?"

Reece was pulling rank. *Crew business* was their motto. It meant that nothing or no one came before the crew. Whatever it took for their crew to win was *crew business*. That was the oath they had built the Crescent Crew upon.

"I remember, bro." Qwess sighed heavily. "I'm just saying, we can't do this shit forever. If we have a way out . . ."

"We ain't trying to do it forever. We just trying to do it for *our* forever," Reece returned.

Qwess turned away. "I feel you," he conceded, then pointed at the TV. "But this shit can't be good for nothing."

Reece shrugged. "It is what it is, bro. We here now. Ain't no such things as halfway crooks."

"True indeed."

The brothers walked outside to Reece's Maserati Cambiocorsa Spyder. Reece popped the trunk and passed Qwess a bag stuffed with cash.

"Take that, Qwess. Smell that money and remind yourself what life is all about," Reece suggested.

Qwess took the bag and tossed it on the back seat of his Benz. "What you got planned tonight?" he asked.

"I got to see a man about a dog," he joked. "Matter fact, two dogs."

Qwess shook his head. "You can't get enough, huh?"

"Brother, you locked down; I'm not. I'm a descendant of Solomon, and I'm going to live like it," Reece bragged.

"Word." Qwess dapped Reece up. "I'll get at you later."

The friends parted ways with their minds on two separate missions, yet one cause—glory for the Crescent Crew.

Unbeknownst to them, there was someone watching their interaction from a distance. This person was on a mission also. Their cause? The demise of the Crescent Crew.

Later that night

Reece lay in amazement as the ladies worshipped him like the god he thought himself to be. Sure, this wasn't the first threesome he'd indulged in, but it was definitely the most memorable. Just the way Cretia was moaning had him rock hard. And oh, that skin . . . that beautiful chocolate skin! He'd normally go for the redbones, but Cretia was next-level fine with thick thighs, nice breasts, and long, wavy hair that she didn't pay for. Besides, the way Cretia had made this proposal, who was he to refuse? Turned out she was right. Chocolate does melt in your mouth!

And how could he forget Vanilla? She was doing her best to make sure he didn't do that. Hell, the way she was sucking him, you'd think his dick was a pacifier. The broad never let up! He had already released himself inside her mouth twice. The first time, she shared the reward with Cretia. The second time, she selfishly kept it to herself.

Reece raised his head from the bed. "Yo, why don't y'all switch," he suggested. "Vanilla, let a nigga breathe this time, though."

Vanilla smirked. "I'll try, 'cause you know that shit be feeling too good," she claimed. "Who would've thought King Reece could eat pussy like that."

"Yo, chill, shorty. They call me King 'cause I get down for my crown in everything," he boasted.

"Well, why don't you get down on this," Cretia interrupted, pointing to her crotch. "My shit is throbbing, and I'm dying to feel that inside me," she stated, pointing at his erection.

Reece slipped on another condom and dived in. Although she was wet already, she was still somewhat tight. With a little maneuvering, he managed to sink deep inside Cretia. As he began a nice, rhythmic, long stroke, he felt Vanilla grab his ass. He knew what she was about to do, but before he could object, she slid her tongue through the crack of his ass. At that point, it felt so good, he figured *fuck it* and let her have her way.

A few moments later, Reece exploded with a powerful orgasm. No sooner than he released his load, both women snatched the condom off and drank of his essence as if their lives depended on it.

As they pleased him simultaneously, Reece marveled at how beautiful the women were, as if truly noticing it for the first time. He had dealt with so many beautiful women in his life that he was somewhat jaded when it came to pretty faces. However, he'd always run into one—or two—that would raise the bar on his personal standard of beauty.

Such was the case this night. Cretia and Vanilla were two of the most desired women in the city. Every hustler in town wanted a piece of them, but they played hard to get. Yet, here was Reece having his way with both of the beauties, doing things that would have gotten them kicked out of the Bible, purely on the strength of who he was.

This is the life! he thought. *Qwess would be a fool to want to give this up.*

For Reece, living any other way wasn't an option. He was true to the game. He would rather rule in hell than serve in heaven.

Chapter 3

Qwess scanned his rearview looking for a cop as he ran yet another red light. He shifted the gear in his SL55 and zoomed down Skibo Road. He was already late for his meeting with Reece and Doe, and he knew how Reece could be about time. For a dude who didn't have any set work hours, he sure stressed punctuality.

As Qwess rolled up to the restaurant, he spotted Rolando, or "Doe" as he was called, sitting on his Corvette, talking on the phone. Reece's first cousin, Doe was the third member of their brotherhood. The three had been friends since high school, and although Doe chose to live on the right side of the law, their bond never wavered. By day, Doe worked as a logistics specialist for a firm that handled accounts for Cape Fear Valley Hospital. By night, he handled most of the day-to-day business operations for Qwess's record label, A.B.P. In fact, it was Doe's expertise that had catapulted A.B.P. to the top of the rap game in the Southeast. He had coordinated the marketing campaign and was responsible for getting the CDs in the hands of the people.

Right beside Doe's car was Reece's Porsche. Qwess

pulled into a parking space a few cars down from Reece's 911 and hopped out, eager to share the great news.

As he got out of the car, he spotted Reece all the way on the other side of the parking lot of the restaurant. He was bent over at the window of a red Honda Accord, spitting game at some chick. Reece spotted Qwess and held up a finger for him to wait. Qwess had to give it to the brother, he pulled more hoes than a dentist pulled teeth.

Qwess and Doe *salaam*ed each other, as they were both Muslims, in theory anyway. Doe checked Qwess's clothes out and nodded approvingly. Qwess was wearing olive-green slacks, an orange Coogi short-sleeve sweater, and olive-green alligator loafers. He topped it off with a thin platinum chain with a charm that read *Allah* in Arabic, along with his signature Versace frame glasses with rose tint.

"You looking real smooth, brother," Doe complimented him.

"Appreciate it. You ain't slacking yourself." Doe instinctively looked down at his gear and knew what was coming next. "Though you could lose the tie," Qwess continued.

"Yo, you always say that!" Doe said, shaking his head.

"'Cause that's word, Ock," Qwess insisted. "You gotta learn how to coordinate."

Just as Doe was about to respond, Reece walked up, interrupting them. "Yo, son, you not gonna believe what happened to me the other night," Reece claimed.

"Here we go!" Both Qwess and Doe said simultaneously.

"Yo, word, word. Check it," Reece said, rubbing his palms together. "You remember ole girl that used to dance at X-tasy named Vanilla?"

"You talking about the short mixed broad with the blond hair?" Qwess recalled.

"Yeah, yeah. Her!" Reece confirmed.

Before Reece could delve deeper into his tryst, the red Honda Accord pulled up next to them. The driver's door swung open, and time seemed to slow down as the woman stepped out of the vehicle as if she was on a photo shoot. Her black stiletto heel touched the pavement and she rose to her full five-foot-six-inch height, allowing everyone to drink in her beauty. Black suede boots encased her smooth, peanut butter–colored skin all the way up to her thick, sculpted thighs, which glistened with oil all the way up to the edges of her short, ripped jean shorts. Her waist seemed to disappear between wide hips and large melons weighing down the fabric of her white spaghetti-strap top. It was evident she wore no bra because her nipples were eagerly trying to get a glimpse of everything around them. Her juicy lips were coated in lip gloss and shined like the chrome rims on Reece's Porsche. Her auburn colored hair was cut in a sharp bob style that was Reece's weakness.

Reece quickly stepped in, wrapped his arm around the woman's slim waist, and presented her to his crew. "Brothers, this is my new lady," he said, staking claim to the bombshell. "Her name is Destiny. Destiny, these are my brothers. This is Doe, and this is Qwess."

"Qwess? That name sounds familiar . . ." Destiny whispered to herself. "Wait! You're Qwess, the rapper?"

Qwess took a slight bow. "In the flesh. Rapper, producer, CEO, etcetera."

"Ahhh, I should've known," Destiny stated flatly. She glanced at Reece with a dejected expression. "The dreads, the Porsche . . ." She shook her head. "I should've known."

"Is there a problem?" Reece asked.

"Problem? Uhhh, yeah," Destiny retorted. She looked down at the business card she had been clutching since

Reece had given it to her just a few minutes ago. "*King Reece*," she repeated, reading the card. "So, you're part of the infamous Crescent Crew?"

"Of course," Reece answered, barely able to contain his smile. He knew this deal was closed now. Most women flocked to the Crescent Crew like birds to bread. He figured he would have her limbs up by nightfall now for sure.

Destiny shook her head emphatically. "Oh, noooo, I can't even get involved with you. I heard about you guys."

"I hope it was the good parts," Qwess quipped.

Destiny extended the business card back to Reece. "Um, Reece, I'm sure you're a really nice guy. For real. But I'm not going to waste your time or mine. From what I've heard, you're definitely not my type of guy."

"Hold up now," Reece objected. "You don't seem like the type to feed into hearsay. I took you as a smart woman. Let me holla at you over here for a minute."

Reece pulled Destiny away from the others and lowered his voice to just above a whisper, kicking the smooth game he was known for. "Listen, Destiny, don't let what you hear stop you from what could be your namesake," he pleaded.

"My namesake?"

"Yeah," Reece said. "I'm talking about your destiny. This thing right here is bigger than the both of us. Let's stop all this beating around the bush and go on with our original plans. That way, if you choose to indulge in the *he say/she say*, you can at least have my perspective in the matter. Feel me? No one can speak for me better than me. And we can at least do it over a nice meal—my treat," he added, flashing his million-dollar smile.

Destiny crossed her arms and gnawed on her bottom lip while contemplating his offer. Reece didn't miss one second to admire her, either. Even the way she pouted was cool and sexy to him. He was smitten. He *had* to have her.

"Well?"

Destiny smirked. "Okay, *King* Reece, I'll give you a shot, but if anything happens to me, you will regret it."

Reece dismissed her with a wave of his hand. "Knock it off. The only thing in danger is that thing right there." He pointed to her chest.

"What? My breast?"

"Nah, shorty, your heart. I'm going to steal it," Reece vowed.

Destiny blessed Reece with a genuine smile. She was impressed.

"Well, I have somewhere to be, Reece."

"Of course." Reece rushed to hold the door open for Destiny. He helped her get into her Honda safely, then stared at her as she adjusted herself inside the safety belt. Destiny looked up at Reece and fell into his dark eyes. Right there in the parking lot, both of their hearts skipped a beat.

After Destiny made her exit, Reece joined his brethren inside the steakhouse for this important meeting Qwess had called. While they waited for their meals, Reece kept the conversation light with the blow-by-blow from his threesome.

"Aww, man, the bitch licked my ass so good I started calling her Charmin," Reece joked, referring to Vanilla.

Doe frowned. Clearly, he wasn't interested in the graphic details. Qwess just laughed. Meanwhile Reece continued, "Yo, on the real, though, the broad had me feeling like I was a bitch. If I would've known it was like that, I would've pulled that a looong time ago."

"I heard shorty was freaky," Qwess cut in. "I just never got a chance to find out. And she was choosing hard," he added, recalling the time Vanilla had caught him in Walmart.

"Man, y'all niggas goin' get enough of fucking with them gold-digging hoes," Doe warned.

"*NIGGA!*" Reece exclaimed, a little too loudly, apparently, because the other patrons were now looking at them. Reece lowered his voice just a bit and dropped game. "All hoes after money, Doe. With a name like Doe you should know. Oh, shit, I'm rhyming again," Reece joked. "Seriously, though, that's what you don't understand yet. You be thinking 'cause a bitch don't live in the hood, or because she talk proper, she ain't a gold digger. Man, them the biggest ones! It's just them cornball-ass niggas raised the price of pussy so high, a regular nigga can't afford it."

Qwess nodded in agreement. "Yo, he ain't lying, D. Bitches thinking they entitled to money 'cause they cute."

"Sheeeit, I'm a handsome mu'fucka myself!" Reece said, more to himself than anyone else.

They were interrupted as the waiter brought their food. When the waiter left, Qwess took the time to change the subject to the business at hand.

"All right, now that I got everyone's attention," Qwess began.

"Not for long, nigga. You already was late. I got shit to do," Reece interjected, checking his Rolex for the time.

Qwess gave Reece a stern look. "Anyway, like I was saying," he continued. "You know I been politicking with AMG, trying to get them to do right. Well, they finally agreed to the terms," Qwess shared.

"Word! When?" Doe asked, excitedly.

"That was them on the phone earlier," Qwess informed them.

"What were the terms?" Reece inquired. "You've been keeping shit all secret like *Mission: Impossible*."

"Remember I told y'all I was gon' try and get the whole crew out of the street?" Qwess reminded them. "Well, that's how. I'm going to use these crackers' money to get us out. All you gotta do is roll with me."

Reece turned serious. "Just how much are they offering you?"

Qwess grinned. "Check it, they want to give us seven for a P and D deal to distribute all of A.B.P.'s recordings for the next five years."

"Seven hundred thousand?" Doe asked, slightly disappointed. He was hoping for more.

Qwess shook his head and grinned even harder. "Seven *million*."

Doe whistled. "That's a lot of fucking money, Ock. I can't believe they offering you that much."

"*Us* that much," Qwess corrected. "It's a package deal. If I sign this deal, y'all rolling with me."

They noticed Reece tense up at the mention of *both* of them rolling. He had yet to say a word since Qwess had first begun breaking down everything.

Qwess clapped his hands together and rubbed his palms. "This is it, baby! We made it."

Doe was excited as well. "Tell us more about the deal," he prodded.

"It's simple. Under the terms of the deal, we—A.B.P.— would keep full creative control, a majority percentage of the masters of our own records, and AMG will foot the bill for the first two big-budget videos," Qwess explained.

In addition to that, they wanted him to go on an international promotional tour for six months to start at the beginning of spring—two months from now. They wanted to re-release his freshman album *Janus* to an international audience and back it up with appearances.

"Basically, we killing shit out here, and they want in on what we got going on," Qwess added, citing their success. They had essentially locked down the Southeast, dominating the radio and selling 50,000 units without a video or major-labeling backing. Now they were poised to reap the fruits of their labor.

There had only been one problem with the deal.

"I been had 'em," Qwess bragged, "But they wouldn't meet my final demands until a few minutes ago."

"Which were?" Doe asked.

Qwess smirked. "You ready for this? I told them muthafuckas they had to cover the salary of my VP for the first two years." Qwess paused to let his words sink in. "Get this . . . at three million dollars total!"

"Get the fuck out of here!" Doe could hardly contain his excitement.

Qwess held up a finger. "And . . . they also agreed to an unprecedented deal that said they would pay a seven-hundred-fifty-thousand-dollar advance to the first new artist signed to A.B.P. once the deal is finalized. To top it off, the advance would have to be paid back over a five-year span, without taking any royalties from that artist's first album."

"Nooooo!"

"Yep. So, you know what that means?" Qwess leaned back and folded his arms. "That means everybody at this table is about to be a legal millionaire off this rap shit. I told you I got us!"

There, it was out there. Qwess had done what they said couldn't be done. He had found a way to get the Crescent Crew out of the streets, and become rich, all in one move. Everyone at the table didn't seem too happy, though.

Qwess looked over at Reece. "Yo, you heard what I said, nigga. I said, we good now," he reiterated.

Reece shook his head. "You don't get it, do you? It's not that simple, bro. I mean, you did good, but what about me and the crew?"

"Apparently you don't get it," Qwess countered. "I negotiated the seven fifty K for *you*! I plan for you to be the new artist to get that money."

"Get the fuck out of here!" Reece threw his napkin on the table. "I ain't nobody's rapper."

"Are you kidding?" Doe chimed in. "You can still rap your ass off! I see how you punish cats on that mic in the studio."

"Yeah, but I just be fucking around. I'm not trying to make no *career* out the shit."

Qwess eyed Reece in disbelief. He had held out for a long time to get these terms. Truth be told, AMG had come to him numerous times with very favorable deals, but he never bit, because he had his whole crew in mind. He had Reece in mind to be that franchise artist, and now it seemed that Reece wasn't going along with the plan.

"Knock it off, Reece. This is the promised land; this is why we started the crew—to get legitimate money," Qwess reminded him. He knew that Reece had been getting major money in the street, especially for the last few months. However, three quarters of a million dollars—legally—was a big step in the right direction. Any crime is only as good as its escape route, and drug dealing was still a crime, no matter how much money was made off it. Reece seemed to be refusing the escape route.

"Yeah, well, shit changed. You not the only one that made moves," Reece informed them. He leaned in to the table and lowered his voice. "I just got linked with the *plug*, plug, straight from Mexico. We getting them thangs right out of papi's hand now, two hundred at a time."

Doe whistled. Even *he* knew that was the big leagues.

"Yeah, but what's the cost of that?" Qwess wondered.

"The price is lovely," Reece assured them.

"No, I'm not talking about the price. I'm talking about the cost! Mo' money, mo' problems," Qwess preached.

"Well, I'm down with you," Doe stated, letting his position be known. "I really don't know what else to say, but thanks. Thanks, bro."

"Yo, Ock, don't even sweat that. You know you want for your brother what you want for yourself," Qwess reminded him.

"Yo, that's love," Doe responded. He felt as if his body was floating as he tried to grasp the magnitude of what Qwess had just dropped on him. He was about to become a millionaire.

Qwess turned to Reece again. He had a look of deep concentration on his face. "What you gonna do?"

Reece deflected. "Ahhh, I don't know."

"You don't know? Reece, you down or what?"

Reece peered out into the traffic riding by, weighing his options. He had achieved the hustler's dream, a plug straight out of Mexico. Yet Qwess was offering him a ghetto dream. To be the crème de la crème of the music industry was what every young boy from the hood desired.

"Yo, excuse me for a second," Reece said. He stood and went to the bathroom to gather his thoughts.

While Reece was in the bathroom, Qwess took the opportunity to clarify some things with Doe.

"Listen, bro, I don't want you to think this is a charity position. I chose you to be VP because you're the man for the job. I couldn't have done this without you. So, I'm gonna make sure you get what you deserve for your part. This ain't a cush job, though. It's gonna be a lot of work, especially if we sign that kid Flame off of Bunce. I heard he is a live wire." Qwess kept his ear to the street. Flame was the hottest thing spitting right now, and he needed him on his team.

"No doubt," Doe nodded. "You already know, whatever it takes from me, I'm there."

Just then Reece reappeared from the bathroom looking a lot more comfortable. He sat back down in the seat directly beside Qwess.

"So, are you down or what?" Qwess asked.

Reece released a huge sigh. "As much as I appreciate it, I gotta decline."

"What!?" Doe and Qwess both exclaimed.

"I have to," Reece insisted, holding firm. "As much as I appreciate you going all out for the crew, I gotta decline. Believe me, it's for the best. My heart is in these streets."

"What?" Doe was confused. "Nigga, you know on your worst day these niggas couldn't fuck with you on that mic! This is the opportunity of a lifetime."

"Yeah, well, I make my own opportunities these days."

"But you know how this game go," Doe insisted.

"Look, it's deeper than that," Reece said. "You know what I do. It ain't no secret. You two know me better than anyone. You know I ain't no quitter. This is the life I chose." He inched in a little closer and lowered his voice to just above a whisper. "Man, we 'bout to lock down this whole state. Charlotte, Greenville, Raleigh . . . all this shit 'bout to belong to the crew. Hell, at this rate, I can probably see that seven fifty you talking about in a week." He shook his head. "Nah, shit is going too good to bow out now."

Qwess spoke low, in measured tones, "You know everything comes with a price."

"Well, it's the price I'm willing to pay. Everyone has their own destiny. I'm just fulfilling mine."

"Man, you know that's bullshit!" Qwess blurted out. "I was in it, and got out. And in my family that's unheard of. Shit, it was like *the* thing to do. So, don't give me that."

"Look, like I said," Reece repeated, "I appreciate you going all out, but I've already chosen my life. Now, I gotta live it. I've gone too far to turn back now. I can't go from being a shot-caller to being controlled."

"Man, you know it wouldn't be like that!" Qwess insisted.

"Yo, brother, please just respect my call?" Reece asked, looking him dead in the eye before continuing, "You know it's nothing but love. Crescent Crew until we die, but I can't go backwards. Now let's just rejoice in the good fortune that we're all about to become millionaires at twenty-five. Regardless of the route we took, we all got there."

At that, he lifted his glass of tea to propose a toast. The others did so as well, albeit reluctantly.

"To prosperity!"

"To prosperity!" they all repeated and clinked their glasses, then drank.

"I gotta go to Charlotte in the morning to sign the papers and it'll be official," said Qwess as they were getting up from the table.

"I gotta give my two-week notice," said Doe.

"I gotta go get my stick dipped," said Reece, and they all laughed.

Before they left, Qwess dropped a thirty-dollar tip on the table for the waiter. They all shook, embraced, and peeled out.

Life was good. Or so they thought.

Chapter 4

The Mobb Deep track banged through the subwoofers, enveloping the car's passengers in a cloud of bass. The weed smoke was pungent and prevalent. The tint on the windows was so dark it was impossible to see through to the inside. The occupants felt safe and secure. It was rather ironic considering they were plotting the assassination of an adversary.

"Yo, are you sure that nigga Qwess don't fuck around no more?" Black Vic asked his driver and right-hand man, Hardtime.

"Nah, he taking that music shit serious now," Hardtime assured his leader. "Ever since he got out, he ain't really touch shit."

Black Vic leaned back in the plush leather interior of the Lexus and listened as Hardtime ran the game down. "Well, shit, I wonder why he reached out to me, then?" Black Vic wondered aloud.

"Shit, matter fact, word is AMG 'bout to give him a big-ass deal, yo. A few mil or something. So, shit, I can't see the nigga taking a chance at fucking all that up over some street shit." Hardtime paused long enough to inhale the potent marijuana deep into his lungs, then passed the blunt to Black Vic.

Black Vic took the blunt and shot him a vicious stare. "See, mu'fucka, you don't understand shit. Listen and take heed," Black Vic schooled. "Once a street nigga, always a street nigga. It's in his blood. All his peoples—his pops, uncles, everybody—they all street. And they all vicious, or was at one point. Most of 'em dead or in the feds now, but the fact remains." Black Vic hit the weed hard, then continued his lesson with the smoke wrapping around his words. "And Qwess and Reece are like brothers; they started that little funky-ass Crescent Crew together. You think he will let something happen to Reece and not retaliate? Would you let something happen to me and not retaliate?" Black Vic posed, illustrating his point.

Hardtime humbled down to his mentor. "I understand," he conceded. "But if you ask me, we should keep our eye on the prize. That nigga Reece is dangerous enough."

"Reece is a dead issue, as far as I'm concerned, pun intended. I took care of that already. Trust. Just be on point for the storm that follows," Victor warned, as they pulled into his driveway. "I'll link up with you later."

Black Vic walked into his house with Ruger in hand. He cleared every room in the three-bedroom home before he finally relaxed. Each time he closed his eyes, a vision of his lieutenant dangling from a high-rise appeared. Alvin had been a good dude, very loyal to their gang. He would be missed, but his death would not be in vain.

Black Vic pulled a plate full of cocaine from under the bed and placed it on the nightstand. Methodically, he diced the coke up into thin lines on the plate. Satisfied with his construction, he pinched one nostril and dunked his head in the plate like an ostrich. He snorted deep then leaned his head back until he felt the drip. High, he was now able to focus his thoughts.

Reece had been a thorn in his side for the past few months now. He was letting work go for too low, so low that no one else in town could eat. In the game, this happened from time to time. Say a hustler scored a bad package. The remedy would be to get it off for the low in hopes of breaking even on his investment before his name became soured for pushing bad product. Although frowned upon, it was still accepted from time to time as a necessary evil of the game. This was different. With Reece and the Crescent Crew, their prices were low *and* the product was top-notch. Now it was beginning to encroach on his money and territory.

Black Vic took the civilized approach. He approached one of the youngsters of the Crescent Crew and tried to get work for the low. He laughed at him. So Black Vic took the work. On another occasion, he approached them on some partnership shit. They hit him with consignment, but the price was too high. So again, he kept it. He concluded that what they had done to Alvin was their clap-back. However, he was determined to get the last laugh.

Black Vic dialed a number on his phone. "Yo, you took care of that yet?" he asked.

"Not yet, but I'm on it," the man promised.

"Don't disappoint me."

Black Vic ended the call and snorted two more lines of coke. His thoughts shifted to Qwess.

He had respect for Qwess because he always showed love. He recalled when Qwess used to come up from Atlantic Beach and spread love throughout the city with the potent work he copped from the Dominicans. Black Vic had been one of Qwess's biggest customers. Then when

Qwess went to prison, all that changed. In a way he was happy Qwess was out of the game. Sometimes he wished he could get out himself, but that wasn't his life.

Black Vic knew that Qwess was still down with Reece. He hated to do it to him, but if Qwess brought drama, he was gonna lay his ass down, too—rapper or not. Bottom line: Ain't nobody getting in the way of his paper. Reece was gonna find out firsthand.

There was a war going on outside, and no one was safe from it.

Chapter 5

A week after Reece declined Qwess's deal, the brothers had just left the *masjid* on Murchison Road after attending Jumu'ah, the Friday prayer service for Muslims.

Attending Jumu'ah was essential for a Muslim staying on the correct path, a ritual that reiterated a Muslim's purpose every Friday. When constructing the Crescent Crew, Qwess and Reece had drawn from the ranks of their Muslim community because they knew the brothers bore allegiance to one another on the strength of Islam. Muslims had rights over one another that included loyalty, protection, and the responsibility to lend aid to their brother when needed. Of course, their initial recruitment of the brothers wasn't nefarious. It started as them lending a hand to a brother, then another, then another, in secret, away from the community. Word quickly spread among the brothers that were already in the streets that Qwess and Reece were the guys to see. After that, it was a no-brainer to cull their soldiers from the ranks they were already in. The rest was the stuff of ghetto legend.

Reece centered the business of the Crescent Crew

around Jumu'ah Friday, since everyone would be in attendance. After the imam released them, hyped up on a sermon, Reece would gather the members of the crew and break bread with the fam. This day was no different.

Except someone was watching their every move.

After Reece hit the crew with their work for the week, he dipped off in his Porsche, headed to his car dealership on Skibo Road. He hung a left on Country Club Road, and a brown Chrysler made the turn with him. Oblivious to the tail, Reece bent down and fiddled with the radio. When he raised his head, the Chrysler was right beside him at the stoplight. The driver of the Chrysler was staring at Reece with a mean mug.

"What's up, homie? You know me?" Reece asked, throwing his hands up.

He never saw the Uzi hanging out the back window until it spit fireballs into the Porsche. The first volley shattered the small back window. A piece of glass ripped through the air and slashed Reece's face. He smashed the accelerator, and the Porsche rocketed forward, leaving the Chrysler in a cloud of smoke.

"Muthafucka!!!" Reece swore. He ducked low and piloted the Porsche through traffic at insane speeds, wiping the blood from his face. He looked over his shoulder and saw that the Chrysler had been reduced to a small dot in the chaos of traffic. Reece wasn't sure if the men in the Chrysler were alone, so he didn't slow down one bit. When he made it to McPhearson Church Road, he hung a left and pinned the accelerator to the floor. The inline-six engine roared to life and carried Reece to safety.

Once safe, he pulled into the parking lot of Red Lobster to assess the damage and phone the goons. There was minimal damage to his $100,000 whip, but the damage to his pride was immeasurable. There was no doubt in Reece's mind who had sent the hit. Reece wiped the blood from his eye and licked it with a smile.

Now he had a reason to get off the chain.

Qwess piloted the big Benz through traffic toward his sister's hair salon. The deal was made, and it was official. He had hustled his way to legal millionaire status. As he maneuvered the Benz onto the expressway, he reflected on how he got to this point in his life.

He was born and raised in Atlantic Beach, South Carolina. Growing up, it was just he and his older sister, Fatima. They didn't really have a hard upbringing, because their father and their uncles had the streets on lock, while their mother mostly remained home and attended to them. Anything they wanted, it was granted. As long as they obeyed the rules, minus the few little infractions that went along with childhood, their parents never gave them any trouble. One thing that was stressed, though, was education. It was absolutely imperative that they learned something new every day. No matter what their father was doing, who he was with, or where he was, at the end of every day he would gather the both of them together, and they would have to explain to him what they learned for that day.

It was on Qwess's eighth birthday that the whole family accompanied his father on a "business" trip to Miami. It was then that two things happened that would affect Qwess's life forever. The first thing was that he saw a black Cuban family speaking Spanish. This was intriguing to him because at that point, the black people he had come in contact with could barely speak decent English. Here, he met a person, a black person, speaking two languages. This intrigued him to a point beyond comprehension. His father noticed his interest and encouraged him to learn Spanish. As he put it, *it could only be good for the family business* later on down the line. So he tackled learning Spanish with the ferocity of a madman. It practically consumed him. Later, upon returning to South Carolina, his father hired him a Spanish tutor. By the time Qwess was ten, he had complete mastery of the language.

The second thing that affected his life forever after was when he and his sister snuck away and stumbled right into an Eric B. & Rakim concert. Well, they didn't actually get in. The concert was on the beach, so they were able to climb onto a balcony of one of the surrounding hotels and see everything. Man, the way those people were going crazy just made his blood pump! His sister, who was twelve at the time, just watched and stared in amazement. She could barely keep her legs still; they kept twitching back and forth for some reason. It was then that Qwess knew exactly what he wanted to be when he grew up. He wanted the power to move the crowd, the power to control masses of people with his wordplay. The only problem was, it seemed he was destined to inherit the family business: cocaine.

When he was ten and his father knew he knew Spanish through and through, he started going with his father on business trips to Florida. His father would introduce him to his Cuban friends as his successor. This would give him esteem in their eyes, because they allowed him to sit in on their meetings. However, he had explicit instructions from his father to never speak Spanish, and never let them know that he understood Spanish. His father told him, "Never show all your cards." He was only to listen and learn, and if they said anything of concern in Spanish, let him know. These trips went on once every two months for two whole years. Sometimes, one of his uncles would accompany them, and this would allow him to write songs. He always kept his dream alive. He knew one day he would make it as a rapper.

When he was fourteen, he experienced another life-altering event. His father and two of his uncles were busted by the feds. His third uncle was shot and killed by the police when he tried to shoot his way out.

The feds had a strong case, and it seemed that the family wasn't going to win. His father and uncles were charged with murder, extortion, trafficking, and any other crime you could think of . . . besides robbery. His father had always taught him that robbery wasn't a viable option. Robbery was a sucka's game, a hater disguised as a hustler. While out on a half-million-dollar bond, his father pumped all he could into him about the streets, but his day came too soon.

When Qwess was fifteen, his father and two uncles were all found guilty and sentenced to life in prison. In order to get a fresh start, his mother packed Qwess and his sister up and moved the family to Fayetteville, North Carolina. He was a sophomore in high school. It was there that he met Rolando and Maurice.

The friends clicked immediately, because Rolando was half Puerto Rican and spoke fluent Spanish. He was originally from New York, and was a Muslim just like Qwess. Qwess showed Rolando that he could rap, and Rolando wanted him to meet his cousin Reece, who at that time had just gotten a record deal.

When he first met Reece, it was inside of a rap cipher. Reece was smashing everyone who stepped up. Then when Qwess stepped into a cipher, he and Reece went round after round. Reece eventually won, but he earned Reece's respect. It wasn't long before the three of them were inseparable.

On a trip to the beach to visit his sister, who had

moved back, Qwess took Reece with him. While there, Reece noticed how all of the drug dealers showed Qwess love and casually hinted that he could make money in North Carolina with the right product. At the time, Qwess wasn't able to keep up the high standard of living he was accustomed to. To add to that, he had become quite popular, courtesy of his skills on the mic. The crew would travel all over North Carolina, rapping at clubs, gaining momentum, with Doe acting as manager. At that point Reece had turned down his record deal, because they were making so much money independently, they figured they would just produce themselves. To finance their music endeavors, they dived in the dope game knee-deep.

By the time they were seniors in high school, everyone knew them . . . either from rapping or their street hustle. On graduation night, not even two hours after they walked across the stage to receive their diplomas, they were busted during a routine traffic stop. They were on their way to deliver a half ounce of powder to some white kids from a neighboring high school, and that's what the cops found: a half ounce of cocaine. Instead of all of them going down for the charge, Qwess took it on the chin. Since Reece was the better rapper and Rolando the manager, he believed if he took the charge, the crew would still be intact.

As luck would have it, he turned eighteen two days before he went to court. The judge gave him an ultimatum: go to jail or join the army for two years. Of course, he chose the army.

He went to basic training, and advanced infantry training at Fort Benning, Georgia. In the infantry, he learned all kinds of survival tactics, as well as numerous ways to assassinate men. He would later use these same skills to terrorize any unlucky soul who got in the way of his crew's money. After schooling he was stationed at Fort Bliss, Texas. It was there that he found the woman he was going to marry.

He was a nineteen-year-old private, she a seventeen-year-old virgin. Her name was Hope. They met and fell in love almost immediately. She was the first woman he ever thought about seeing more than once. She was the first woman, other than his mother and sister, whom he actually respected. It was rather uncanny the way they clicked, but like all good things in life, it would eventually end. She went off to college, and was supposed to meet him back in Fayetteville, North Carolina, where her parents were from. During the time, he started venturing off to Mexico, first for fun. Then, while he was over in Mexico, he met someone he presumed was a regular local. He started talking to the guy in Spanish one night while drinking. The guy liked the fact that he had a healthy appreciation for Spanish culture (or so he was told), and got close to him. When the guy found out a little about his background, the guy revealed more about his background. Turned out his name was really Poppo, and he was a middleman for a Mexican cartel. Needless to say, they hooked up, and before long Reece was coming out to Texas to pick up cocaine and marijuana. Rolando was in school studying accounting and management. Turned out that one brush with the law was enough for him.

At the end of his two years, Qwess returned to North Carolina and visited Hope at Fayetteville State University often. He eventually took her virginity, and he grew real close to her family as well. However, as each day went by, he and Reece grew stronger in wealth and power. Because they were still dealing with Poppo out of Mexico, the other dealers couldn't compete. For those who tried with violence, they were met with violence. One guy in particular woke up one morning, cranked up his brand-new BMW, and was blown all over the neighborhood. They found his head in the neighborhood preacher's backyard. It sent a message: Don't mess with the crew.

At the ripe age twenty-one, Qwess and his crew, who encompassed a gang of young, hungry, loyal hustlers, were major players in the city. To top it off, he was engaged to be married to Hope when she graduated from college the following year. However, that was not to be. One night he was supposed to be delivering a kilo of cocaine, along with one of his crew members, when they were ambushed by would-be robbers. The robbers aired the car out with automatic gunfire, killing his partner, Paco. Qwess was also hit, but managed to get away. He found out who it was and went to exact retribution. On his way to the spot where the robbers were, he ran into the police. This time when they searched the car, they found a grenade as well as an unregistered Glock pistol. He was by himself, believing all dirty work should be done alone. After spending fifty thousand dollars in legal fees, Qwess received five years, federal time. He was still only twenty-one years old.

His incarceration devastated Hope, because she never knew about his street endeavors. She tried to be by his side as much as possible, but when she graduated college with a degree in public relations, she felt her career was more important than he was. She moved away to Baltimore, and the lovers lost contact, although Hope and his sister kept in touch.

While in prison, Qwess rediscovered Islam, as well as his passion for music. He told himself he was going to go straight, and prepared himself by giving fifty thousand dollars of his stash money to his sister to open up the hair salon she always wanted. It became an instant success. He also planned to use the music industry to maintain a way of living. He figured he'd be killing two birds with one stone: He'd be appeasing his hunger to make music and appeasing his hunger to make money. To him, the only way to do music was on his own terms. So while in prison he studied every music management book he could get his hands on, like *All You Need to Know about the Music Business* by Donald S. Passman, and other books as well. He also read *EQ* magazine religiously. It was teaching him all about production equipment, since he planned to self-produce.

Qwess was released from prison after three and a half years, partly due to good behavior. When he came home, he noticed his whole crew—now going by the name Crescent Crew because they were all either five-percenters or Muslims—had grown in stature and money. Reece had whipped the crew into shape, and with him as the head, the Crew flourished. Ever since Reece had orchestrated the killings of the guys who tried to rob them before Qwess went to prison, no one questioned his authority. They offered to let Qwess get right in at the top, but he declined. Instead, he built a studio in his home, made an album, and sold it himself out the trunk of his car. He initially started selling in Atlanta, then spread throughout the whole Southeast. Now, a week before his twenty-sixth birthday, he was about to become a legal millionaire. His only wish was that he could help the others in his crew.

Qwess's phone rang, interrupting his reverie. He answered. "*As-salaam alayka.*"

"Hello, handsome." It was Shauntay, his steady girlfriend.

"What's up, love?"

"I'm just calling to see what time you'll be home. I don't want your dinner to get cold."

"I gotta stop by the salon. I'll probably be there about seven."

"Seven?" she asked anxiously. "That's four hours from now!"

"Yeah, I know. Fatima wanted to see me."

"Well, come when you can."

"Why, is something wrong?" he asked.

"No, I just miss you."

He sighed. "Oh, well, I'll be there sooner than you know."

"Okay, I'll see you then. Love you."

"Yeah, all right." He clicked off his phone and exited the expressway.

Qwess changed the disc from Sade to Dead Prez, and cracked his window, getting into the mood. His phone rang again. He thought it was Shauntay, but when he saw Reece's number he quickly picked up.

"Peace! What's up, Reece?"

"They got me, brother," Reece said, with pain in his voice. "They caught me slipping and wet me up."

"What?! Who? When? Where?"

"You know who. Meet me at the studio."

Qwess sighed heavily with the world on his shoulders. It never ended. The drama, the violence, the uncertainty.

But he couldn't walk away from his brother.

Chapter 6

It was just after midnight when Qwess pulled his Benz into the garage. He waited for the wrought-iron gate to close, making sure no one came in behind him. His nerves were on edge after the evening he'd had. He rested his head on the steering wheel and tried to stop his world from spinning. Everything was coming at him so fast. AMG, the Crescent Crew, the upcoming tour, and Reece's war . . . For the first time in forever, he felt over-whelmed. He guessed it was true: more money, more problems indeed.

The door to the garage opened, and Shauntay was standing there in a beautiful purple satin robe. A faint glow from the house framed her beautiful face, giving her an angelic appearance. He could hear the music of Floetry drifting from inside the house. This was exactly what he needed, a soft dose of femininity to balance out a rough day.

"Hey, honey, you okay?" Shauntay called out. She stepped into the garage and retrieved Qwess from his car. "Come on inside. I got just the thing to make you feel better."

After she had received the call from Qwess as he rushed to Reece's aid, she could sense his mood was tense. She knew exactly what he needed. Shauntay went all out preparing a dinner for Qwess. Afterward she planned to bathe him and give him a nice, long hot-oil massage. She wanted to show him how proud she was by pampering him and making him feel like a king.

She had the kitchen sectioned off from the rest of the house because she didn't want him to see the trail of roses that she had laid for him leading from the kitchen to the bedroom. She wanted him to be surprised. Just like she wanted to surprise him with the roses floating inside the garden tub in the master bathroom. She even had a silver platter filled with a variety of fruits. She was going to feed him dessert inside the tub. After this, she was sure that whatever plagued his mind would be a thing of the past.

"Damn, baby, you went all out, huh?" Qwess said, taking in the arrangements.

"Yeah, I already had dinner made, but when you called me back I figured you needed something extra to get you back to yourself."

Qwess took a seat at the bar in the kitchen and sighed. "Yeah you wouldn't believe the night I had."

Shauntay placed the baked potato on his plate. "Reece?" she asked knowingly.

Qwess nodded. "Yeah."

Shauntay placed his plate before him. "Baby, I love Reece like a brother, you know I do, but . . . you have to learn to let go. You just signed the deal that is going to change your life. You can't do the same things you used to do with the same people, hun."

Qwess nodded. "You right, but how am I supposed to turn my back on him?"

"If he's truly your friend, you won't have to. He

wouldn't *let* you get involved in his shit anymore. A *friend* protects a friend."

"Exactly."

"Exactly."

Qwess dropped his head and closed his eyes. An image of his friend bleeding flashed across his eyes. "Reece was shot at today," he whispered.

"Ohmigod! Is he all right? Did he get hit? Are you okay?" Shauntay rushed over and cradled Qwess's head into her bosom.

"He's fine," Qwess mumbled into her chest. "Just caught some glass in his face."

Shauntay breathed a sigh of relief. "Thank God!"

Qwess stroked Shauntay's thighs beneath the robe. He needed to shift his mind from the carnage of the streets, the drama, the bloodshed, and hits. He needed her.

"What you got on under this robe?" Qwess asked.

Shauntay grinned and opened the robe. Beneath it, she wore a purple thong with no bra. Her hair was pulled into a coil of curls on top of her head and held in place with a chopstick.

Qwess moaned. "Niiice!"

"You like this?"

"I love it."

She knew Qwess would love this. She maintained the sexy by switching up styles on the regular because she knew the quickest way to kill a relationship was to get complacent. Furthermore, Qwess had so many women coming at him, if she didn't keep him interested, she knew what would happen.

Shauntay slipped from his grip long enough to retrieve the chilled wine from the freezer and set it onto the glass table.

"Now follow me," she commanded, taking his hand, leading him to the dining room table. She sat him down in a chair and told him not to move. As she walked into the kitchen, he silently admired the sway of her hips. Moments later, she returned with a platter of fresh-cut vegetables. He knew this was an appetizer because he smelled the shrimp the second he walked in.

Shauntay straddled him face-forward and began feeding him. He started to say something, but she took her perfectly manicured finger and placed it on his lips.

"Sshh," she whispered softly. "No more talk. This is your time. Just bask in the moment."

Qwess obliged and continued eating. He inhaled her scent, something feminine and erotic, but he couldn't place what it was. All he knew was it smelled good. He looked deep in her green eyes as she fed him and basked in the love he found there. This inwardly warmed him, and he started to get an erection.

Shauntay smiled, leaned into him, and whispered into his ear, "You want to feel me, huh?" He nodded. "Not now, you haven't eaten your meal yet," she teased him, all the while grinding back and forth slowly.

"But I want to eat you," Qwess pleaded.

"Hmmm, promises, promises."

Shauntay slid from his lap and went to the kitchen. She came back with a bowl of sautéed shrimp over pasta, some breadsticks, and chopsticks. She placed the bowl on the table in front of him. Then, she walked around the back of his chair and whispered in his ear while at the same time blowing in it. "I want you to get comfortable," she said before leaning over to take off his Coogi sweater. He was now bareback, except for his platinum chain.

Shauntay came back around and sat on Qwess's lap, half facing him and half facing the table. She dipped the chopsticks into the bowl, spun them a couple of times, and came up with food. She slowly put the food in his mouth. As she was doing so, some of it fell onto his chest.

"Oops." Shauntay giggled and bent to suck it off with her mouth.

"Ahhh," Qwess moaned.

She then put the glass of wine to his mouth for him to drink, spilling some of that as well. She licked this off, too.

By the end of the meal, Qwess was rock hard. Shauntay could feel it. She was wet herself. In fact, you could wring her panties out like a dishrag at this point.

As she was getting up from the table, she conveniently dropped a chopstick. She pushed Qwess's chair back from the table while still in front of him. She turned with her back facing him and bent way over to get the chopstick, exposing all of her business.

Qwess was so horny, he was ready to bust on himself, but Shauntay continued to play the game. She grabbed his hand, leading him to the bedroom.

"Word, that's what I'm talking about," Qwess mumbled. Shauntay looked over her left shoulder, smiling as she led him down the hallway to the bedroom.

The lights were low inside the bedroom, consistent with the rest of the house. Shauntay led him to the bathroom. As they walked past the back wall, which was mirrored from floor to ceiling, Qwess glanced at himself. There was nothing but pure glee on his face now where a mask of confusion had lived before. Before they went inside the bathroom, Shauntay began tugging at his pants.

"Sorry, mister, but we have a no-clothes rule in there," she mocked.

"Oh, excuse me, miss."

Qwess stepped out of his pants. Shauntay pointed at his boxer briefs. "Those too," she instructed.

"Well, what about you?" he asked, stripping down to his birthday suit.

"I'm the help. The rules don't apply to me."

They went into the bathroom, where candles were burning at each of the four corners of the garden tub. Qwess could see the steam coming from the water. He also smelled Egyptian musk; apparently Shauntay had sprinkled some of the oil in the water. Last, he noted the fruit tray.

Qwess stepped into the tub and looked at Shauntay questioningly. She looked back at him, nodding her head. As soon as Qwess sat down in the water, she slowly removed her robe. Qwess's eyes got big as he noticed the tattoo above her navel that read *Qwess* in pretty cursive script.

She returned his gaze and said, "It's all about you, daddy. Anytime a man sees my navel, he's reminded of whose this is." She patted her crotch. "Now lay back and let me give you a massage."

Qwess obeyed. Shauntay rubbed his shoulders and began feeding him fruit. First, she tasted a strawberry by sucking on it vigorously before putting in into Qwess mouth. Then she did the same thing with a slice of watermelon, all the while trying to mesmerize Qwess with her green eyes. It worked. Suddenly, Qwess couldn't take it anymore. The sight of Shauntay's erect nipples was too much. He snatched her into the water with him with a big splash.

"Ahh! You brute!" Shauntay screamed.

Qwess just laughed heartily. "Now let me feed you," he said as he pulled her onto his lap. He only fed her two grapes before she straddled him face-forward. She pushed her thong to the side and let Qwess enter her. However, she wouldn't let him move. She just slowly sat all the way down on Qwess's penis, enveloping all of him into her.

"Ah, shit, baby," Qwess moaned.

"Sssh, don't move. Just feel me . . ." Shauntay hissed.

She squeezed the inner muscles of her vagina, and Qwess closed his eyes in pure ecstasy. "Baby, look at me."

Qwess did, and was at a loss for words. Her eyes were so enchanting with the light from the candle reflecting in them. He cupped her face in his hands and kissed her deeply. He rubbed one of his hands through her hair. When it got stuck on the chopstick in her hair, he snatched the chopstick out, letting Shauntay's hair fall down to the middle of her back, into the water. As Qwess tried to take control, Shauntay stopped him by pushing him back against the wall of the tub. She stood, dripping wet, nipples erect, and allowed him to drink her in.

"Let me please you, daddy. Let me take care of my man," Shauntay pleaded. She stepped out of the tub, pulling Qwess's hand with her.

As they walked into the front of the bedroom, Shauntay still had on her thong, and Qwess admired the way the string ran up into her cheeks, making her butt look like a split apple.

Damn, he thought. *That's a nice ass.*

As they walked past the floor-to-ceiling mirrored wall again, Shauntay stopped directly in front of it with her back facing the mirror. Her eyes were on Qwess as she grabbed his penis in her hand. She felt it throbbing intensely. She stroked it a few times before dropping to her knees and taking him into her mouth.

Qwess peered down at her, then to the mirror, where he could see her beautiful ass spread open like a flower. He looked down into her eyes as she sucked him off. As each stroke intensified, he couldn't take it anymore. The scene was too much for him. Her beauty intensified by the ambient lighting, her warm mouth expertly moving on his penis, the erotic perfume in the air, coupled with the sweet scent emanating from her center . . . It was too much.

Qwess exploded into her mouth. Shauntay swallowed every single drop and continued sucking. Before long Qwess was hard again.

Shauntay stood up. She turned around with her back facing Qwess, looking directly into the mirror. Her eyes met with his eyes through the mirror, and she whispered softly, "Get you baby, tear this pussy up."

Qwess bent Shauntay over, gripping each cheek in a hand, and buried his nine-inch cock deep into her warm, wet center. Shauntay cried out and shook uncontrollably as orgasm after orgasm gripped her body. She was shaking so badly she could barely stand up. Qwess scooped her up and carried her to the bed.

On the bed, Shauntay wrapped her legs around Qwess's waist as he plunged in and out of her, long-stroking her with his love. He flipped her over on her stomach and sank deep inside her tightness. His gentle strokes became more and more powerful, until he was pounding her into the headboard viciously. He wrapped her long tresses around his hand and pumped furiously, grunting and growling like a wild animal. Suddenly, his thrusts sped up. He pumped into her like a rabbit on steroids until he exploded deep inside of her, painting her walls with his lust and angst.

Qwess collapsed onto Shauntay's back, with his flaccid penis still lodged inside her.

"Damn, that was good!" Shauntay gushed. "I love you, daddy!" she cried out.

Qwess moaned in satisfaction, but he never returned her sentiment.

Later, as they lay in the afterglow of sex, Qwess vaguely informed Shauntay of the day's events and what the upcoming weeks should hold. Shauntay informed Qwess that she had something to tell him, but it would have to wait until his birthday the following week. He playfully tried to extort information from her. She playfully eluded him. She straddled him, laying her head on his chest, where she fell asleep.

Qwess played in Shauntay's hair, his mind moving a million miles a minute. Tomorrow was a big day.

Tomorrow he and Doe were going to see the kid, Flame.

Chapter 7

The next morning Qwess woke up, took a shower, and made *salaat*. It had been a while since he did this, but he felt he needed guidance now more than ever. He had been off his *deen* for a while, but he still knew where his blessings came from.

Just as he completed his prayers, Shauntay woke up moaning in pain. He went to her side immediately, but she waved him off, told him it was just cramps. He got dressed and called Doe to let him know he was on his way. Before he left, he checked on Shauntay once again, kissed her, and left.

When he arrived at Doe's house, he noticed a familiar car in the yard. Qwess shook his head and honked his horn. Doe ran out in a hurry as if Qwess had saved him from an uncomfortable situation.

"Yo, brother, you all right?" Qwess asked Doe as he got into the Benz. Qwess had a knowing smirk on his face.

"Yeah, I'm cool."

"Shit, I can't tell! You look like you escaping from prison," Qwess joked, as he backed out into the street.

"You know how that is. Brother call for a booty call, and she wanna talk marriage."

"Yeah, but y'all got history," Qwess rationalized.

"Yeah, and her ass is history. I ain't got time. I'm single, and I'm ready to enjoy life."

"I hear that."

"What's up with Shauntay? She good?"

"Yeah, man, she did it up for me last night when I got in. After the day I had, I needed it." Qwess sighed.

"Ole trusty Shauntay always been your ride-or-die from day one, huh?"

"Yeah, man, that she has," Qwess replied, recalling how he and Shauntay had first met.

Shauntay was in Atlanta working at a travel agency, where she was director of sales. He had come in asking about special rates the agency could provide. Said he was an entertainer, and would be doing a lot of traveling. She had spotted him way before he saw her. He looked so cute, she'd thought back then. He was wearing slacks and a dress shirt. His three-sixty waves were spinning from where he'd obviously gotten a haircut. She was in the back entering data about a new client. When she came to the front, their eyes met. So much was said in that one instant. He asked her out then, but she declined, because she had just gotten out of a relationship. However, he was persistent. He told her he was from North Carolina and would be leaving soon . . . but that he'd be back for her. He sent her flowers every day until he left. When he did go back to North Carolina, he sent her roses.

Qwess finally broke her down, and she agreed to go on a date the next time he was in Atlanta. He was there two days later. They went out, and he was the perfect gentleman. They went to a comedy show. Though he was dressed conservatively, there still was an underlying street element in his demeanor. It wasn't just his bottom row of diamond-encrusted teeth, either. It had more to do with the way he casually observed his surroundings at all times. Or the way people gravitated toward him. He had a commanding presence. Kind of like you sensed him when he walked into a room. You felt him way before you saw him. These traits were what made him irresistible to her, she'd confided later. She slept with him after only one week, though if he had tried the first night, she would have given in. They just clicked.

As he sold more records, he showered her with more lavish gifts. He eventually convinced her to take some time off from work. "When I want you by me, I want nothing in the way. I'll take care of you," he had told her. He had made good on his promise. She didn't want for anything, except to hear him say he loved her. Years later, he never said it.

"You heard about Reece ass?" Qwess asked.

"Yeah, man," Doe said. "I mean, how did this shit come about? Why niggas trying to wet him up now, though?"

Qwess looked away. "You know how it is out here in these streets," he answered evasively. Doe was privy to a lot of things pertaining to the crew, but they drew the line on informing him of murders they committed. For one, they wanted to ensure he maintained plausible deniability. Two, murder was murder. No statute of limitations, automatic life. One just never knew . . . .

"Yeah, man, I hope you not getting dragged back into this street shit."

"Nah, never that," Qwess hoped.

They conversed a lot more on their ride across town, mostly about signing Flame as their new artist to fill the void created by Reece's decision.

Little did they know, Flame would help them create hip-hop history.

* * *

It was an unseasonably warm day in North Carolina, and hustlers were out enjoying the weather. Chicks strutted up the street in skin-tight clothing hoping to attract the attention of the hustlers on the block. However, hustlers were only focused on one thing—getting to the money. While dealers waited on their customers to come through and pay them a visit, they entertained themselves with a game of craps. While some of the gamblers were playing, one of them was dead serious. He was kicking ass and taking names.

Joey Devon picked up the dice to roll again. "Yeah, nigga, watch that fever," he barked at the spectators and opponents, shaking the dice feverishly. He nodded his head vigorously. "When I hit this fever, you better not cry." He rolled the two dice. The squares tumbled around in slow motion for a few seconds before a two and a three showed up.

"Fever!!!" Joey yelled.

"Awww, damn!" the crowd screamed.

"Yeah, mu'fucka! I told you. Pay me!!!"

They were on Bunce Road, one of the dope strips in Fayetteville, North Carolina. Everyone was passing time shooting dice. Some to pay bills. Some to just double money already made. Joey was in the latter crowd. Since graduating from high school a couple of months ago, he had become heavily immersed in the streets. The money he was now doubling was the booty from a robbery he had committed in the wee hours of the previous morning. It was now the middle of the day, and everyone was out in full swing. The drug dealers. The drug users. The jack boys, and their unsuspecting victims. Just another day on Bunce Road.

"Yo, nigga, quit hogging the blunt," Joey said to

8-Ball, his chubby, trusty companion. "Let me smoke right while I gut these fools."

8-Ball took another toke and passed Joey the blunt.

"Aww, nigga, you need to stop hogging the goddamn rocks, and roll." That was J.D. He was a main player on this strip, and he had already let this young buck beat him out of eight hundred dollars.

"Oh, I'ma roll these mu'fuckas. You just roll my dough up out your mu'fuckin hand when I hit," Joey bragged.

All the other lookers-on placed side bets while everyone popped slick. Joey rolled again.

Seven.

"Muthafucka!"

"Yeah nigga, I told you. Pay me!" The block erupted!

The lucky young buck hit again. There were a lot of salty faces. Money exchanged hands. Everyone settled down for another run at the dice.

Suddenly, everyone's attention was interrupted by a thump in the distance. The thump drew closer and got louder. When it was too close to be ignored, the dice game was temporarily suspended while everyone looked up to see the source of the music. When the car was close enough to be identified, some mouths dropped, some mouths twisted. Everyone stared.

"Damn, that Benz is fuckin' hot!" 8-Ball conceded.

When the black AMG Benz came to a stop directly in front of the crowd, a few of the gang reached for their pistols but didn't pull them out. Everyone was on edge because the car windows were rolled up airtight, and the super dark tint prevented anyone from looking in. The passenger window rolled halfway down revealing a light-skinned dude with a ponytail. They could vaguely make out the driver reclined all the way back in the seat.

"Yo, who this broke-ass Ice-T looking nigga?" someone from the crowd snickered.

Doe spoke up from behind the wheel, "Yo, anybody seen Flame?"

"Who wanna know?" That was J.D., who still had his hand in his pants.

"Yo, dawg, a friend wanna know."

"Oh, a friend, huh?" J.D. inquired. He was obviously the alpha male, because everyone on the block remained quiet.

Seeing the conversation was going nowhere, Qwess stepped out of the car wearing a black two-piece Steel G jean set and mustard-colored construction Timbs.

"Yo, yo that's the boy, Qwess," someone whispered. J.D. recognized him also, but he still didn't give any ground.

"Peace, brothers," Qwess greeted. "Be easy. We come in peace." He walked over to J.D. while Doe pulled the car out of the street. Doe slipped from the Benz and joined Qwess. He was wearing black jeans and a white t-shirt along with Air Force One sneakers.

They stuck their fists out to give J.D. a pound, obviously knowing who was in control of this block at the moment.

"Yo, dawg, I know who you are," J.D. told him. "But laws of the street still apply to you, too. You can't roll on this block any kind of way asking for my li'l homie."

Qwess returned his steely stare right back, "True dat. You know I got mad respect for the streets. I want to do some business with the li'l brother, though."

"Oh, yeah? What kind of business?"

"I'm trying to fuck with him on that music tip."

J.D. paused as if taking his answer into consideration. Then he called out, "Yo, Flame, check this!"

Joey, the young buck who had been taking their money all day, stepped out from the crowd, joining them.

"You know this cat?" J.D. asked him.

"Yeah, I know who he is," Flame answered.

"Well, he says he want to do some business with you."

"Yeah, I heard him. Good looking out, J.D., but we got it from here," he said, motioning toward 8-Ball, who had joined them. "We gonna holla at him, see what he talking 'bout."

"All right. Cool." J.D. responded, somewhat hesitantly. The he added, "Ock, *salaam alaykum*." Qwess and Doe looked at him with a puzzled expression. J.D. pointed to the necklace with the Arabic script around Qwess's neck. Then he pulled out his own chain from underneath his shirt. It had the same charm on it, but was iced out. "I was just fucking with you. Gotta keep my brothers on point," J.D. told them, and he busted out laughing as he walked back over to crowd to continue the dice game.

When it was just Doe, Qwess, Flame, and 8-Ball, the conversation resumed.

"What you two getting into?" Qwess asked them.

"Nothing."

"I want to get at you. You want to go get something to eat?"

"Damn right," 8-Ball offered, rubbing his stomach. "Always!"

They all laughed.

"Word. Let's take a ride then."

They all climbed into the Benz. Doe was driving; 8-Ball was in the passenger seat. Qwess and Flame sat in the back.

Inside the Benz, everyone got comfortable. 8-Ball

pushed buttons adjusting the front seat. Flame sat in the back with his arm on the rest all relaxed, as if he rode in a ninety-thousand-dollar car every day. 8-Ball started touching buttons on the center dash display, until Doe slapped his hand.

"Ow, nigga! Chill, you don't know me like that."

"You better keep your hands off them sounds!"

"All right, nigga, damn!"

Qwess spoke up from the back seat. "Yo, where can we sit and blaze in the car? I know y'all get down."

"Damn right!" 8-Ball answered. "It's a spot over by the park. The rollers don't never come by there."

"All right, cool, show the way."

As they were en route, Qwess pulled out some rolling papers and an ounce of hydro-weed. He meticulously rolled a joint. Flame just looked on, enjoying the ride. He felt like he was in a forest by all the rawhide and wood inside the Benz.

8-Ball looked in the back, noticing Qwess rolling a joint, and immediately spoke up, "Ah, nigga, you rolling a joint! All the paper you sitting on, I know you can afford to roll a blunt."

Qwess shot a glance at Flame. Flame shrugged his shoulders in surrender.

"Yo, chill, nigga," he told 8-Ball.

"I'm just saying, though. The nigga come round here on some ballin' shit, and got the nerve to roll a joint. Nigga, please."

Qwess had had enough. "Nigga, how often do you blow dro?" 8-Ball looked surprised. "Yeah, I thought so. Your li'l young ass probably can't take this much. Now you need to turn your ass around and show where to go before you get an unwanted workout—walking."

8-Ball recognized real and turned around to find Doe gritting on him as well.

Doe tapped him playfully. "Man, calm your big ass down."

8-Ball smiled in return. "All right, I'm cool. Turn here."

Moments later, they reached their destination. They pulled into a spot on the edge of the woods. As Doe turned the car off, Qwess passed him a CD to put in. Then he lit the joint.

"Yo, check this out," Qwess began, talking to Flame. "I'm feeling your shit. I hear you on the radio all the time. I even came to the talent show you did a few months back. You nice. Real nice. You remind me of when I was your age. What you, seventeen?

"Nah, I just turned eighteen."

"Yeah, I been clocking for a minute."

"Aw, nigga, you the man. Stop fronting."

Qwess chuckled. "I like your style."

"I like your style."

Qwess passed Flame the joint. Flame took a pull and started coughing, "Goddamn, this some strong shit!"

"Yeah, all we blow is dro. Give it to your man. Let him taste it."

Flame passed it to 8-Ball, who hit the joint and coughed also.

"Come on, tough guy," Doe told him, laughing. "Man up!"

8-Ball waved his hand in surrender. He passed it to Doe, who declined. It went back to Qwess. Qwess inhaled deeply and started talking again.

"Yo, Flame, I'm talking about us putting you on, nigga. Changing your situation. Making you a star. Only thing is . . ." Qwess paused to blow out the smoke. "I keep hearing you down with that jack shit. See, if we put you on, and you do some bullshit, we all look like fools, and I done been a lot of things, but a fool ain't one."

"Word!" Doe affirmed.

"So, if you doing bullshit, why should we put you on?"

He passed the joint to Flame. Flame took a hit and held in the smoke.

"See, I'm a product of my environment," Flame explained. "I gotta get it how I can. Ain't nobody giving me shit." Flame blew out some smoke. "I ain't never seen my dad, and I don't hardly see my mom. She always working. So, if a nigga can show me a better way to make it, I'll do it. The only thing I know how to do is hustle and rap. My rapping ain't paying bills, so for bread and butter I catch niggas in the gutter."

"Thank you, Biggie Smalls," Doe joked. "Seriously, though, we talking about putting you in a situation where money is your last worry. At eighteen, nigga, you driving a Benz. What you know about that?"

"Sounds good."

"Sounds good? Nigga, that should sound great! We talking 'bout making you a star. Going all over the world. Boning the baddest broads. Ménage à trois style. All you gotta do is listen to the guidance we give you, stay out of trouble, and do what you do: rap."

Flame took it all in, realizing for the first time how serious these cats were. He noticed the music bumping through the speakers. The music was a beat CD that Qwess had recently made.

"Damn, that beat is hot!" Flame said, bobbing his head and rapping to himself.

"No, it's not hot," Qwess told him. "It's missing that Flame. It's missing you. I made that beat with you in mind."

Flame sucked his teeth in disbelief. Qwess sat up in the seat looking directly at Flame and got his full attention. "Yo, straight up, no bullshit. I been hearing about you for a while, so that means you got drive. I like that. It seems like all you need is a chance. Now we willing to give you that chance, but you got to want it. You got to want this music shit like you want your next breath, nigga. You can't slack up for a minute 'cause that's when you lose your edge. You got to be willing to do what it takes to get where you want to be. You got to be professional. You understand that?" Qwess leaned back in his seat and continued. "See, I ain't have nobody to throw me a bone. I wish I did, but I didn't. The only reason why you see my shit in stores is because I put it there. I paid outta my pocket. I hit the highway. I got on my grind. You know why?"

"Why?"

"Because I wanted this shit! Now do you want it?"

"Hell yeah, I want it!"

"How bad do you want it, though?"

"Bad enough."

"You can't want it bad enough, because a brother trying to put you on, and you acting like you offended."

"Nah, it ain't like that. It's just that, in my experience, anything that sounds too good to be true usually is."

"See that's what I'm talking about," Qwess said, nodding his head. "You sharp. I like that, but listen," He looked him dead in the eye. "All I got is my word and my balls. I don't break 'em for nobody. So if I tell you something, you can bank on it. Ask any nigga in the street about me. They'll tell you. They may not like me, but they'll tell you: I don't break my word."

"I kind of heard about you," Flame admitted.

"All right then, listen. Word is bond, if you give me one hundred percent, I'll do the same to you, and we'll smash this muthafucking game. We'll put Carolina on the map like it's supposed to be."

"Word, that's what up," Flame said, looking at 8-Ball in the front seat listening intently.

"I only ask one thing, though," Qwess informed him. "Never lie to me. I gotta be able to trust you to an extent, feel me? We gonna be all over the world. The last thing I need to worry about is the loyalty of the dudes in my camp."

"I can dig that."

"All right, so you with us or what? You gonna help us put Atlantic Beach Productions on the map?"

"Damn right!" 8-Ball answered from the front seat. Doe playfully slapped him on the arm again.

Flame thought for a brief second and answered, "Where do I sign?"

"Word!" Qwess said. "We'll get to that later. I got to put you to the test first. I got make sure you the nicest in the Carolinas."

"Nigga, I'm the nicest in the world," Flame arrogantly assured him.

"We'll see at my party next week. All the top shottas gonna be there. If you smash them, we'll sign the papers and give you your advance."

"Advance?"

"Yeah, advance," Doe threw in. "You think it's a game? We serious about this thing."

Flame nodded his head, "All right then."

8-Ball interrupted, "Aye man, I thought somebody said something about some food. I'm hungrier than a muthafucka."

Everyone agreed. "Let's get some Chinese food," Flame suggested.

"I said I'm hungry, not desperate," 8-Ball joked. "I don't eat nothing I can't pronounce." Everyone broke into laughter.

"We'll get some Captain D's," Doe told them, cranking up the car.

Qwess reached in his pocket, pulling a knot of money out. He counted out six hundreds, six fifties, and five twenties. He slid them to Flame on the low.

"This should keep you out of trouble 'til next week," he told Flame. Flame put it in his pocket without counting it.

"Learn how to budget your money," Doe suggested. "You going to have a lot of it soon. Trust me."

"All right."

"By the way, tell J.D. he's invited to the party. It's Thursday. One week from today."

Flame nodded and kicked back, enjoying the ride. This was the chance he had been waiting for. No way was he going to mess up. He always said the world was going to know his name. He was finally on the brink of his destiny. As of today, he was retired from crime. He was finally getting the chance that he thought everyone got at least once in a lifetime. He was going to run with it. He refused to be denied.

The world was going to be calling his name.

Chapter 8

Reece looked in the mirror one last time, tucking his long locks under a knit cap. It had been three days since the attempt on his life, three days since they had awakened the warrior in him. At this moment, he was in his spacious yet modest home outside of the city waiting on Samson, as he was known in the streets. They were going to spend the day collecting money from his various spots. He had to see this one unscrupulous fella in particular. Reece had broken his own rule and given someone outside the Crescent Crew some work. Now this fella was having "problems" coming up with the money. Reece figured there shouldn't be any "problems" coming up with the money. He damn near gave him the kilo at twenty thousand dollars. Reece knew the guy from way back, which is why he had decided to put him on his feet. Now he wanted to get cute? One thing Reece couldn't stand was for someone to take his kindness for a weakness. If the guy didn't have the money, he was going to find out the hard way, which was why he was bringing Samson.

Samson was six foot seven, three hundred pounds of solid muscle. As if that wasn't enough, he had a twin brother named Wali, whom everyone called Hulk because of his beefy six-foot-six, three-hundred-thirty-pound frame. Together these two had been the muscle for the Crescent Crew since its inception. Back when Qwess came home from the army, he had brought them back with him. They were originally from Mobile, Alabama, and countrier than catfish and grits. Qwess had met them both while in the army. They had brutally assaulted their company commander after he called one of them stupid—in front of the whole platoon. The commander wasn't completely off his assessment; however, neither brother was too fond of it. So, when they were kicked out, they had nowhere to go. They definitely didn't want to go back to Mobile. So Qwess offered them a job with him. As long as there was money involved, they didn't care what the job was. They weren't the most morally adept men. They figured if they could kill for a country, they could do whatever was necessary to obtain a certain lifestyle.

Qwess bought them back to the Carolinas with him. He introduced them to the burgeoning crew. Their orders were simple: Samson went with Reece on pickups (since they clicked) to watch his back, and Hulk shadowed Qwess. Over time, as the Crescent Crew grew in stature and money, Samson and Hulk grew in rank. Now Samson was Reece's lieutenant, keeping all of the others in check; and Hulk still rolled with Qwess everywhere. Only this time, it was on frequent trips out of town to promote his album. Hulk and Samson were both paid to the bone, and loyal to a fault.

Reece checked his Movado for the third time in as many minutes. He was trying to keep schedule because he had a date later that night with Destiny. She was the woman he had met at the restaurant the day Qwess had offered him a record deal. He remembered her like it was yesterday. Her smooth brown skin and thick, slightly bowed

legs. When he first saw her, it was like she was waiting
on him to approach her. Almost like she was profiling in
her coochie-cutters. Surely, he didn't disappoint her. He
had only spoken with her once since then to confirm their
date. Now, for the first time in a long time, he was looking forward to going out with a woman. There was something different about her. She seemed different, a
challenge. She was feisty and firm, as if she didn't give a
damn about who he was out here in these streets. This excited him. After all, every man loved a chase.

He looked out the window and saw Samson's black
Yukon roll up. Actually, he'd heard the pipes rumbling
before he saw it. He double-checked to ensure he wasn't
leaving anything behind, grabbed his pistol, and left out
the door.

Samson got out of the truck and greeted Reece as he
walked out. Samson was dressed identically to Reece:
black cargo pants, long black polo shirt, and black Tim-
berlands. War attire. Samson's jet-black skin and bald
head were in direct contrast to Reece's light brown com-
plexion and long dreads.

"Peace, God." Samson greeted Reece with dap and a
hug.

"Knowledge," Reece responded, getting into the truck.

Inside the truck, *Thug Life: Vol. 1* quaked the four
twelve-inch speakers. Reece leaned the seat back a little
and rode in silence as they headed into the city. He loved
to bump Tupac's music when he put in work. It was as if
he was speaking directly to him, exhorting him to ride out
on his enemies and bomb first. 'Pac never failed to put
him in that zone.

As they were riding down the long, winding country
roads, Samson interrupted Reece's thoughts.

"Yo, God, I heard you turned down the deal Qwess
got for you. What's up with that?"

Reece let the question linger for a moment before he answered.

"See, it's like this," Reece began, lifting his seat up. "I'm in too deep. I've done too much dirt in the streets to seriously pursue a career in the music business." He chuckled. "I mean, picture me being on somebody's TV nationwide. Niggas would flip! I can see it now, *'Yo, that's the nigga that sold me those bricks!' 'That's the nigga that shot my cousin.'* Shit, and we ain't gonna talk about concerts and touring. You know how many families I ruined behind this shit? I'd never feel safe!" Reece shook his head and shuddered at the thought.

"Them niggas you hearing rapping nowadays talking about they did this, and they did that, and woo woo woo, are straight faking. Either that, or them niggas who they claim they did it to are more pussy than them for letting them get away with it. Nah, hell nah! Not me. You won't catch me slipping."

Samson took in what Reece was saying and weighed the words before he responded. "I feel ya, but Qwess facing the same dilemma, and he going through with it."

Reece laughed loudly, pointing his finger at the air, shaking his head. "See, that Qwess is different. He sneaky as shit and he smart. He always dealt exclusively with the crew when it came to handling the work. We all know the fam is mad loyal."

Samson conceded, "True, but what about when he got grimy and had to handle business?"

"He always went by himself!" Reece exclaimed, as if he had made his point. "And the niggas he would go see were never seen again. So, he can do as he pleases. At best, all anyone has is speculation. With me, I like to get down and dirty and leave somebody to tell the tale. Feel me? When I act a donkey, I want the word to spread."

With that point being made, they rode in silence until Reece had another thought.

"See, me, I'm in this until the end. I've been tainted by these streets. I've done too much to ever look back. Plus I'm paid. Shit, the whole crew is paid! What other way can a black man in the United States make the money we're making at our age. Fuck telling me I can't drive a Benz until I'm thirty. Says who? I made up my mind a long time ago. I'd rather die rich than live poor. Ya feel me?"

"Hell, yeah."

Samson turned onto the expressway leading into the city. As they drove closer to the city, an issue that was weighing on his mind kept resurfacing.

"Yo, word on the street that nigga Black Vic dropping salt on you. Talking about he going to shut us down for killing his man. Said he ain't gonna stop until you're dead."

"Man, fuck that nigga!" Reece exploded. "Them niggas got that shit off the other day, but I will *never* get caught slipping like that again. Mu'fucka must be crazy. I'm going to get him right, though. And wait a minute, why the fuck whoever said this shit felt so comfortable saying it to you?"

"Some guy at the gym said he had some info for me about you, so of course I had to see what he was talking about. Said he fucked with you because you gave his kid a backpack when you did your back-to-school drive for the community last year. Anyway, he said his cousin was a part of Black Vic's crew and that they beefing with you because you disrespected Black Vic when you turned him down a few weeks ago for some work."

Reece remembered the incident all too clearly. Just a few weeks ago Black Vic had approached him about partnership. Said it was enough money for everybody. There was no need to go to war. Reece dismissed him in a not so flattering way. Reece knew he had all the cards in his favor. He had the whole Crescent Crew with him, which had expanded throughout the Carolinas. All of them, thoroughbreds, proven in bloodshed. Then he had the better connection. With his new connect, he was getting kilos at ten grand a pop. So, of course, he spread the love to his crew. He would give them to his crew for fifteen grand a pop. Exclusively. At those prices, the other dealers—including Black Vic—would go broke trying to compete. He knew this. Reece also knew it was only a matter of time before they had to go to war. He honestly felt like the Crescent Crew was too strong. So, if Vic wanted a war, he'd get one. In Reece's eyes it would only make it easier to monopolize the Carolinas. With rival crews out of the way, the Crescent Crew would run North and South Carolina.

"Oh, yeah?" Reece asked. "So then what? What happened to the messenger? You broke him off?"

Samson chuckled. "Shole did—right in his runny mouth. Told him don't bring no bullshit to me about what another nigga said about you, unless he bringing him with him."

Reece smiled. "My nigga. That's what the fuck I'm talking about."

Samson glanced at Reece. "So, you absolutely sure you don't want to get in with Qwess?"

"I'm already in," Reece said.

With Qwess getting his deal, it would also make it easy to clean up dirty money. Unbeknownst to everyone else, it was Reece who had actually given Qwess the money for his studio on Bragg Boulevard, and the money to set up A.B.P. So Qwess was actually in his debt. However, Reece didn't sweat it. That's what brothers are for. Truth be told, Reece would be happy to continue laundering money through his car lots and funeral homes, but they hadn't been around long enough to be million-dollar enterprises. With this new connect, Reece was definitely about to touch millions. The music business would be the perfect Laundromat.

"Yo, you got that thing I asked you to bring?" Reece asked.

Samson nodded. "I got that thing you wanted me to bring."

"Good, good. When we get there, just follow my lead. We gon' show these niggas what time it is." Reece turned the music up, leaned back into the seat, and let the music put him in the zone.

"Thug Life. Y'all Know the Rules. Gotta do whatcha gotta do . . . Stay true!"

When the black Yukon pulled onto the block, the hustlers who were out there paused. The first thing they noticed was the license plate on the front. It was actually a designer plate that had a crescent star and two C's between them. Everyone on the block knew that this was the Crescent Crew's coat of arms, or sign. They just didn't know why anyone from that crew would be here. This wasn't their block.

Reece stepped out of the truck and set the block ablaze with his presence. Onlookers' mouths were agape. It seemed Reece had fallen off the loot, because the last time they had seen him, he was stepping out of a Benz coupe in a silk suit. Silk suits were his trademark. To see him in the uniform of the streets could only mean one thing.

"Yo, anybody seen Tyrone?" Reece asked everyone and no one in particular.

There were some kids eagerly anticipating the ice-cream truck, which was coming up the street. There were a few adults out as well, but the block was mostly filled with young hustlers.

Reece walked smoothly up to the kids, now at the ice-cream truck. He pulled out a crisp one-hundred-dollar bill, passing it off to the ice-cream man. "Everything's on me. No disrespect, Pops," Reece said to an older gentleman.

"None taken," the old man responded, holding up his hands in surrender.

As Reece was waiting to make sure the kids got everything they wanted, one of the kids pulled him to the side. He informed him that Tyrone was inside a soul food restaurant located just up the street. Reece thanked the little boy, sliding him a hundred-dollar bill, and proceeded up the street. As he walked past the truck, Samson got out and fell in step. He was holding a small briefcase in his left hand.

The restaurant was a small mom-and-pop type deal. Reece and Sampson entered and spotted Tyrone immediately. He was sitting at the bar obviously waiting on some food. He didn't notice Reece and Samson at first. Then he felt a huge shadow at his back. He turned around in time to catch Samson's massive hand under his throat.

"Hey man, w-what's up?" he gasped.

"You know what's up," Reece spat. "Time to pay the piper, mu'fucka!"

Samson snatched him off the stool with one arm and cradled him with the other as he carried him out the door. Reece picked up the briefcase and followed him.

When they got outside, all of the hustlers saw Tyrone in the air and looked like they wanted to interfere. However, Reece shot them all a menacing stare, palming his Glock in his waistband.

"This ain't about you all," Reece told them. "Don't waste your life over a bad paymaster."

The hustlers reluctantly backed off. Reece noticed the children coming back from the ice-cream truck, and motioned for Samson to throw Tyrone in the Yukon. Samson did so, joining Tyrone in the third-row seat. Reece jumped into the driver's seat and peeled off.

Inside the truck, Tyrone uselessly tried to cop pleas. Samson had palmed the back of his neck at this point.

"Y-yo, king man. I got your money!" Tyrone cried. "W-well, not all of it. Something came up, but word is bond, I got you!"

Reece remained silent as he pulled into an alleyway. When he pulled far enough from the street, he stopped the truck and got out.

Inside the alleyway, there were overturned crates and boxes. Reece sat one on top of another, forming a make-shift table. Samson and Tyrone joined the party. Samson had Tyrone in a yoke. His massive biceps were entrenched all around Tyrone's head.

Reece opened up the briefcase and pulled out a small black tarp. He gently laid it on the table. Next he pulled out a twelve-inch, single-edged blade. It was razor sharp.

Tyrone's eyes bulged as the realization of what was about to happen hit him. Samson grabbed Tyrone's skinny arm and brutally slammed it onto the table. His right hand conveniently fell right onto the tarp. His feet still dangled in the air, as Samson's large frame smothered him from behind. Once again he tried to cop pleas.

"K-king man, I wear I'll have your money . . . with interest," Tyrone stammered.

"Quit bitching and man up!" Reece screamed at him. Spittle was forming in the corners of Reece's mouth. He was seemingly about to lose it, but he remained calm.

"I tried to give your bitch ass a chance to get on your

feet. I hit you with consignment, and you decide to keep shit," Reece chastised. "You want to take my kindness for weakness? Now you gotta learn."

"Man, I—I just need more time."

"Nigga, you had my shit three weeks. What kind of hustler are you? Can't get a few grand in three weeks!"

"I—I just need a little more time. Come on, man! We go way back."

Reece remained calm, but began to chuckle.

"Oh, I am gon' give you more time. I'm just going to give you a little motivation. You stealing from my pot with your tardiness. When you deal with Crescent Crew, the penalty for stealing is a hand. Can you afford that, nigga?"

"Oh, God, Lord, please." Tyrone begged.

"Stop it. You flatter me," Reece joked. He referred to himself as a God-body. "You took my shit like a man, now take my shit . . . like a man."

Reece knew the anticipation was killing him. He had seen men pass out from the thought of losing their hand. You would think Tyrone would've heard about him by now. Oh, well, he'd definitely remember him now.

Reece placed his hand over Tyrone's extended wrist and held the blade in the other hand. Instead of pulling the blade to Tyrone's wrist, Reece put it over his middle finger. Tyrone's attempts at moving his hand were futile. Samson had a vice grip on it.

Reece held the blade past the second joint on Tyrone's middle finger, almost to his knuckles.

"From now on," Reece told him, slowly applying pressure on the knife, "every time I see you and you don't have my money, I'm taking one of your fucking fingers as collateral!" Reece chopped the blade down the rest of the way. Tyrone's finger came off as easily as cutting cold butter with a hot knife. His bloodcurdling scream could be heard for blocks. Reece wiped the blood from the blade onto Tyrone's sweater and watched as he crumpled to the ground with blood spurting from his hand.

The hit on Reece had brought the worst out of him. Now he was on a warpath to ring his name in the streets like the Liberty Bell. The streets were going to run ill with bloodshed until someone coughed up Black Vic.

Reece exited the shower, looking at the clock. It was a quarter after six. He had plenty of time. He wasn't supposed to meet Destiny until seven. He was meeting her at a neutral location because she didn't want him to know where she lived. Reece couldn't believe the audacity of this chick. Like he was some sort of pervert or something! If anything, he had so many broads he had to turn down snatch. Fuck was *she* thinking?

He walked around his spacious bedroom stark naked. He enjoyed it, as he was an exhibitionist at heart. The events of that afternoon were still fresh in his mind. It didn't bother him, though. It was the price of doing business. Reece understood that, in the streets, fear is the strongest emotion. The minute people didn't have some amount of fear of you, things were going to go wrong.

Reece walked into his closet and pulled out a bag straight from the cleaners. Inside the bag was a dark green two-piece suit. The fabric was a cotton-silk blend. He bent to retrieve a t-shirt out of his drawer. Next, he selected a white mock-turtleneck silk sweater. He topped the ensemble off with burnt-orange alligator loafers and matching belt.

He dressed in no time. He put on some Issey Miyake oil and pulled his long locks straight back into a ponytail. This accentuated his strong jaw line, as well as his chin-strap beard.

Reece checked his perimeter cameras to make sure they were functioning. Then he pressed record. No one could even come by his house without him knowing. He went into the garage.

While some people struggle and strive, his hardest choice was which car to drive. He selected his Acura RL, with its snow-white interior.

Reece arrived at the designated meeting place—a gas station—at five to seven. He immediately spotted Destiny's red Honda. He pulled in right beside it. He noticed Destiny sitting on the passenger side talking to a woman whom he presumed was a friend. Destiny hadn't noticed Reece yet, because she didn't know what he would be driving.

Reece smoothly exited the car and tapped on the window. Destiny and her friend both jumped.

"Boo! I scared you," Reece joked.

Destiny covered her heart with one hand and waved her face with the other.

"Wooh. That you did," she admitted.

Reece opened the door the rest of the way and held it as Destiny sensually got out of the car.

"I'm good, Deb. Thanks," Destiny told her friend, who cranked up the car and left.

Reece escorted Destiny to the passenger side of the Acura and opened the door for her. As she carefully sat in the car, Reece admired her slip dress. It stopped just above her knee and was hugging her curves something serious. She wore matching black sandals with diamond studs adorning the straps that led up to her ankles. Her brown hair was wrapped into a short beehive. She wore diamond earrings that extended an inch from her ear. Around her neck was a matching choker. Her flawless skin was glistening like it was wet. Destiny truly was a sight to behold!

"Damn, you are beautiful," Reece whispered more to himself than to Destiny. She still heard him.

"Thank you," she told him. "You look damn good yourself. I didn't realize you were as tall as you are."

Reece's shoes added about two inches to his height, making him six-three, if only for the night.

He closed her door and got in on his side. He glanced over at Destiny. She looked right at home in the plush leather seats. As he was pulling out, an SUV quickly pulled up behind him, blocking his way out. The day's events were still fresh in his mind, so he calmly reached for his pistol so smooth that he was sure Destiny didn't notice.

Luckily, it was a false alarm. It was Qwess. He was driving his Cadillac Escalade. The window rolled down to reveal Qwess laughing hysterically.

"Aha, I got you!" Qwess joked. "You shook like dice, too!"

Reece didn't like it, but he had to admit it: Qwess had got him good. Qwess jumped out of the truck, walking over to Reece's Acura. He leaned into the driver's window and peered in.

"Damn, bro, who is that?" Qwess asked.

Reece, obviously uncomfortable, answered, "This is Destiny. You remember from the other day?"

"Oh, yeah! She looks different."

Destiny mumbled under her breath, "You got so many, can't keep count, huh?"

"Hey, hey," Reece chided. "Cut that out."

Destiny giggled.

"Yo, where you going all dressed up?" Reece asked Qwess. Qwess had on a suit similar to the one Reece wore. However, Qwess's suit was black, and he was rocking a derby hat with it.

"We about to see this play."

"Who that? Shauntay?"

"Yeah."

Reece stuck his head out the window. "Aye, girl!" he yelled.

"Heeey, Reece!" Shauntay yelled back. "What's up!"

"Chillin'!"

"All right, I'll see you later." Shauntay rolled the window back up.

Qwess gestured for Reece to get out of the car. "Let me holla at you a sec." When Reece got out and stepped a few feet from the car, Qwess continued. "Yo, you heard about the tour already, right?"

"Yeah."

"So what's up? You wanna roll with me? You can use the break. It might be good for you to get a change of scenery. I heard about what happened today."

Reece sucked his teeth. "Man, don't start."

"Nah, I ain't tripping on that. They did what they did so you gotta do what you gotta do." Qwess shrugged. "I'm talking about *you*. I think this will be a good look for you, give you a chance to clear your head. So, you want to roll or not? We are going all over Europe, places in the motherland . . . everywhere. For free! It won't be right if you not there. I couldn't be doing this without your help; it's only right that you come."

Reece paused a moment to contemplate. "I don't know, man. I told you I just started this new thing. I gotta keep my eye on things, you know?"

"Man, Samson and the Crew can handle things for a few. It'll give you a chance to get your mind right," Qwess coaxed.

"I don't know right now. I'll get back with you, though."

"All right. You coming to the party, right?"

"You kidding? I wouldn't miss it for all the gold in

the world. Matter of fact, the whole Crescent Crew gonna be there in all our splendor."

"Word?" Qwess asked. He was surprised, because the crew had expanded all over the Carolinas, as well as parts of New Jersey and Florida.

"Well, you know. The Carolina fam anyway. You know we gotta see our man off right. This party is like your official retirement from the trap. Even though you not in the trap no more, we still look at you as a boss. You helped us start this shit, nigga, Crescent Crew for life, baby! Ride or die!"

A horn blew, interrupting the moment. It was Reece's car. "Reece, what time are the reservations?" Destiny yelled from the passenger seat.

Reece took the hint and bid farewell to Qwess. They jumped in their respective cars and drove off.

When Qwess got back in the Escalade, Shauntay was wearing a look of concern on her face. When Qwess asked what was wrong, she evaded him until she couldn't anymore. She finally came out with it.

"How many hoes does Reece have?"

"What?" Qwess asked, unbelieving. "Why would you ask me something like that?"

"Because every time I see him, he with a different girl."

"Sooo?"

"Sooo, birds of a feather flock together. How many hoes you got?"

Qwess couldn't contain his laughter. "You trippin', Shauntay."

Shauntay was determined. "No, I mean seriously. I know hoes be trying to holla, so what's there to stop you. Especially with Reece condoning it." Qwess didn't respond. "I mean, you never tell me you love me, and I know I gained a few pounds. Do you still find me attractive, Qwess?"

Qwess sensed she needed validation. That's what was wrong. She was already starting to feel insecure because he was now playing with a different kind of money.

"Baby, of course you're beautiful," Qwess assured her.

"Then why you never tell me you love me?"

Qwess didn't answer. How was he supposed to tell her that he was incapable of love? The streets, and all that came with them, had bred love out of him.

"Shauntay, I could tell you anything I want, but it's my actions that should matter."

That apparently did the trick because she left the subject alone. Instead, she turned up the radio. It was playing *Mind Sex* by Dead Prez. How ironic.

Reece and Destiny arrived at the Japanese restaurant five minutes after eight. The hostess was eagerly anticipating their arrival. This was apparent by the look of relief on her face when Reece announced they had reservations under the name Kirkson. The hostess was immaculately dressed in a white satin kimono with red trim. Her face was painted in a traditional Japanese style with white base and red accent. It seemed exaggerated, but to one who understood Japanese customs, it fit just fine. It was the uniform of geisha.

She led Reece and Destiny to their table, which was secluded from the rest of the restaurant. The restaurant was divided into sections. On one side there was communal sitting, and the other was more couples oriented. This was the side Reece and Destiny sat in. All of the tables had candles on them. With the candlelight flickering throughout the room, it created an ambience of extreme comfort. Each table had a complimentary cup of sake for the patrons. This was intended to be an appetizer.

The hostess sat Reese and Destiny at their tables. Reece pulled out Destiny's chair for her, then bid the hostess farewell. Menus were on the table, and as they perused the menus, Destiny couldn't hold it in.

"This is nice, Reece, or should I call you King?" she asked sarcastically.

"You can call me what you want," he responded. "Just don't call me too late for nothing good."

Destiny smiled, but she still didn't let up. "So, do you bring your hoes—oops, I mean honeys—here often?"

Reece saw where this was going and decided to play along.

"Nope, you're the only hoe—oops—I mean honey that I've been out with in a while," he said, never looking up from the menu.

Destiny conceded. "O-kaay. Point taken," she said. "But seriously, do you come here often?"

Reece lowered the menu momentarily, looking at Destiny. "Destiny, I'm serious. Most of the women I meet are really not deserving of this type of date."

"So, what makes me different?" Destiny shot back.

"Well, for starters, when you found out who I was, you didn't try to push up on me, trying to fuck me."

"Ooh."

"I apologize if I'm too blunt, but I'm a realist. I deal with the actual factual. If my language offends you, let me know."

"No, it's not the language," Destiny assured him. "It's the statement itself."

Reece placed the menu down and got serious for a moment. "I'm serious," he told her. "If a woman isn't trying to trick straight up, she's trying to play all kind of cute games to get a brother to spend anyway."

Destiny listened and responded. "Well that doesn't say much about the vibes you put out."

"Excuse me?" Reece asked unbelievingly.

"I'm saying, for these women to feel like they can get in your pockets so easy says something about the message you sending."

Reece reasoned with her. "Maybe."

Destiny nodded her head. "Of course."

"Or," Reece continued, "maybe they go by what they hear, like some other people I know." He shot her an accusing look.

"Who, me?" Destiny asked innocently.

"Yeah, you. By the way, what was it you heard? 'Cause, damn, the way you acting, you'd think I killed Kennedy." Reece laughed at the thought.

Destiny threw a breadstick from the basket on the table at him playfully. "It's not funny. I did hear some crazy things about you."

"Oh, yeah?"

"Yeah."

"Like what?"

"Well, for one, I heard that you sell drugs . . . lots of it, too. Then I heard that the Crescent Crew,"—she accented quotation marks with her hands—"are nothing but a bunch of murderers, drug dealers, and notorious playboys. And you're the leader."

Reece mockingly shuddered his shoulders. "Whew, they sound like a rough bunch! Got me scared just thinking about them," he retorted.

"I'm serious, Reece," she insisted. "And I heard that your guys had something to do with the body that was found hanging from a high-rise downtown a few weeks ago."

At the mention of the murder, Reece perked up, but he was too much of a vet to let it show on his face. "Well, that shit sound crazy," he said, sipping some of his warm sake. "I'm just glad you don't believe it."

Destiny raised her eyebrows. "How do you know I don't believe it?"

Reece jumped to answer like that was the million-dollar question. "If you believe it, why are you here with me alone? For all you know I could kidnap you, and no one would ever see you again." He smiled confidently, raising his eyebrows.

Destiny spoke in slow, measured tones. "You know I thought of that."

"Oh, yeah?" Reece challenged.

"Yeah, that's why I got my girlfriend to get your tag number. So if I'm not home by twelve, she going to call the police." She smiled and arched her eyebrows this time. Checkmate.

The waitress came to take their orders. She was dressed as a geisha as well. Reece ordered yakitori. It sounded so good, Destiny ordered the same. The waitress brought more sake and bread before she left them alone again. When they were alone, round two began.

"So, Reece, let me get this right? You don't sell drugs, but you drive around in ninety-thousand-dollar Porsches, wear silk on the regular, and you're wearing a Rolex that probably costs more than the average person's house." Destiny paused for emphasis. "May I ask what do you do for a living?"

Reece leaned farther back in the chair, sizing her up, deciding how much of himself he wanted to reveal. "Well, I own a few car dealerships," he casually admitted.

Destiny looked at him, pleading for more. She obviously didn't believe owning a few car lots could accurately account for the lavish lifestyle he lived.

"So let me get this right," she questioned. "You have three cars, none of them costing less than fifty grand, a home in the country—"

"Hold up!" Reece interrupted. "Fuck are you, police?"

"Yeah," she answered unflinchingly, before breaking into a laugh. "I'm just kidding, man," Destiny assured him. "Relax, Reece, don't be surprised. We live in the information age. You can find anything you want to know about someone right off the Internet. All you really need is a name, if you know where to look. I must admit, I looked you up. I apologize, but I was curious."

She looked deeply into Reece's eyes, silently begging forgiveness. Reece stared back into her eyes intensely, as if trying to read them. After a short while, he broke the stare down.

"Don't sweat it," Reece told Destiny. "I guess there's not enough information on the Internet to hurt me. If anything, it proves my case. I'm not a drug dealer." Reece made a mental note to check the Internet as soon as possible to see what it held about him.

"Score one for Reece. I guess you're right," Destiny replied.

"So, what do you do for a living?" Reece asked, taking the subject off of him. He sipped his sake while she talked.

"I'm a student. I take criminal justice at UNC. I'm in my second year this semester."

Reece looked from side to side as if he missed something. "What do you do for a living?" he repeated. "You drive around in a Honda Accord, wear slip dresses with diamond-dipped sandals, keep your do freshly dipped . . ."

Reece was turning the tables. Destiny was agitated and charmed at the same time. She hated to admit it, but she was actually feeling Reece. His sense of humor was a plus.

Destiny turned her mouth up at him. "Real cute," she said.

"Hey, I'm just saying, I need to know, because for all I know you could be a drug dealer," Reece taunted, innocently shrugging his shoulders.

"Hee-hee-hee. You made your point. I'm a daddy's girl. My father takes care of me."

"Your father? How old are you, girl!? I ain't down with the R. Kelly thang."

Destiny was in stitches. She was really enjoying this. "Boy, I'm twenty-four."

"Oh, whew!" Reece remarked, playfully rubbing his forehead.

Their conversation was interrupted as their cook, who introduced himself as Haiku, rolled his whole cooking apparatus in front of their table.

This was a restaurant where you were entertained as well as fed. The cook cooked the whole meal in front of them. He spiced things up by flipping food, chopping different ingredients up with huge knives, eyes closed, all the while telling you each dish's name and origin.

Haiku held a broiled shrimp to Destiny's mouth on a chopstick. She ate it off the chopstick and complimented the chef. She was having a ball.

Reece was enjoying himself as well. This was the most fun he'd had with a woman in a while. Just pure fun, no sex. This was an anomaly for him. Because he was so eccentric, he rarely found a woman he had chemistry with out of bed. However with Destiny, it was different.

After they ate the main course, they talked over dessert. Destiny was abreast of world politics. To her surprise, Reece wasn't just abreast of world politics; he was fluent in history, world economics, and especially world wars. He completely broke down the cause of World War II and all but declared Hitler a genius. He could even break down the number of miles to the sun and how much the planet weighed . . . though Destiny questioned his estimates for lack of proof. She was genuinely surprised. Reece was a regular Renaissance man. To say she was impressed would be an understatement.

When the night was over, he dropped her off at her girlfriend's house. They promised to do this again soon. Real soon, as Reece didn't like long-term plans. He was a live-for-today type of guy.

Chapter 9

The cars rolled into the storage garage off Hope Mills Road one by one, single-file. There was a black Lexus LS 430, followed by a Jaguar S-type. They were followed by two black 4Runners. Standing on his 350Z, at the end of the garage, was Black Vic. He was coked up and eagerly anticipating the arrival of his guests.

Each vehicle came to a stop just a few feet from where Black was parked. The occupants exited the car and Black greeted each of them.

"What's up, Scar." He drove the Lexus.

"What's the deal, D." He drove the Jag.

The occupants of the 4Runners were never referred to by name, only by their title: Blood Team. There were four of them in all, two per truck. They were known in certain circles, but Black had never met them personally until now. They had been enlisted by the gentlemen in the first two cars, Scar and D, who were business partners of Black. They all shared a common problem: They couldn't make any money because of the Crescent Crew. They all agreed the best way to get rid of the problem was to eliminate Reece, in the hope that with the head cut off, the body would fall. Then all could make money again.

Black jumped off the car, joining the rest of the crowd. "Yo, I'm glad you could make it," Black opened.

Scar nodded. "Of course. We need to deal with this problem." Scar was short and stocky. He resembled a penguin, but his nice clothes and charisma made him attractive. He was thirty-six years old, and for the last fifteen years had had a strong hold on the west side of town, off Cumberland Road. Until now, any major weight came through him. He owned businesses and was well-respected in every hood.

"Preferably as soon as possible." That was D. He was short also, but he had a muscular, athletic build. His curly hair and light skin made him a ladies' man. It also made him suspect to the other dealers. They thought him too soft to deal with tough issues. Little did they know, when prodded, he was more vicious than the most vicious. He owned businesses as well and was so far removed from the streets, he only saw his product once in its route to the inner cities of the Carolinas. D was twenty-eight years old.

"Of course, that's why we're here," Black said, pinching his nose. "We've been doing business for a long time. Too late to let this nigga come in and stop it."

"Uh, Black, did you go to him with the proposal like we suggested?" Scar asked, always the businessman.

"Yeah."

"What did he say?"

"Told me they were self-contained. They didn't need me for anything. Damn near spit in my face. I started to shoot his ass right then," Black relayed. He was getting more heated by the minute.

"Calm down, Black," D cooed. He was always smooth.

"Yeah, calm down," Scar agreed. "We're glad you didn't do that. We don't need any extra heat on you or your crew, which is why we hired the Blood Team here." He gestured to the four men in the back. "I know you can handle it, but to be safe, we want them to handle it. They're professionals."

Right on cue, one of the four men stepped forward. Black presumed he was the leader. He carried himself with assurance. It's just something about being there when someone meets their maker that gives one certain poise. Especially if you caused it.

The man spoke, "For twenty-five K, we'll bring his head to you, if that's what you want." He was dead serious. There wasn't a hint of amusement in his voice. He waited on an answer on the decapitation, which tripped Vic out when he realized it.

"Oh, nah, man. That won't be necessary," Vic replied. "Just make sure he's dead, that's all."

"Now, Vic, listen. We're not trying to say we can handle your business better than you," Scar clarified. "We're just trying to help you. Everybody wins this way."

Vic understood exactly what he meant. Scar supplied Vic cocaine, and D supplied Vic heroin. If Vic didn't make money, they didn't make money. Everybody loses. If they lent Vic this hit squad, the competition would be eliminated. Everybody wins. Vic's hands would never get dirty. In fact, he was going away to the Bahamas for two weeks Monday morning for an alibi.

As long as Vic wasn't implicated in a murder, they wouldn't be implicated by Vic for anything. It was simply business. Vic had been dealing with D and Scar since he was twenty-three years old. He was twenty-six years old now.

"I understand that," Vic told Scar.

The hit man spoke. "Look, man, all we need to know

is what kind of car he drives, what he's called on the street. All of that."

"I know you heard of him. His name is King."

"King?" The hit man asked, shocked. "As in King Reece?"

"Yeah, mu'fucka! Why? Is there a problem?" Black asked, agitated. He felt offended that the killer was giving Reece so much respect.

"Hold on, dawg. Be easy," the hit man pleaded. "It ain't a problem, as long as the money ain't a problem."

"I got the money." Black whistled, and his right-hand man, Hardtime, emerged from the shadows with a brown bag. He spread the contents of the bag onto the hood of Scar's Lexus. There were five stacks of money carefully wrapped.

"It's all there. You can count it," Hardtime told him.

"Wait a minute," D interrupted, looking at Scar. "Put the money up. We got this. Right, Scar?"

"Yeah, we got it."

"Hold up. I carry my own weight," Black protested. He never wanted to appear weak.

Scar walked over to him and put his arm around his shoulder. "Come on now. Don't be so testy. What's a favor between friends? This is *all* of our problem. Let us handle this." He whispered in Black's ear, "Remember, everybody wins."

That did the trick. Black reluctantly agreed. He reasoned, *Hell, if they want to spend twenty-five grand on that, more money for me.*

"All right, cool," Black said aloud.

"Good, now when do you want it done?" the hit man asked.

"Listen, all you have to do is have it done this week. I know he's going to be at that party Thursday. That's the best time."

"Are you crazy? Everybody in the Southeast is going to be at that party!" Scar exploded.

"Exactly, which will make him an easy target," Black reasoned.

The hit man watched them go back and forth for a moment. Then he spoke. "Don't worry, we'll handle it. If it's the party you want, it's the party you'll get." Then he added with a smile, "After all, the customer is always right."

That concluded the meeting. Everyone loaded into their cars and headed to their respective parts of town, except Vic. He stayed inside the garage with Hardtime. They poured a big bag of cocaine onto the hood of the 350Z and snorted for the rest of the night. Vic inwardly rejoiced. He was close to solving his dilemma and getting back to the money.

He warned the streets before. Now, they were going to learn about messing with Black Vic.

At the exact moment Black Vic was plotting Reece's demise, Reece and Samson sat in an old Chevy across the street from a single-story family home in Hollywood Heights. It was just after midnight, and there wasn't a car on the block. Samson had backed the Chevy up in the carport of the empty house about a half hour ago. They had been watching the house across the street ever since. The home belonged to the shooter who had taken aim at Reece that day in traffic.

After the incident, Reece had put a substantial amount of money in the street to track down whoever had the audacity to take aim at his life. It took a few weeks for the money to dance and do its thing, but in the end, the info moonwalked right back into Reece's lap.

Now he was here to right a wrong.

"How much longer we gonna wait?" Samson whispered, looking around. Even though the windows were rolled up airtight, Samson's mood still had him whispering. "You know how these neighborhoods are, they can spot something out the ordinary like a bloodhound can a coon."

Reece glanced at his partner, confused. Sometimes Reece forgot Samson was just a country boy at heart. He was a dangerous country boy, but a country boy nonetheless. "Just a few more minutes," Reece replied, never taking his eyes off the light in one of the bedrooms. "A few more minutes."

Reece's two-way buzzed to life, scaring the shit out of them both. He checked it. A message from Destiny. He smiled as he replied to the message.

"Damn, what got you cheesing over there?" Samson wondered.

"Huh? Ohhh, ole girl just hit me up."

"Which one?"

"Destiny, the one I went out with the other night."

"You must be feeling this one. I haven't never seen you smile like that."

Reece smiled, recalling some of their conversations. Since their date, they had talked every day, three and four times a day, long, thought-provoking conversations. "Yeah, this one seems different, bro."

"Oh, yeah? How so?"

"I can't put my finger on it, but she just seems different. The more time I spend around her, I'll figure it out." Reece was actually looking forward to spending time with Destiny. He had already invited her to Qwess's party. Her message asked if her uncle could tag along with her.

"Yeah, this is definitely different," Samson joked.

"Chill with that, bro. Matter fact, let's go."

The two men walked across the street, casually holding long objects in their hands, as if they were simply enjoying the weather. They walked up onto the porch, and Reece held the screen door open. Samson raised his big boot up and crashed it into the door.

The door burst open, nearly splintering off the hinges.

Samson rushed in with Reece close on his heels. A man was lying on the couch in the front room. When he saw the giant rush in, he hopped off the couch—right into Samson's clutches. Samson hoisted the man high into the air and slammed him into the wall, nearly throwing him clean through the drywall. "Where you think you going? We need to talk to you."

The man's legs dangled in the air like a baby. "You got the wrong guy!" he pleaded, kicking and struggling to free himself from the grip around his neck. "I didn't do nothing to . . ."

His words trailed off into deep space when he saw Reece step around Samson.

"What you say?" Reece taunted, touching the bandage on his face. "You didn't do what?"

"Reece, man, they told me if I didn't do it, they would kill me!" the man lied.

Reece smirked and shook his head. "And yet here you are about to meet the same fate."

"Reece, man, please! Wait, I got information, man!"

Reece gestured for Samson to put him down. As soon as his feet touched the ground, his mouth opened. "I know where Black Vic lives, I know where his mama live, his baby mama, too."

Clunk!

While the man was snitching, Reece swung the tire iron from the old Chevy and caught him right on the side of the head. A sickening thud echoed throughout the room, and the man crumpled to the floor gripping the knot that had instantly popped up on his head.

"We know where he live, too, snitch-ass nigga!" Reece barked. Samson checked the other bedrooms while Reece waited for his victim to recover. "You really thought you were going to get away with shooting at me? Do you know who the fuck I am? This my motherfucking city!"

Reece was so amped up, he raised the tire iron high into the air and brought it crashing down across the man's back again and again. Samson returned from his search of the house just in time to see Reece deliver the final blow to the back with the tire iron.

"Is he dead?" Samson asked.

Reece paused a moment and stood tall over the beaten man, his chest heaving. He raised the tire iron high into the air and split his skull open with the steel.

"If he wasn't, I'm sure he is now."

Chapter 10

Shauntay dried Qwess off with the towel. He had just gotten out of the shower stark naked. Shauntay was wearing nothing but a thong and a smile. When she got down to his dick, she spent extra time drying it off. She caressed it with her hand before bending down to kiss it.

"You keep doing that and we won't be going nowhere," Qwess said.

"Promise?" Shauntay purred.

She finished drying him off and disappeared into the other room. When she came back, Qwess was half dressed standing in front of the mirror putting Sportin' Waves pomade in his hair.

Shauntay took a moment to admire her man. She thought he looked so handsome with his cream slacks and cream colored ostrich-skin boots. He wasn't wearing a shirt, which was perfect for Shauntay. She walked in front of him carrying a long, gift-wrapped rectangular box. She passed Qwess the box. "Happy birthday!" Shauntay said, clapping her hands in mock amusement.

Qwess thoughtfully caressed the box before tearing the paper off. He opened the box. Inside was a diamond-encrusted A.B.P. pendant about three inches long. Beside it was a square-cut diamond earring. Qwess was ecstatic! Baby girl had gone all out! He enjoyed it more because it showed Shauntay wasn't selfish. He knew she knew he was in the position to buy himself anything he wanted for his birthday, so gifts weren't a biggie to him. However, the fact that she went out and got this was a testament to her selflessness. He was impressed and told her so.

Shauntay coolly responded by helping him put the jewelry on. It complemented the birthday present he had gotten for himself: a one-and-a-half-inch-thick diamond-encrusted bracelet. Shauntay loved the way the light reflected off the diamonds, making Qwess's neck glow. To her he looked like a king in regal splendor. Qwess pulled on his V-necked, ribbed, short-sleeved cream shirt and left the room.

When Qwess left the room, Shauntay quickly dressed. She was wearing a cream-colored strapless tube dress, with matching Xena sandals. The straps nearly came up to her knees. Simple yet elegant. She wanted to shine and show all the bitches what Qwess was working with. She posed in the mirror, very satisfied. Her curves were prominently on display. She knew that tonight every broad would want to be her, and every dude would want to be with her!

Let the party begin.

At 15,000 square feet, 919 Live was a large club by any standards. It boasted two levels, the second portion being mostly the VIP section. Half of the floor was encased in glass, allowing the occupants of the VIP section to look down on the rest of the club. There was a sunken dance floor on the first level, so one could look down in there and admire the dancers.

Tonight was a special night. It was evident by the kaleidoscope of guests in the crowd. You had ballers from as far away as Greensboro, North Carolina, all the way to Atlanta, Georgia. There were numerous Carolina Panthers football players in the house, too. The DJ from the local radio station was broadcasting live. News was out about Qwess signing with AMG, so this was more than a birthday party. This was a celebration. One of Carolina's own had made it, and everyone came to pay homage to one of their own.

"Damn, this shit is thick!" 8-Ball said to Flame, as they pushed their way through the crowd. They had just arrived to the club along with some of Fayetteville's finest, including J.D.

It was a little after eleven, and the club was packed already. However the guest of honor hadn't arrived yet, though Reece was in the house early.

Reece wore a green two-piece suit with four buttons and a mock collar. Of course, it was made of silk. The Crescent Crew colors were cream and green, which represented cocaine and money. Since this party was a big event for one of their own, everyone agreed to fly the flag by wearing either green, white, or a combination of the two. There were members coming from all over the Carolinas. The crew was going to be thick! Reece tugged at the platinum chain around his neck. On the medallion was the Crescent Crew logo: a star and crescent with two C's in the middle. There was going to be no mistaking who was in the house tonight.

"Yo, what the fuck is this, a St. Patrick's Day celebration or something?" 8-Ball joked to Flame. "What's up with all these niggas in green?"

He was referring to the Crescent Crew, who had hogged

a spot by the bar. They were about forty deep at this point. Everyone from the top shot callers to their young squads were present. They were all surrounding Reece and Samson, who never left Reece's side in public settings such as this.

"I don't know. I think that's the *crepit* crew or some shit like that," Flame guessed, butchering the name. "I believe that's ole boy them peoples. But I ain't know they was that deep. Gotdamn."

8-Ball sized the crew up before speaking again. "Hell, yeah. All them niggas in the game, and it look like they all winning, too." He laughed.

The DJ was playing everything out of the Wu-Tang Clan's arsenal. He knew this crowd liked that real hip-hop. He gave shout-outs to the whole Crescent Crew. He worked the crowd into a frenzy and back down. Then he noticed Qwess coming through the door accompanied by Hulk, Doe, and Shauntay.

"Big up to my man, Qwess. Happy birthday, nigga!" DJ Mike Technique screamed over the music. It was official. The party had started.

Qwess threw up a hand in salute. The crowd noticed him and instantly gravitated toward him, only to be met by 330 pounds of muscle. Qwess navigated his way through the crowd to the bar where his crew was posted, with Shauntay between him and Doe.

Qwess and Doe were met with a phalanx of pounds and hugs. Qwess took note of everyone who was there. He knew each and every one well. There were about four Universals, eight Alis, a few Borns, and too many Muhammads to count. Yet he knew them all. They all showed him love. It was this camaraderie that Qwess missed most about the streets. In no other way of life is the camaraderie so strong. Maybe it was because of the life-and-death chances taken every day, or the fact that they thought outside the box. Whatever the reason, they were all accepted for who they were. That's what made the bonds so strong.

Qwess whispered into Shauntay's ear over the pounding music for her to go in the VIP room upstairs. He told her he'd meet her there in a few. He sent her with a bottle of Cristal champagne.

Once she was out the way, he was able to get down and dirty with his brethren. They laughed, joked, caught up on events, and did what brothers-in-arms do. There were so many women in the place, it was unreal. They were in their finest splendor, too. Leather, silk, satin, rayon, or hardly nothing at all summed up their attire.

Doe surveyed the crowd looking for something to take home. He was definitely in King Solomon mode. He was young, rich, and unattached. While looking through the crowd, he spotted Flame. He tapped Qwess and pointed Flame out. They both chatted for a few more minutes and excused themselves, with Hulk following closely behind.

Flame was trying to spit at some older chick when he saw Qwess and Doe coming through the crowd.

"I'm telling you, baby. I'm about to be large. You better get in now. It may not be enough of me to go 'round later." The lady walked off, not bothering to look back.

"What's up, Flame. Everything all right?" Qwess inquired, walking up.

"Yeah, we cool."

"Sup, J.D." Doe spoke.

"As-salaam alayka," J.D. greeted

"Hey, if y'all need anything, let me know. There's plenty of food. No pork, of course," Doe offered. "Where you sitting? We'll send you a bottle of something."

"Over in the corner." J.D. answered.

"All right, cool. Check it. We need to holla at the li'l homie. We'll get up, though. Enjoy yourselves."

With that, Doe, Qwess, and Hulk left with Flame and 8-Ball in tow. They went straight to the DJ booth. The others waited outside while Qwess went in to talk to DJ Mike Technique. A few minutes later, Qwess emerged with a smile on his face, looking directly at Flame.

"Yo, you ready to earn this deal or what?" Qwess asked Flame.

"Damn right!"

"We about to see."

Flame looked puzzled, but confident.

"What he talking 'bout?" 8-Ball asked, chewing a wing.

"I don't know." Flame shrugged.

Qwess tapped Flame and led him to the dance floor. When they got there, Qwess looked to the DJ booth, and the music stopped. DJ Mike Technique spoke:

"All right, muthafuckas! It's midnight and it's party time! Check this out. All you rappers in the house. It's a rapper in here named Flame who says he's the hottest in the Carolinas. My man Qwess want to see. So it's a thousand dollars up for whoever can beat him in a freestyle battle!"

Flame was stunned, but ready to accept the challenge. Some of the club staff emptied a space on the dance floor and stood there waiting with a cordless mic. A line of hungry rappers formed in front of them, including some females. A circle formed around the dance floor as everyone waited to see this. On cue, DJ Mike Technique spoke:

"All right. Here's the rules. You gotta freestyle. No written shit here. My man Dino will give you a topic and you spit about it in a battle form. The crowd decides the winner. Fair enough?"

The crowd roared.

"All right, show time," Qwess told Flame. "Show me what you got."

Flame stepped into the arena. The DJ put on the instrumental to Mobb Deep's "Shook Ones Pt. II," classic battle music. Flame had five people to knock off. Contestant number one started it off. Dino told him to rap about money.

> *Money is my bitch*
> *I need money to live*
> *I got a gang of money-hungry niggas that kill*
>   *kids*
> *And be in spots where you can't go*
> *all on a mission to get that Doe . . .*

The crowd gave him a mediocre response. He passed the mic to Flame.

> *If money is your bitch, then I guess you broke*
> *'Cause money is the reason I just jacked yo' hoe*
> *You don't know*
> *Nothing 'bout this kid named Flame*
> *Who used his tongue as cash and bought your*
>   *dame*
> *And if money is the root of all evil*
> *I gotta change my name 'cause I bring hell to*
> *People . . .*

The crowd met Flame with better response, though it was obvious he was still cold.

Round two went much the same. As did round three. When round four came, Flame was battling a female. Her name was Saigon. She was pretty and nice. So nice that in the end, it was Saigon and Flame engaging in a tense battle for a thousand dollars.

Flame, I'm glad to see you got skills wit yo'
  tongue
'Cause after I beat you, you can lick me 'til I'm
  numb
When I cum, I put out all the Flames in a fire
I flip the script and have you calling me sire
Wit' a mic, I'm too hot to handle
So I'll burn you and smear your
Name just like a scandal . . .

The ladies in the house erupted! Here was a rapper's rapper representing for the ladies.

8-Ball was all in Flame's face barking, "Nigga, handle yo' bidness. Handle yo' bidness!"

Flame was unfazed. "I got it. I got it."

Flame grabbed the mic, and the crowd got quiet. Everyone wanted to see what he'd come back with.

Yo, I rep Fayetteville, better known as Fayettenam
'Cause niggas pull guerilla tactics on Saigon
I freeze minds like o-pium
Niggas call me Flame cause I stay roastin' 'em
Like rotisserie
Only way a bitch'll do me
Is if her and her girlfriend is down with the three
It's history, right here in the making
'Cause I'm for real about this shit, and this bitch is
Faking . . .

Flame dropped the mic in Saigon's face. It was over. He was clearly the victor by the crowd's reaction. There wasn't a closed mouth in the house. Even Qwess and Doe were going bananas!

"That's what I'm talking 'bout! That's what the fuck I'm talking 'bout!" Qwess roared. He pumped his hands in the air and began a chant of "A.B.P." Before long, the whole Crescent Crew was shouting *"A.B.P."* Then the whole club was shouting, "A.B.P.!" This went on for a good seven minutes before the applause died down.

Saigon, for her part, held her head up high in the face of defeat. Doe pulled her to the side and slid her a thousand dollars anyway. She deserved it. She had held her own against a formidable opponent. He also slid her a business card and told her to get at him.

When Qwess sifted through the crowd, he found Flame and 8-Ball in the middle. Flame was on 8-Ball's big shoulders while 8-Ball carried him around as if he had won the championship. 8-Ball was yelling and screaming, "This my nigga! This my nigga!"

Qwess signaled for Flame to get down and meet with him in the VIP.

They walked up the stairs to the VIP section: Qwess, Doe, Flame, 8-Ball, and of course Hulk. They settled into a table by the window so they could see the floor below. Apparently, there was a prettiest ass contest ensuing.

The server brought a chilled bottle of Cristal over to the table. Qwess briefly spotted Shauntay sitting with her best friend, Meka, in a corner. Meka had joined her in VIP earlier. He motioned for her to bring the papers she had inside her Hermès Birkin handbag over. She did so, and left them alone.

Qwess poured everyone drinks, except Hulk, who was standing post in front of the table, and got to business.

"Yo, you look good out there. You had me worried for a minute. Ole girl was holding it on your ass," Qwess joked.

"Psst. I got that!" Flame responded confidently.

"That's what's up. I knew you had it in you. Now you 'bout to get paid," said Qwess, pulling out some papers, giving them to Flame. As Flame perused them, Qwess kept talking.

"We want to sign you to a five-album contract. We are an independent label, so you'll be getting better points than average. We gon' start you off giving you ten points. Depending on how you sell, we'll raise them with each album."

Flame was oblivious to what Qwess was saying. The only thing that registered to him is that he was getting out the hood. He had realized his dream with a bona fide record deal. He didn't care if Qwess was telling him he had to cut fifty albums. For the amount of money he was looking to gain at the end of the contract, it was done.

"S-so when do I get this advance?" Flame asked, shuddering. The magnitude of the moment was taking effect. Anxiety was ripping through his gut.

"Immediately," Qwess answered pulling a $375,000 check out of his pocket.

"It's actually double that, but I gotta wait 'til you get some insight into managing it. You know 'a fool and money will soon part company."

Flame was in another world. "Where do I sign?" he asked. Qwess passed him a pen and pointed to signature lines. Flame rushed to sign the contract before he awoke from this dream. Although he was living in the moment, he still felt as if he was dreaming.

Qwess perused the contract then folded it in thirds. "Do you have a bank?" Qwess asked.

"No."

Qwess just shook his head. "Check it. I want you to spend a couple days with us, so we can get you set up. We need to help you get your business in order real quick. You gonna be going on this promo tour with us starting next month. We gonna introduce you to the world. Things are going to move really fast out there. All we need you focusing on is rapping and performing. You can do that better if you know your business is in order."

This was music to Flame's ears. He definitely couldn't see himself putting $375,000 under a mattress. "I'm down, but I'm riding with J.D. and them tonight. They're my transportation right now."

"I thought about that," Doe said, flashing a big smile.

Doe motioned for everyone to follow him. They all trekked down the back stairs to an exit. When Doe opened the door, parked in the alley was a brand-new BMW 645 convertible awaiting them. The metallic green paint sparkled beneath the streetlamp, and the snow-white interior glowed behind the frosted glass. The Bimmer was sitting on twenty-one-inch chrome Breyton rims.

Doe held the keys up to Flame. "Congratulations, Flame, welcome to A.B.P." He tossed the keys to Flame. Flame kissed them, then ran to inspect his new fifty-thousand-dollar ride.

Satisfied, Qwess and the others returned to enjoy the party.

There were four people seated inside the 4Runner, two in front, two in back. The two in back caressed the triggers on their sawed-off shotguns, eagerly waiting to use them. The two in front held HK-433 assault rifles with collapsing stocks. They all wore black. The two in back were getting uneasy.

"Gotdamn, where this mu'fucka at?" Nino inquired, looking at his watch. "It's two o'clock." Nino was in the back, behind the passenger seat.

"Just be patient, man." That was Murda. He was drinking. He was the unofficial leader of Blood Team. "We know he in there. It's only one way in and one way out.

When we see that little black Porsche roll out, we roll out."

"What if he got a bitch with him?" That was Shooter. He sat on the passenger side. He asked this because they were parked at the top of the road that led to the club. They couldn't see who got in the car; however, they knew every car leaving had to come this way.

"Nigga, I don't give a fuck if Oprah Winfrey in the car wit' him. She gotta die tonight!" That was T. Gunn, the resident hothead in the Blood Team. He sat behind Murda. "We follow this nigga 'til we got him isolated, and then we murk this nigga! End of story."

T. Gunn passed the bag of cocaine he was using to Nino, who dipped his quill inside and picked up a clump of the white stuff. He hit both nostrils and passed it around. They were passing time waiting for their mark. They would wait until Christmas if need be.

They were professionals, and murder was their trade.

Reece was at the bar talking to Jersey Ali when someone tapped him on the shoulder. He turned around to find Destiny standing there with a smile on her face. When Reece looked her over from head to toe, he didn't know whether to smile or frown. Destiny was wearing a red velvet cat suit with four-inch stilettos. "Dayum!" was what Reece muttered. Jersey Ali openly lusted as well. Destiny was flanked by a short, balding black guy, who looked clearly out of place. When Destiny saw Reece glance at him, she introduced him.

"Reece, this is Lieu . . . ah Lou Jenkins. He's like my older uncle. He knew me before I was still a crush in my father's mind," she joked. "Lou, this is Reece."

They shook hands. Reece noted the firm handshake.

He also took note of how Lou observed his surroundings like a bird of prey. He didn't miss much.

After the pleasantries, Reece dismissed Lou with a bottle of Moët and pulled Destiny into a corner where they were by themselves.

"Hey, you. I missed you," Reece told Destiny.

"Yeah, right. With all the women you got, I'm surprised you noticed I'm gone."

"Ah. Cut it out. I'm serious. I missed your conversation more than anything," he said seriously. He grabbed both her hands in his and looked at her affectionately.

Destiny returned his stare before breaking his hold. "Quit gaming, Reece. I'm sure you have more than enough people to give you conversation." She motioned to his crew at the bar.

"I don't talk about much with them. Plus, they ain't as cute as you."

Destiny blushed.

DJ Mike Technique was taking the party to the islands. He was doing an old-school Buju Banton set. Destiny could barely keep still in her seat. Reece finally caught the hint and pulled her to the dance floor.

"Whatchu taken pon di river?" he teased, in a faux Jamaican accent, as they danced.

"Bwoy, chu not know nuttin' 'bout dat," Destiny teased back, winding her hips.

"Come on then, let's see." Reece gripped Destiny's waist and rode her groove.

Qwess had just come out of VIP with Shauntay, who wasn't feeling well, when he ran into his sister, Fatima, at the bottom of the stairs. She smiled broadly and stepped aside. Qwess ran right into a roadblock. It was Hope, looking him dead in the face.

"Congratulations!" Hope said.

"Thank you," Qwess returned. He tried to push past, but Hope stopped him.

"Unh-uh, Qwess. Not tonight. We need to talk. There's some things I need to get off my chest, and I'm not leaving 'til I do."

Qwess heard her and tried to push on past, but Hope grabbed his arm tighter. She would not be denied.

"Look, either you talk to me, Qwess, or I will make a scene!"

Qwess didn't know what type of shit Hope was on. He hadn't seen her since he had come home from prison. Although he knew she kept close ties with Fatima, he hadn't spoken to her. Now she wanted to crash his party? This was some bullshit.

Qwess wanted to tell Hope to go fuck herself, but after some prodding by Fatima, Qwess relented and gave her a few minutes. He and Hope slid into a booth so he could hear her sob story.

"Listen, Qwess. Don't say nothing. Just listen," Hope said, holding his arm down. "You owe me that."

"Owe you? Owe you!" Qwess flipped. "What do I owe you? I don't owe you shit! You the one who left me in that sweatbox by myself with nothing but time and the feelings I had for you eating me. You the one who left me! I'm the one who had to hear about you dealing with fuck-ass niggas while I'm in the joint. But guess what? I learned to deal with it! You chose, and I had to deal with it. All you ever lent me was time, so I don't owe you shit!"

Hope calmly sat and accepted her rebuke. She could tell he really needed to get that out.

"Qwess, all I ever did was love you. I thought me leaving would give you time to focus. Give you time to realize what you had in me, so you could straighten up, because your previous lifestyle I didn't approve of."

Qwess interjected, "Funny, that lifestyle wasn't so bad when it funded your lifestyle. You didn't care when I was lacing you with shit." This was true. Hope definitely reaped the benefits of his criminal lifestyle.

"No! Don't do that. It was never about money with you and me. It was just so real. I mean, of course, I enjoyed the gifts and things, but I didn't know what you did. In fact, I didn't know until I left you. Only then did I know. I used to hear girls at my school talking about a Qwess. I only knew you as Salim, so it didn't dawn on me."

Hope was on the verge of tears. Qwess wanted to console her, but his anger and pride got the best of him.

Hope continued, "Qwess, I always loved you. I just couldn't deal with what you did. I mean, the stories I heard about you! Please just understand, I never meant to hurt you. I just had to make a stand. You understand, don't you? Qwess, look at me." He did. "You understand, right?

For the first time in three years, Qwess allowed himself to look at her, the woman who had stolen his heart like a very skilled cat burglar. She hadn't changed a bit, either. Her chocolate skin was smooth as ever. Her petite size-six frame was still intact, as was her curvy, beautiful booty. Qwess could see it spreading in the chair, falling over like soft clay. Hope wore a green satin dress with a plunging neckline. Her shoulder-length hair was coiled under into a china bob. Obviously, she intended to gain Qwess's favor. When Qwess didn't say anything, Hope continued.

"Look, I don't want anything from you," Hope claimed. "I just want my friend back. You bring out the best in me." Hope reached over and stroked Qwess's beard lovingly. When he didn't flinch, she thought he was giving in.

Qwess finally spoke. "Look, I don't hate you, Hope. I just gotta look out for *me* now. Love is an emotion I can't deal with right now. Love weakens a man, and I can't be weak again. Ever!"

"So what are you saying, you don't love your little girlfriend? You buying her Benzes and shit," Hope asked, unable to pass up the potshot.

"First of all, that was supposed to be your Benz, but you couldn't weather the storm." Qwess looked at Hope sternly. "Secondly, I repeat, love weakens a man. I can't be weak. Ever."

Hope sized up the answer before speaking. "Point taken. Can we at least be friends again?"

Qwess shrugged. "Okay. I guess we can try it."

"Good, can I give a friend a birthday hug?" She reached over and gave Qwess a hug. All kinds of feelings washed over him. Memories of their good times flooded across his mind. He closed his eyes to savor the moment. When he opened them, he was looking right at Shauntay.

Shauntay narrowed her eyes into malicious slits, then turned and stormed off. Hope never even saw her.

Qwess broke the embrace and went after Shauntay. He found her in the back of the club, near the bathroom.

"Yo, what's wrong, baby?" Qwess asked, tugging Shauntay's arm to turn her around.

Shauntay palmed her forehead. "I-I don't feel well. My stomach has been hurting all day."

Qwess looked into her eyes. "Are you okay? You've been feeling bad a lot lately."

"Who was that woman? Is that Hope?"

Qwess dropped his head. "Yeah, that's her, but trust me, it's not what you think."

Shauntay frowned. "Oh, really?"

"Really."

Qwess was, in fact, telling the truth. While it was true

he would never love a woman like he loved Hope, it was also true that he would never love Hope the same, either. She had abandoned him when he needed her most. That was an unforgivable sin in his book of life. Regardless of how fine a woman was, or what she had going on, if she couldn't be loyal, she was useless to Qwess. Loyalty was its own aphrodisiac, and Hope didn't turn him on.

Shauntay searched his eyes for the truth. "Qwess, I don't feel well. I . . . I just want to go home. How much longer are we going to be here?"

Qwess frowned. "Ahh, I got a few loose ends to tie up, but I tell you what, you can take Reece's car, and he can ride with me."

Another pain zipped through Shauntay's stomach. She grimaced. "Okay. Hurry, please?"

Qwess searched the club for Reece. He found him by the bar talking to Destiny.

"Yo, what you getting into tonight?" Qwess asked.

"Nuttin' really. Me and Samson gotta go see this dude about my cake later on. Why?"

Qwess was hesitant before speaking. "Ahh, 'cause Shauntay ain't feeling too good, so she ready to go. But I can't leave because I still gotta handle some business with Technique and some more stuff."

Reece frowned at Qwess. "Nigga, don't tell me you done fucked up. I saw you and ole girl Hope over there reminiscing like lost lovebirds and shit. Did Shauntay catch you?" Reece asked.

"Something like that," Qwess admitted. "But she was already feeling sick."

"So anyway, what you want from me?" Reece asked, confused.

"I want Shauntay to take your car and go on home, and you ride with Samson," Qwess proposed.

"Oh, that ain't no thang. She can get it," Reece said.

He nodded his head at Qwess. "Playa, playa. You trying to hit something strange tonight, huh? You gone tear Hope back out. Ahh, I knew you still had it in you."

"Nah, go ahead with that shit, man." Qwess blushed. Hope *did* have some of the best pussy in the world in his eyes, but it took more than good sex to lock a boss down. Besides, he had already crossed that bridge. He was ready to settle down and be with Shauntay, maybe even make her his wife. She had earned that spot.

Reece glanced at Destiny and imagined what he was hoping to get into later. He quickly passed Qwess the key to his Porsche. "Here's the keys. I'm neglecting my date. Just bring it to me sometime tomorrow."

"All right, cool. Thanks, bro." Qwess and Reece dapped up and parted company.

Inside the 4Runner, Murda and the others couldn't believe their luck. They were prepared to wait until the club closed so they could follow Reece home and get him on the country road. They were monitoring the party via the live simulcast on the radio, and knew by the numerous Crescent Crew shout outs that Reece's crew was still inside real thick. They knew it would be a task to get him isolated from the other members long enough to make their move. They knew from the bevy of luxury cars that it was highly unlikely they'd catch him by himself tonight. They were already kicking around contingency plans to get him at a later date when the heavens opened up and shined favor upon them. At least, that's how they saw it.

Like a godsend, they observed the little black Porsche roll out of the club all alone. They couldn't believe their luck. Initially, they thought their cover had been blown, and they were being set up. *No way would the leader of the Crescent Crew roll out all alone and at this time of night knowing there was still a bounty on his head.* Then again, they thought, *that's exactly what King Reece would do.* His arrogance preceded him. Riding the high from the murder he had committed last night that once again had the streets talking, he would roll solo to flex his muscle.

"A'ight, fellas, there the nigga go right there. It's showtime," T. Gunn informed his crew. "Mount up."

While Murda waited for the Porsche to pull out from the side road, everyone readied their weapons. The 4Runner crept out and maintained a safe little distance behind him. Everyone already had their assignments and was prepared to execute their orders. As they neared the car, Shooter and Nino pulled down their masks, as did T. Gunn.

The Porsche stopped at the red light and idled. Seconds later, the black truck eased up beside it on the driver's side. As they pulled beside the car, they peered through the dark tint and made out only one silhouette. Good, he was alone.

The windows on the 4Runner slowly glided down. Shooter and Nino simultaneously stretched their bodies out the windows, aimed their weapons, and let them rip!

The night lit up hotter than the Fourth of July, as huge blasts from the double-aught buckshot rocked the small Porsche, almost turning it over. Shooter sprayed the car with the high-powered assault rifle in a sweeping motion, left to right. The rounds were so fast and furious it sounded like a chopper was landing on the street. The balls of fire seared through the metal of the Porsche sending smoke streams up into the air, as the Blood Team fulfilled their mission. The cacophony of sounds was deafening in the early-morning hours. The assault seemed as if it went on for minutes, though it was only a few seconds. Only when the hammers clicked against the metal did the team let up.

Before Murda could make a hasty retreat, T. Gunn exited the truck and walked around to inspect what was left of the six-figure sports car. In his hand, he held the shotgun. As he raised the weapon toward what was left of the door and attempted to see into the car through one of the craters, something strange caught his eye. He struggled to pull the driver's door open and peek inside. What he saw stopped him dead in his tracks.

A huge hole gaped where an eye used to be, and blood gushed from three holes in the neck. All along the chest were entry wounds from the assault rifle. He saw another hole where a bullet had ripped through the side of the face.

Under normal circumstances, this would be the part where T. Gunn and the Blood Team rejoiced. Unfortunately, they had fucked up. Oh, they had carried out a hit. But it wasn't Reece at all in the car.

It was a woman.

Back at the club, someone heard shots and went to alert security. When one of the security guards went to investigate further, he immediately recognized Reece's Porsche. What was left of it, anyway. There was a woman present already. She informed the security guard that an ambulance was on the way. The victim was still alive.

The security guard went to alert the rest of the crew at the club to what had transpired. When Qwess and everyone arrived, the ambulance had come and gone. They all rushed to the hospital.

By the time Qwess and company arrived, it was total pandemonium. News crews were there, as well as what looked like the entire police force. They were questioning the woman who had called the ambulance, and mean-mugging the whole Crescent Crew, who mean-mugged right back. Qwess, Reece, and Doe led the way straight into the emergency room. The doctors tried in vain to stop them, but Qwess would not be denied. When one of the doctors brushed against Hulk, he felt his pistol through his shirt and went ballistic. He immediately alerted the police. When the police came to apprehend Hulk, they were met by a solid wall of muscle, steel, and pure, unadulterated aggression. When the police reached for their guns, so did the entire Crescent Crew . . . right in the emergency room. The police, seeing they were outgunned, hesitated in confusion. One of the doctors, possibly the head doctor, came to defuse the situation.

"Gentlemen, please. This is not the place or time. We have a young lady valiantly fighting for her life. Please let's not have any more senseless bloodshed," the doctor reasoned.

The police sergeant in charge took the opportunity to save face and regain control of the situation. He boldly stepped into the middle of the fracas.

"Everyone calm down. Calm down," he began authoritatively. "Now if we can just retain some order. If you gentlemen will please take all your firearms outside and please just retain control, I promise no charges will be filed. I understand this is a trying time, but this is getting no one anywhere."

The officers and the crew continued to grit on one another until Reece spoke up. He calmed everyone and told them to walk outside. Once outside, he instructed them to put away their weapons, then go to his funeral home and wait on him. He instructed them that Samson was in charge until he got there. Then, he rejoined Qwess, Doe, and Hulk back in the emergency room.

Qwess was zoned out as he stood in a corner awaiting word. His heart felt as if it had been ripped from his chest. Deep regret buried him standing, as a million questions rampaged through his head. *Why did I have to send her in Reece's car? Why didn't I go with her? Why didn't I send Hulk with her? Why didn't I tell her I loved her?* He knew that he loved her now for sure. There was no other way to explain the feeling. It felt as if his heart had melted onto his soul. Thankfully, no one said anything to him. They allowed him to stew in silence as everyone awaited word with him.

Reece was on the phone. He had been on the phone since the incident occurred, barking out orders, preparing for the get-back.

Doe was in utter disbelief. After the carnage he'd witnessed at the scene, he knew it was just a matter of time before Shauntay gave up the fight. He was actually surprised she had made it this far. For his part, Doe had been out of the streets a long time. This level of savagery had been nonexistent during his block tenure. He couldn't fathom how anyone could do this to a woman. He had already taken the liberty of calling Shauntay's parents before he left the scene, and they were on their way from Charlotte. He couldn't imagine what they were going through or how they were going to take it. The situation was gruesome.

A surgeon walked into the room, grabbing everyone's attention. It was evident that she had tried to clean herself up, but there was still blood on the cuffs of her shirt.

"Who is Qwess?" she asked. Qwess quickly stood. "Well, Ms. Simmons is requesting to see you." She paused dramatically before continuing. "Sir, I'm sorry. It doesn't look like she's going to make it. We gave her medication to keep her conscious as long as we can. She's in a lot of pain, but she wants to see you. In fact, she insisted."

Qwess held his head high and followed the surgeon into the room. He was not prepared for what he saw.

"*A-stag-fir-allah*!" he growled, as he broke down to his knees. Tears flowed freely from his face as he turned away from the grotesque sight before him.

Shauntay was lying in the bed with tubes coming out of every possible orifice. A huge bandage cloaked her head, and an enormous patch covered her eye. Her whole body had swollen to double its normal size. The doctors had operated on her for hours. She had drifted to the other side twice, but each time she fought to come back. It was as if she still had one more mission to do here on Earth.

Qwess stood and walked slowly over to the bed. The steady beep from Shauntay's heart monitor hypnotized him as he forced himself to her side with heavy steps. "Baby . . ." he called out to her, not sure if she could hear him.

She felt Qwess's presence, and her eyes fluttered open. Covering Shauntay's mouth was a transparent oxygen mask. She tried to speak, but her words never made it past the plastic. Qwess placed his hand over hers to console her. Shauntay tried to speak again, but it was too much of a feat. Instead, she led Qwess's hand to her stomach. When he let it rest there, she looked deeply into his eyes, trying to send a message.

"Who did this?" Qwess croaked.

Shauntay bravely tried to speak. On the second try she was successful. Qwess's ear was way down, touching the mask. Shauntay murmured, "I s-saw Tommy!" she coughed. "My cousin, Tommy." She finally got it out, and as she said her last words on earth, she began coughing, each time harder and harder. Eventually, she coughed so hard, blood filled the entire oxygen mask. Next, the monitor beeped into a solid flat line. Doctors rushed into the room, but it was too late. Shauntay was gone.

When Qwess walked back into the waiting room, his face was void of emotion. Now waiting with Reece and the others were Fatima and his mom. Fatima, knowing her brother well, slowly walked over to him and embraced him. He didn't have to say a word; she already knew Shauntay was gone. A somber vibe hogged the air . . . until Shauntay's parents arrived.

"I know you had something to do with this! You drug-dealing bastard! I told my baby you weren't shit!" Shauntay's mother screamed at Qwess before she even made it into the waiting room. "What happened?!"

"Calm down, Irene!" Shauntay's father grabbed his wife and attempted to calm her down. She broke down in his arms.

They were all interrupted by the head surgeon walking out. He asked who the parents were, as if it wasn't obvious already. Once he identified them, he broke the news.

"Ladies and gentlemen, I'm sorry, but we did everything we could. She was a fighter, but we lost her and the baby."

Qwess perked up. "Baby? What baby?!"

"Yes, she was pregnant. Ten weeks. You didn't know?" the doctor asked, but from the strange looks, it was obvious no one knew.

"Ooh, lawd, lawd, lawd!" Shauntay's mother cried. She turned her venom on Qwess. "You! You! You! You did this to my baby!!!"

Mr. Simmons saw that things were getting out of hand. He pulled Qwess aside.

"Son, no one believes it was your fault," he explained. "Give Irene some time, she'll come around. Thank you for being here, but it may be best if you leave now. We got it from here. Go on and leave. We'll call you later."

Qwess wanted to refuse. There was no place he wanted or needed to be besides right by Shauntay's side. However, there were more pressing matters to tend to. He gathered up the remainder of his crew and walked out of the emergency room.

Once outside the hospital, Qwess was met by a phalanx of reporters all clamoring for a story. Qwess was big news now. He was the local rap star who had gone major. He was becoming the toast of the industry. A street rapper with gang ties, a shooting at his birthday party? Of course they were hungry for this story. The mob grew so large that Hulk was forced to act as a wall between the reporters and Qwess as he ushered him to his truck. Hulk stuffed Qwess in the passenger seat of the Escalade and took the wheel. They led the convoy out of the hospital, followed by Doe and Reece in Doe's new BMW 745.

They headed straight to Reece's funeral home on the other side of town.

Chapter 11

Inside of Eternally Yours, the Crescent Crew was kicking back, puffing dro, waiting on Reece. Everyone's mood had changed from festive to demonic. They all had come up to celebrate the arrival of one of their own. Instead, they were all witnesses to the first strike in what was definitely going to be a war. They all knew Black Vic was behind this hit. Reece had explained the situation to them weeks ago. Now everything had come to a head.

Lights flashed in the glass picture window, and they all stood, hands on weapons. Moments later Reece walked in followed by Doe, Hulk, and a grief-stricken Qwess. They could tell from Qwess's expression that Shauntay didn't make it.

They were seated in Reece's office, which, though spacious, wasn't enough to accommodate the huge entourage. Therefore, the brothers made space by standing around the wall and sitting on the floor. Like loyal soldiers, everyone awaited their orders.

When Reece didn't say anything, one of the Alis took it upon himself to open the floor.

"Yo, that nigga done fucked up! We are eliminating

his whole crew," he vowed. "His whole bloodline. Black Vic is dead!"

Ali's sentiment was followed by more affirmations of murderous mayhem before Reece interrupted.

"Hold up, hold up." Reece raised his hand. "Something ain't right. I've been talking to my man on that side of town all night since this happened, and he said Black Vic been out of town all week."

The crew looked at him, puzzled. "Your man on that side of town?" a couple of them asked in unison.

"Yeah. I got a few niggas on that side of town. Money well invested," Reece quipped. Even in times of grief, his dynamic personality shined bright. "Like I was saying, Vic's been out of town, so it couldn't have been him."

Muhammad spoke up. "That don't mean nothing. He could've had it done. You know the nigga pussy."

Reece contemplated a brief second before responding. "Nah, he ain't soft, and paying people ain't his style."

"But listen, though. Who else had a beef with us?" Universal asked.

"Could be anybody at the rate we letting thangs go for," Samson reasoned. "We hurting 'em out here."

"Yeah, but ain't too many niggas stupid enough to fuck wit' the crew. Everybody know we go hard," Born stated, obviously feeling himself.

Reece twisted one of his locks that had fallen out of place from his ponytail. This was his habit when he was in deep thought. Suddenly his eyes lit up as he came upon an epiphany.

"Wait a minute, Vic is backed by some old heads," he recalled. "And if we cutting Vic throat where he can't make money, they damn sure can't make any money," Reece deduced, trying to put the pieces together. "Now sending hits ain't Vic style, but them old heads definitely 'bout that type of life. So, it's possible they ain't want to get their hands dirty."

"Shit, then they would've used Vic," Ali reasoned

"Nah, god, if Vic catches a case, they still don't make money," Reece explained. "Which might be why Vic bounced? Nigga think he slick. His man Hardtime didn't go, though. I know this for a fact. Hardtime could be the shooter."

"Well then, that's it. We hem his ass up 'til we find some answers," Samson suggested.

"He ain't talking," one of the Borns disputed.

"Oh, he'll talk!" Samson assured him.

Someone's two-way pager went off, and the whole room checked theirs. It was Reece's. Destiny was paging him. He had left her at the club by herself when he ran out. He filed away the message, which read, *Where are you?* and turned the pager off. This was time for business.

Qwess stood in the corner looking off into space while his surrogate family put the pieces together. Regardless of whether they solved the mystery or not, his Shauntay would never come back. The mere thought of that sent him into shock.

Doe sat in a chair near the window, amazed at what he was hearing. He was surprised to be privy to this type of meeting. He didn't realize his cousin wielded this much power, nor did he realize how heartless the streets had become. Here these men were discussing murder as if they were selecting a salad from a menu. The contrast was both intoxicating and scary. Finally, he heard Reece speak.

"All right. We'll pick Hardtime up and go from there. Samson will handle the details. That's all for now. I take it you all aren't going back home tonight?"

There was a loud murmur emanating through the room.

From it, Reece gathered they were all staying for at least a couple days to attend the funeral.

"Good. Get with Samson, and he'll get with me. I'll get at you. Peace, gods. *As-salaam alaykum,* brethren."

Everyone filed out the room besides Qwess. Reece gestured for him to remain behind.

When everyone was gone, Reece doused all the lights in the office except his table lamp. He then rolled a nice, fat joint in complete silence while Qwess stood by the window.

Reece lit the joint, took a few tokes, and then passed it to Qwess. Reece remained seated at his desk but threw his feet on the table.

"Talk to me, Blackman. Where your mind at?" Reece asked Qwess.

Enamored with the potent marijuana, Qwess's words were slurred when he spoke. "Just thinking, man. Shauntay was a good girl, you know? She didn't deserve to go out like that. And the baby . . . I didn't even know she was pregnant."

"I know, man." Reece went over to comfort his brother. He put his hand on Qwess's shoulder. "I kinda feel responsible. The cocksuckers were gunning for me." Qwess started to stop him, but Reece put his hand up. "No, no, really. I feel it's my fault." Reece paused. "Which is why I'm asking you to let me handle it."

"Man, I know you ain't thinking I ain't gonna do—"

Reece interrupted him. "Listen brother, I know your soul is crying out for revenge, but you have to stay focused on the big picture, man. You made it out. You got signed. You a made man now. As such, you got made-man responsibilities." Reece paused and inhaled the weed while his words sank in.

Reece continued, "You can't afford to come back to the streets. You don't need that. You out. Stay out. Let me handle this. Besides,"—he pointed to the television on the wall—"it's all on the news that your girl got killed, so you know they gon' be watching you. These people ain't stupid. They know exactly who you are. The best thing you can do is go ahead on this tour, and let shit cool down. When you come back, I'll have handled everything. Trust."

A single tear crawled down Qwess's cheek. "Man, I can't sit back and do nothing. How can I live with myself? I'm a muthafucking thoroughbred! I can't let that shit ride! They did this shit! Not me; them!" Qwess's tone softened as he released a whimper. "I can't let them get away with doing my girl like that, my baby . . . Nah, I can't let that go."

"Calm down, man. Calm down." Reece whispered. "You know me better than anybody. Do you actually think I'm going to let this go? Man, I'm going to do them niggas so dirty they gonna be begging for me to kill 'em when I'm done."

Qwess spoke softly. "Tommy."

"What?"

"Tommy. That's what Shauntay told me. Her cousin, Tommy, shot her."

"Tommy . . . Tommy . . ." Reece searched his mental Rolodex for the name of all the street players named Tommy. Then, it hit him. "Tommy! What the fuck?" Reece said, as he smacked his forehead. "Now it makes sense!"

"You thinking what I'm thinking?"

"Definitely."

Reece was referring to Shauntay's cousin Tommy aka T. Gunn. Everyone knew of him as a hired gun. Back in the day, Qwess and Reece was going to hire him to hit the lead investigator in Qwess's case before he took the plea deal. They hadn't heard much about him since, except that he was now mobbed down with a bunch of heartless hired guns. They all spelled trouble with a capital T.

"So Black Vic hired Tommy to kill me 'cause he was too pussy to do it himself, but they got Shauntay, thinking it was me?" Reece clarified, more to himself than Qwess.

Qwess nodded.

"I'm sorry, bro," Reece offered. Armed with the new information, it was time to devise a plan. "I tell you what, work with me. Give me a couple days to see how everything pans out. If after I find out more details, you still want in, then we'll see what's up. Fair enough?"

Qwess mulled the proposal over in silence.

"They missed, and I'm going to make sure they know. Just give me a couple days to let me check out my theory. Like I said, if you want to come on after that, then you're welcome."

Finally, Qwess nodded. "Fair enough."

"All right, Qwess, I'm serious. No vigilante shit. Crescent Crew is self-contained. Let us handle this. I know you, nigga. Give me your word."

"Word is bond," Qwess reluctantly agreed.

Reece grabbed Qwess in a tight embrace and patted the back of his head. "I got you, my nigga. I got you."

They sat on the leather sofa together, and smoked joint after joint for the rest of the night.

Shauntay was laid to rest on a Sunday, in an elaborate ceremony. Reece's funeral home took care of the arrangements, so no expense was spared. Her family came from all over. Qwess was there, along with key members of the Crescent Crew strategically placed throughout the congregation. They didn't want to draw too much attention, but they were at war, so security was extra tight. Even

Flame was present at the funeral, along with his trusty sidekick, 8-Ball. Flame had taken up with Doe ever since the party. Doe was showing Flame how to organize his money, as well as explaining, in detail, the ramifications of his contract. Doe was taking extra care to make sure Flame didn't get out of hand. There was a lot riding on the young buck, and he didn't want things to go sour.

Reece was a no-show at the funeral service, though he promised to make an appearance to pay his respects.

Qwess was standing at the burial site consoling Shauntay's mother when Reece approached him on his right side. Reece stood quietly while the priest committed Shauntay's body to the ground. After the service was over, he pulled Qwess aside and told him he had something for him. Qwess said his goodbyes to the family and left with Reece. They climbed into the back seat of the middle vehicle in a three-truck Range Rover convoy, all black. Samson piloted this particular truck, while his twin crushed the passenger seat. In silence, they began the long trek into the country.

Following the shooting, the Crescent Crew had launched an all-out offensive with Reece at the helm. On the night of the shooting, two spots known to be frequented by Black Vic's crew were raided SWAT style. Only the raiders weren't police. At each spot that was raided, no one was left breathing.

The following day, Reece personally tailed Hardtime, Vic's right-hand man, to his mother's house. Before Reece could follow Hardtime inside, Hardtime quickly reemerged. So instead, Reece continued to follow him, but broke off the tail when he thought he was made. Later that same night, another one of Vic's spots was raided by the Crescent Crew. A gunfight ensued, but it was cut short when the squad, led by Samson, seemingly retreated. Moments later, the building exploded from the grenades left so cleverly behind by Samson, the ex-infantryman. The streets were still smoldering with beef, but for now the Crescent Crew held the upper hand.

After an hour of driving, the convoy pulled into the yard of a log cabin, deep in the woods. They all stepped out of the truck. Qwess noticed that the cabin was guarded by four of Reece's hundred-pound pit bulls, placed at various intervals around the perimeter of the cabin. As if that weren't enough, Jersey Ali was standing at the entrance with an AR-15 assault rifle on his shoulder. He greeted Qwess with a devious smile as they went inside.

Once inside, Qwess realized what all the extra precautions were for. Sitting in the middle of the unfurnished cabin was Hardtime. He was gagged with a bloody rag, and his hands were tied to the arms of a metal chair. The part of Hardtime's face that was exposed was swollen beyond comprehension. There were no definitive lines on his face. It looked like one big circle of bruised flesh. Upon closer observation, Qwess realized he was already missing a middle finger on each hand. Courtesy of Samson, no doubt. Standing on either side of Hardtime were Understanding and Muhammad, the other part of the frontline trio of the Crescent Crew's first responders team.

Reece spoke to the crew. "This nigga still don't want to talk?" They all shook their heads. "That's all right. He will." Reece gestured to Hulk. Hulk stood in front of Hardtime and slapped him awake. Hardtime awoke in a stupor. "You ready to talk yet?"

Hardtime fixed his one good eye on Reece and tried to burn him off the face of the earth with his gaze.

"Samson, go get my tools," Reece instructed. Samson left the cabin briefly, only to return with Reece's "tool kit."

"String this punk mu'fucka up, son!" Reece ordered.

He was quickly losing it. His nostrils were flared, and spittle formed in corners of his mouth. It was a striking contrast to the neat green suit he wore.

As Samson slung a rope over one of the ceiling beams preparing to string Hardtime up, Reece ranted aloud. "Protecting this nigga. I can't believe this shit. Nigga would've been sold you out, stupid mu'fucka! That's all right, though. You don't want to talk? Nigga, you gon' die! And her, too." Reece threw a picture of Hardtime's mother, taken earlier that day, in his face.

Qwess was shocked. Reece had gone too far. They had an unspoken code among the crew that family members were noncombatants, especially mothers. Qwess pulled Reece to the side and attempted to check him.

"Yo, what's up with this, bro? I thought we had rules?" Qwess hissed. "Fuck is you doing?"

Reece hissed back. "Fuck that! This is crew business." The others caught the last part of Reece's words and repeated them.

"Crew business!" they yelled.

Reece stood against Qwess's chest. "That's what I was telling you. Shit has changed out here. These li'l nigga is savages. They don't respect civility, so every now and then you gotta get medieval on a nigga ass. Ain't that right, Hardtime?" Reece called over his shoulder. "Shit is real in the field. Don't let a broad draw you back to this. She is gone. All the killing in the world ain't gon' bring her back," Reece reasoned. He turned and prepared his kit.

Qwess took it all in. The blood, the gore, the hardcore truth of what Reece was saying. Reece kept talking, and it was then that Qwess knew Reece had set him up. He was testing him, going hard to make or break him.

"You know," Reece said, as he removed tools from his kit, "a man can't occupy both sides of the fence.

Eventually, it'll come crashing down on him. So you let me handle this retribution for you, but I want you to witness this and know we treating every nigga involved the same way or worse. This way, you live vicariously through me, as I do the same through you. You think I don't want to be on stage ripping shit up. Bitches sucking my dick in foreign lands and shit. I do, but I chose my life. I gotta live it. You? You have a chance. This ain't for you no more."

Samson broke up the moment, telling Reece he was ready. Reece and Qwess joined the others. Hardtime was now strung up, hanging from the ceiling by his arms overhead. He was barebacked and still gagged. His legs were tied at the knees and ankles.

Reece placed his tool kit on the floor, then took his time to snap on a pair of rubber gloves. The sound echoed around the cabin with a loud *snap* as Reece popped the ends of the gloves. Next, he took out a twelve-inch double-edged blade. He held it up to the light emanating through the windows of the cabin, admiring it as if for the first time. All of the grand gestures were done to unnerve Hardtime, who was barely conscious.

As Reece walked to him, he began talking to himself. "What a nigga that don't talk need a tongue for?" he asked rhetorically. Reece snatched the gag from Hardtime's mouth and pried it open. Hardtime got the hint and clamped his mouth shut, just missing Reece's hand. Reece struggled with him all the while talking shit.

"Nigga, what you guarding your tongue for? You ain't using it, so you don't need it. I'm getting that!"

Hardtime shook his head side to side, and suddenly spit blood right in Reece's face. Samson pushed Reece aside and cracked Hardtime in the mouth, instantly breaking his jaw. Hardtime yelped out in pain, and Reece smiled when he saw Hardtime's lower jaw dangling.

Reece resumed his position in front of Hardtime. He gripped Hardtime's lower jaw and squeezed it as if he was trying to break it in two.

"Raaaaaaaa!!!" Hardtime's ear-splitting scream bounced off the walls. For Qwess, it was the sweetest music he had heard in a long time.

"You got nuts, nigga," Reece told him. "I give you that." Suddenly, a more sinister idea popped into his head. He began a low cackle. "Or should I say, you *had* nuts."

Reece unbuckled Hardtime's pants and pulled them down to his ankles. He stuck his blade next to Hardtime's exposed genitals. "Last time, nigga . . . Who. Did. The. Hit?" Reece asked.

Hardtime groaned and sucked up the pain as he maneuvered his head to look Reece in the face. *Fuck you, nigga,* is what he tried to say. Instead, with his jaw separated, it came out as air. Still, Reece caught the intent of his statement.

"Nah, you ain't equipped to fuck nothing!" Reece snarled. He pushed the blade up and sliced Hardtime's nut sack open. His balls plopped out of the sack and rolled onto the floor. Reece squished them under his alligator shoes. Surprisingly, Hardtime didn't feel much pain.

Reece dug into his tool kit again and pulled out a handful of M-80 firecrackers. The others cleared the way. They knew Reece was in torture mode. There was no stopping him now. They had once seen Reece cut a man's heart out while he was looking at him. The man was dead a full ten minutes before Reece realized it and ceased his torture tactics.

Reece walked up to Hardtime and gripped his broken jaw again. "It's up to you how long this last," he told

Hardtime. "Tell me who did the hit and you can float on peacefully. No? Okay."

Reece took his blade and methodically carved a hole in Hardtime's stomach, just underneath his sternum. When he was certain the hole was large enough to accommodate the firecrackers, he carefully placed one inside the hole. After that was done, Reece taped another firecracker to Hardtime's flaccid penis.

Hardtime's eyes grew larger than flying saucers. He vigorously shook his head.

Reece twirled his hand and cupped his ear like Hulk Hogan. "Huh? You got something you want to tell me? Stop me anytime by telling me what I want to know. Trust me, it only gets worse from here."

Hardtime had had enough. The thought of his precious jewels exploding was enough to convince him. Broken jaw and all, he told everything, including who turned Black Vic on to the hit squad: D and his partner, Scar. In pain, words barely decipherable, he gave them addresses, spots to find them, where their businesses were. He even offered them a spare key to Black Vic's house and informed them that Black Vic was returning the following day. He told them everything he knew to spare his jewels and save his life, all to no avail.

After Hardtime finished spilling his guts, Reece lit the firecrackers anyway. As the stems sizzled and sparked, just before the mini explosives ignited into a rain of crimson, Reece looked at Qwess.

"Rest assured," he said. "This is crew business."

Chapter 12

The following day, Black Vic walked into his home from his vacation. He dropped his bags at the door. He was pissed. He had been calling Hardtime to pick him up from the airport, but he couldn't get through. In fact, there was no answer at any of his spots. He couldn't wait to pound the streets and show everyone he was back. Out of sight, out of mind was right. His own crew wouldn't return any of his calls. He had been calling to get a confirmation on the hit on Reece, but no one took his calls. He wasn't worried because he knew the Blood Team were professionals, and no news was good news. Besides, Black Vic would know by the reaction on the street when he went out if the hit had been successful or not.

Eager to pound the pavement, he walked into his room to change clothes and hit the street. He was not prepared for what he found.

In the center of his bed sat the bald head of his right-hand man, Hardtime. Even in death, his face was grotesquely disfigured from the intense beating he had taken. His mouth gaped open permanently from where the rigor mortis had kicked in. It was obvious he had been in tremendous pain at the time of his death.

Black Vic adjusted his eyes and blinked, as if doing so could make the image go away. It didn't work. Black Vic regained his composure and slowly approached the bed to get a closer look. That's when he saw the note attached to Hardtime's gold bicuspid tooth. The words were written in blood, the message crystal clear.

It read: *Crew Business . . . You missed!*

A few days later, Black Vic was driving down Main Street with the top dropped on his Lex coupe. He was in better spirits because he had just had a sit-down with D and Scar. They were aware of the botched hit, and they assured Black Vic that the original hit was still on, and it should be executed in the coming weeks. This was music to Black Vic's ears because he knew that a pissed-off Reece was hazardous for business, not to mention health.

Black Vic never anticipated that the Crescent Crew would strike back so hard, so quickly. Vic had lost a major part of his team. To him that was no problem, though. Once the heat died down, he could mold a new squad, probably a tougher squad. All except Hardtime— he was simply irreplaceable. They had been through a lot together, and a part of Vic wanted to kill Reece personally. However, he understood the big picture. It was business, never personal.

Black Vic pulled up to a four-way intersection right in the middle of the downtown business district. It was noon, and the sun was beaming bright on this early spring day.

Black Vic scanned his surroundings for something to get into, a possible fling. This time of the year the women flaunted all their assets and were ready to mingle. Not to be disappointed, almost on cue, a motorcycle pulled up on his left side. The driver was huge, but nondescript because of the dark tinted sun visor on his helmet. However, the driver wasn't what caught Black Vic's attention. It was the passenger: a very dark-skinned woman with shiny black, glistening legs. She was hunched over with all of her ass-ets tooted up in the air. Her thong was clearly visible, for her shorts barely covered her voluptuous ass from the top or bottom. Cakes busted out of the shorts like bread from a biscuit can.

While at the light, she raised her visor and eyed Black Vic the whole time, while her main toyed with the throttle on the bike. Women checking him was common for Black Vic, but the intensity was heightened because she was choosing with her man right there. She winked at Black Vic, and he winked back. For a moment, it seemed the two of them were the only people that existed . . . until another motorcycle pulled up on Black Vic's right side. He saw the passenger of that motorcycle toss something into his car, then speed off through the red light. It took Black Vic a moment to recognize what had happened. Yet it became clear when he saw the dreadlocks flapping out of the helmet of the passenger on the second motorcycle.

Reece!

"Mutha . . ." Black Vic swore. On pure instinct, he floored the throttle and gave chase to the motorcycle before he remembered something had been tossed into his vehicle. He frantically searched the vehicle until he found the grenade that had rolled beneath his driver's seat. He palmed it and prepared to throw it out of the car.

That's when he spotted the second one . . . a second too late.

The grenade exploded inside Black Vic's hand, eviscerating him and the Lexus.

Main Street erupted into a ball of flames. When the second grenade exploded seconds later, it blew out the windows of the entire first floor of a bank on the corner. The cop posted outside the bank never knew what hit him. He saw his legs—now separated from his body—go limp in front of him. Initially, he thought it was a terrorist attack, but he recalled seeing two motorcycles speed through the red light just before the explosion. More important, he distinctly remembered seeing dreadlocks flapping from the helmet of one of the riders. This was a hit.

All of this ran through Officer Cureton's head as he lay on the sidewalk bleeding out. However, he could only focus on the pain. So much pain. He could faintly hear the sirens in the distance as he finally embraced the peaceful darkness that enveloped him.

Qwess sat in the plush leather sofa in his mother's den watching the huge sixty-inch screen. He had purchased the TV for his mother as a birthday gift, knowing full well he'd watch it more than she would. This was where Qwess went to gather his thoughts and think things over clearly. It was something about being in the presence of his mother that made everything in his life small by comparison.

Qwess flipped the channels on the television, and sure enough the same story was broadcasting there as well, the same story that had dominated headlines for the past two weeks.

Someone had blown up a car in the middle of downtown Fayetteville, and in the process severely injured a city policeman. According to reports, the bank that the car was blown up in front of had unclear surveillance photos of the whole thing. The DA was confident that with those photos, and the cop's testimony, he could bring the perps to justice.

Qwess shook his head in disbelief. "This nigga is crazy!"

Qwess's phone rang. It was Doe. He answered, *"As salaam alayka."*

"Do you see this shit?" Doe asked.

"I'm watching it now."

"Bro, this can't be good. I hope this wasn't him."

For Qwess's part, he knew more. Two weeks ago when the incident first occurred, he remembered Reece two-waying him with a message that read: *Qisas. Watch the news.* Qwess knew that *Qisas* meant an eye-for-an-eye in Islam. What Qwess didn't know is how extreme things had gotten . . . until he watched the news. Again and again. The sheer brazenness of the act had garnered national attention, and before long the feds had descended upon Fayetteville.

"This has gotten out of hand. Let me call you back. I need to speak with him ASAP."

It was two days later before Reece came to see Qwess at the studio.

"Congratulations!" Qwess told Reece, as he walked in and took a seat behind the console.

"For?" Reece asked.

"Your victory. It's been all over the news."

Reece scoffed. "You think that's it? This shit ain't over."

Qwess thought for sure that the war was over since Black Vic was dead. He was astonished and a little worried when Reece informed him that he intended to hunt down every person who had had a hand in his planned assassination. Qwess was worried because of the look in Reece's eyes. Qwess had never seen it before. Personally, he thought enough was enough. They should stop there. However, Reece wasn't having it. Reece reiterated that he intended to take out everyone. One look in his glassed-over eyes, and Qwess knew resistance was futile. It was then he made his decision and offered monetary support—which Reece declined.

"Again, I appreciate it, brother, but once they're out the way, money will rain from the heavens like divine confetti."

There was too much on Qwess's mind to dispute with Reece. He had the tour coming up, he had meetings with accountants, label owners, promoters, etc. Plus, he was still mourning the death of his lady and unborn child.

"All I ask is, be safe, though," Qwess asked.

"For sure."

Once Qwess made his decision, he began concentrating on the business at hand: prepping for the tour. He met with the "Uncle Tom" from AMG records to discuss their itinerary. At the meeting, Qwess was informed that before they went overseas for the second half of the tour, they would shoot the video. Qwess was gaining momentum on the charts since his party when Shauntay had been killed, so they wanted to capitalize with a video.

It was not surprising. America had always had a healthy penchant for violence. When word spread out of the tragedy that had knocked on Qwess's door, people flocked to the stores to buy his albums, either to empathize, or to listen to see if his musings on record were authentic. Bottom line, controversy sells, and Qwess's record was selling exponentially. So the heads at AMG wanted to capitalize on this rise and introduce Qwess to the world, not just the Southwest. A video would do that.

The tour was scheduled to start in three days. Everyone was more than ready. During the time Qwess was stuck in his rut, Doe was proving to be a worthy business partner, as Qwess suspected. Doe had made sure Flame and 8-Ball had passports. He also had made sure that Flame's money was well taken care of. He even left Fayetteville to help Flame select a house so he wouldn't become a victim of predatory lending. Ultimately, Doe had personally taken Flame under his wing to make sure things continued to run smoothly. For that Qwess was eternally grateful.

He and Doe were becoming closer than ever.

It was a little after midnight when Doe was ushered into Reece's office at his funeral home. Ever since the war broke out, Reece was using the funeral home as a base. Various members of the Crescent Crew rotated guard shifts at the funeral home. However, Samson never left Reece's side. So he was the only person present with Doe and Reece. When Doe signaled he wanted privacy, Reece dismissed Samson.

"What's up, cuz?" Reece slurred. Doe had noticed the stench of marijuana when he first walked in, so he already knew Reece was high. In fact, Doe could never remember Reece being so high all the time. He even suspected he was doing more than weed.

"Just chillin', man."

Reece slumped down in his leather desk chair, chuckled. "So, what brings you to the dark side, cuz-o?"

"Just came to see you, man. You know we leave tomorrow. Well." Doe hesitated. "Check it, man. I've been watching the news, man. And I'm worried. The DA seems serious, cuz!"

Reece whispered, barely audibly. "Yeah, well, I'm serious, too."

Doe spoke louder as if Reece wasn't getting it. "Yo, I'm serious, cuz. This shit ain't no joke."

"So whadda you want me to do!" Reece exploded. "Stop? Hell naw. I didn't start this shit! But I will end it. Oh, yeah, I will end it."

"It doesn't have to be like this," pleaded Doe. "You can take a break, man."

Doe tried to convince Reece to chill, because in his mind he knew the system wasn't going to let anyone get away with injuring one of their own. They believed that one of their lives was more precious than anyone else's, especially a black one.

"How?" Reece scoffed. "How can I take a break from destiny?"

"You can come with us tomorrow. Get on that bus and leave all this shit behind."

Reece leaned back in his chair, as if contemplating the offer. Then, he reached into his desk and pulled out a blunt already rolled. He took his gold lighter and lit the pine, inhaling deeply. Reece stood, walked over to a shelf in the corner of the room. He removed a fourteen-carat gold crown from the top of the shelf and placed it neatly on his locks. Then he returned to address his cousin.

"See, cuz, I'm a king. Destiny has ordained me to be a king. So, I accept!" Reece crossed the room and slid right up in Doe's face. His eyes bulged from his head as he continued. "As a king, I must defend my kingdom against infiltrators! They crossed me. Now they shall feel my wrath!"

Doe didn't know if it was the drugs or what, but he was certain Reece had lost it. The nigga was talking crazy! All this kingdom shit. What Doe couldn't possibly know is that once you stare a man in his eyes as he takes his last breath, it empowers you with an unparalleled feeling of omnipotence. Reece had done this several times in the last few weeks. So the drug that intoxicated him at the moment wasn't weed. It was pure power in its rarest form. The power of holding life and death in the palm of your hand.

Doe attempted to pacify Reece again. "Look, cuz, all I'm saying is you can take a break. Go with us on the road. Hell, even that li'l broad you been kicking it with can go."

Reece smiled at the mentioning of Destiny. Every moment that he wasn't in the field, he was spending with her. Rarely would a woman keep his interest that long, but Destiny was truly special. She was wise beyond her years. Reece enjoyed spending time with a woman who could match him wit for wit. Plus it seemed like they had known each other forever. She could read him so well.

Reece stayed focused on the conversation at hand, though. "Cuz, by the time y'all come back from tour, I plan on having this shit wrapped up. Hell, we planning right now to get them old heads. We gon' get the Blood Team, too."

A thought occurred to Doe, so he had to ask. "Aye yo, this isn't just revenge, is it?"

Reece paced the room, dragging the blunt deeply. "Hell, naw. I'm a businessman. I'm always thinking about business. With these niggas out the way, the Crescent Crew will run the streets. No competition. I would have done it sooner, but I didn't want to transgress bounds. Now they left me no choice."

"Nigga crazy," Doe mumbled.

Reece heard him and stopped pacing. He looked at Doe with the coldest look he could muster, and told him, "Nigga, when I say I'm a king, I mean that shit! I AM A KING! And all of Carolina will be my kingdom!"

It was official. The nigga had lost it. Doe knew there was nothing he could do but sit and wait for life to humble Reece. So he took the easy route.

"All right, I just came to holla at you before I leave.

I'm 'bout to dip. I don't gotta kiss your ring or no shit, do I?" Doe joked.

Reece didn't think it was so funny. "Laugh now, but I'm telling you: The way we gon' bring the heat to these niggas, it'll go down in history, watch!" Reece walked Doe to the door. "Tell Qwess good luck. Who all going?"

"You know we travel light. Me, Qwess, Hulk, the kid Flame, and his man 8-Ball."

"That's it?" asked Reece.

"Yeah, you know the label gon' send some scrubs wit' us, but we self-contained."

Before Reece opened the door, he touched his cousin's shoulder affectionately, getting his attention. "Hey, cuz, I'm proud of you. I always knew you had it in you. Fuck slaving for them crackers. This ain't 1803 and shit. Doing for yourself, that's what's up. It feel good, don't it?"

"Hell, yeah."

"I know. Let me tell you something. And think hard on this while you on the road."

"What, nigga? You act like you bout to give me the Holy Grail or something."

Reece chuckled. "Something like that. Here goes." He paused for emphasis. "You are a king, too. All you have to do is accept it and demand mu'fuckas treat you like a king. Remember, power concedes nothing without demand. So, when you realize it's only one greater than yourself—and he ain't never been here—then you on your way."

Doe looked at Reece, expecting more. "Is that it?" he asked.

Reece was offended. "Yeah." He sucked his teeth. "Don't worry 'bout it. I'll show you what I mean. Watch. By the time you get back, I'll show you how a king supposed to live."

With that, he opened the door to let Doe out. Then he returned to his desk and opened the bottom drawer. He pulled out a bag of cocaine. He placed it on the desk, separating the fine white lines of the powdery substance. He dipped his head twice, ingesting all of the drug into his system. He then replaced the bag in the drawer, wiped his nose clean, and met Samson in the hallway.

Samson regarded Reece speculatively. Reece just responded with a shrewd look and said, "Let's go."

"Where?"

Reece chuckled. "On to our destiny."

Part 2

The Next Level . . .

Chapter 13

The auditorium was wall-to-wall packed. All of the lights were off in the building except one: the lone spotlight highlighting the emcee on stage. There was a constant murmur in the crowd that steadily rose as the emcee fell further and further into his verse . . .

> *I drop jewels, but this an ode to the streets*
> *For cats carrying that heat trying to make*
>   *ends meet*
> *Righteous men at heart, playing the cards*
>   *they dealt*
> *On a mission for that paper trying to stack*
>   *that wealth . . .*

As Qwess continued to work the crowd into a frenzy, Flame waited at the side of the stage waiting for Qwess to call him on and introduce him.

They were in Houston, Texas, performing at a Memorial Day concert. They were initially supposed to be an opening act. But thanks to AMG's fierce promotions department, they were added to the list of performers straight-up and as a result earned a fee for this concert.

Doe couldn't believe how helpful AMG proved to be. Much to the chagrin of Qwess, Doe agreed to let AMG re-promote Qwess's album on an international level. The result was remarkable! They had been on the road for a little over a month, and when they drove into every town west of the Mississippi, they were greeted with posters of Qwess. Radio was playing Qwess's single, "Street Life," religiously. In fact, it was averaging 350 spins a week in some places. They were even hearing it was huge in fickle New York City.

So far everything was going well and problem-free, with the exception of an altercation they had had with a nationally known Mississippi artist, who had his goons surround the tour bus they were riding on. The situation was quelled when Hulk pointed his shotgun directly at the artist, who miraculously humbled himself instantly. Other than that episode, the tour was operating successfully.

For Flame, he had never known tired like this! They were hitting two, three major cities a day. And in some instances, they were taking groupies on board the bus with them to the next town. The boy had never had so much head! It was unbelievable what chicks would do to and for a rapper. Even 8-Ball's fat ass was fucking every night. They were blowing the best weed money could buy, fucking every chance they got, and shopping like money was water. This was definitely the life he envisioned. Plus, to top it off, the niggas he was down with were cool as hell, though he wasn't too comfortable around the big dude by himself. He was too quiet for Flame's taste.

On stage Qwess was continuing to command the audience as he said his last chorus:

> *Street life everywhere is the same*
> *The only thing that change is the everyday*
> *   slang*
> *You got thugs pumping drugs*
> *No holds barred busting slugs*
> *One struggle, one blood, to all my brethren . . .*
> *   one love!*

On cue, fireworks exploded. Qwess motioned for Flame to join him on stage.

"Yeah, yeah! This my li'l nigga Flame repping Fayette-nam. Show some love, H-Town!"

DJ Technique, who was the tour DJ, busted into an instrumental by a legendary Houston rapper named after a drug kingpin in a movie. The crowd erupted just from the mere playing of the record from their hometown legend. That is, until Flame started freestyling off of it. At first the audience was apprehensive. Then as the smooth flows gushed through the speakers, they had to give up props. Hip-hop was definitely in the house!

Flame went to the edge of the stage and attempted to pull a young lady on stage. Security denied him, so Flame jumped into the audience himself. The spotlight moved with him. He wrapped the thick Houstonian into a tight embrace and began rapping seductively in her ear . . .

> *I been peeping you all day*
> *They way them hips sway got me fiendin' for*
> *   a day*
> *That I could touch you, and see what's really*
> *   going on*
> *Tease you until I make you saturate your thong*
> *Then push it to the side as my tongue just*
> *   glide*
> *Up and down your clit, then slide inside.*

The young lady was damn near cumming in her skin-tight riding pants. Flame taunted her for the remainder of the verse, then joined Qwess back on stage to raucous applause. There wasn't a woman in the crowd who wasn't feeling the brash, raunchy youngster.

Qwess exhorted the crowd to buy the new album, and they left the stage to a standing ovation.

A.B.P. had conquered Houston, Texas.

D lay in the hotel bed looking down at the beautiful young lady between his legs. Her name was Vanilla, and she used to be a stripper. D rarely messed with strippers, but this chick was an exception. She had been pursuing him for the last few weeks, coming by his spot all dressed up and shit. All the fellas were dying to hit it and couldn't believe he hadn't hit. It wasn't that he didn't dig her. He just didn't like when bitches came on too strong. He felt like they had ulterior motives. However, when Vanilla invited him to dinner—her treat—he couldn't resist. Never in a million years did he think she would floss like this! Bringing him to a rented villa, then cooking for him in a lace-up teddy with matching thigh-high boots. It didn't take long for him to decide, he'd rather feast on her rather than what was in the pot.

Presently she was sucking his dick like she was trying to pull his spine through his dick head, and he was in another world because of it. He didn't know which aroused him more, the head itself or watching his joint get surrounded by those beautiful lips. Just as he was about to cum in her mouth, she stopped.

"Aw, damn, girl! What's up?" he asked.

"Ay, papi, I want you to fuck me in my ass," she demanded.

He wasn't used to taking the "brown road" so at first

he hesitated. Then he reasoned that if he wanted regular sex, he could've gotten it at home. So, if this li'l young chick wanted to get her asshole bust open, he'd happily oblige her.

Vanilla got up and told him to wait while she went and got some Vaseline from the cabinet near the front door. She returned a few seconds later, Vaseline in hand.

She began stroking his manhood, then rubbed Vaseline all over the condom on his penis. She then lay on the bed on her stomach, with her ass poked up.

"Go slow, papi. It's been a while," she told him.

As D was spreading her shapely ass cheeks apart, he could've sworn he heard a noise. He paused a moment.

"Come on, papi. I'm waiting!" Vanilla prodded.

Against his better judgment, he proceeded. When the head of his dick penetrated the tight, hot hole, all concerns were thrown to the wind. His only thought was going deeper into Vanilla's orifice.

He was halfway in when he noticed a huge shadow on the headboard. The shadow was more like an eclipse as it darkened one half of the room.

"What the fuck?" It was all D could get out before he felt himself being suspended in the air. His back hit the wall so hard he almost went through it. When the blinding pain subsided enough for him to see, he looked right into the face of a huge bald-headed black man, who punched him in the stomach as he lifted him onto the wall.

D attempted to speak, but he had no air. In a brief moment of recognition, he knew what had happened. The broad set him up. Stinking bitch!

Reece walked into the room, followed by Jersey Ali, Muhammad, and Born. They were all clad in black with masks on. They didn't even acknowledge Vanilla.

Reece walked in front of D, and he immediately started

copping pleas. Reece literally smacked the piss out of him. It leaked out onto his leg.

"Stop bitching, nigga. Time to die!" Reece taunted. "Born, get the girl."

Born walked over to Vanilla, who was curled in a ball at the corner of the bed. He pulled out a silencer-equipped pistol, which made Vanilla start begging for her life.

"Please, Reece. I got kids to feed. I know you make niggas bleed. I don't need that type of shit. Please!"

"Stop begging!" Reece yelled. "I hate that shit. Now tell me why I shouldn't kill you?"

"B-because I did what you asked," stammered Vanilla. "And I ain't gon' say nothing. This shit never happened, Reece. I didn't see nothing!"

Born wasn't convinced. He put the gun to her head, ready to pull the trigger. Vanilla closed her eyes waiting to hear the gunshot. It never came. Instead, she felt a hand under her chin. She closed her eyes tighter. She heard from seemingly far away, "Look at me. Open your eyes. Look at me."

She did, looking Reece eye-to-eye. It's funny how a person's sense of detail sharpens during life-and-death situations, for all Vanilla could think about was how handsome Reece looked in his glowing menace. She thought she was dreaming when she heard him say he was going to let her live.

"Huh?" she asked.

"I said, as long as you give me your word this never happened, you got my word nothing will ever happen to you. You go back on your word, I go back on mine," he explained.

Vanilla assured Reece he had her undying loyalty and got up to gather her things. While she was in the bathroom, she heard what sounded like a loud cough, accom-

panied by ear-piercing screams. At first she thought D
was dead, then she heard Reece talking to him.

"It's not up to me whether you live or not," Reece
said. "It's up to your punk-ass partner. If he can't set up a
meeting with these Blood Team niggas, you die. It's just
that simple."

Vanilla peeked out the door and observed that D had
been shot in the knee. He was crying like a newborn
baby. She had never seen such a powerful man reduced to
tears by another man. In a way, she felt sorry for him.
Better him than her, though. She keenly observed how
Reece directed his squad as they tied a tourniquet around
D's leg, then bagged and gagged him. To her, Reece was
the embodiment of power. Even in his killer black, he still
looked . . . regal. His mannerisms were so kinglike. It
was like he was a part of the action, but still above it.
Frankly, that shit turned her on! The more she studied
Reece, the more her pussy throbbed.

So, when Reece walked to the front, let everyone out,
came back and said to her, "V, take a shower and get
right. All this bitching got my dick hard," it was only fitting that she obliged him.

That night she sucked, fucked, and bucked on Reece
like her life depended on him.

Actually, it did.

New York, New York! Bright lights, big city. The
A.B.P. tour had arrived in New York, and everyone was
high on adrenaline. It was early December, and they were
on the last leg of the tour. They had been all over the
United States performing, and were now back on the
good ole East Coast. Everyone knew the importance of
gaining a following in New York, so after they performed

at club Spotlite, they headed to a radio interview. Radio interviews were only done in the most important cities like Los Angeles, Chicago, Detroit, and St. Louis. Thus far, there was no official format, so everyone played the interviews by ear.

On this particular Friday night, as Qwess and company arrived at the Flava 103.1 studios, no one knew how New York radio got down. They would soon find out.

Diane the Diva was eagerly anticipating her guests. She had been hearing a lot about these Carolina cats from her sister radio affiliates. From what she had heard, they were on point.

When Qwess and crew walked in, she didn't recognize them. They didn't look like southern cats at all. In fact, the light-skinned guy looked like he could be related to her. She was Dominican and could easily spot another Latino. He introduced himself as Rolando, VP of Atlantic Beach Productions, and then introduced the others to her. She recognized Qwess from the advance photos on the Internet, now that she got a closer look. His rose-colored spectacles had thrown her off initially.

It was nearing prime-time for the night show, so Diane wanted to get everyone situated before they went on air. She ushered everyone to their seats at the mic with urgency. They all were ready just as the show went on air. Diane the Diva opened up.

"What up, what up, NYC, stand up!" She played the pre-recorded drop for her show. Then she opened the show.

"This ya girl Diane the Diva, and I have a treat for you tonight. In the studio with me I got ya boy Qwess, representing A.B.P., all the way from the Cackalack. Qwess, say what's up to the people."

"Yo, yo, New York. What's up."

"All right. Now in case you haven't heard by now,

Qwess sold fifty thousand records *independently*! So you know what that mean *cha-ching*! Okaaay." She pushed a button on the computer, and it made a cash register sound, much to everyone's amusement. Then she continued. "Okay, Qwess has been touring the entire last quarter."

Diane the Diva gave her spiel about who, what, when, where, how, and why he was in New York. Then she decided to get creative and open up the interview.

"So, Qwess how is the touring going? I know you can't keep the ladies off you, huh? Ladies, Qwess is *guapo*! You hear me?"

Qwess saw she wanted to play, so he played. "Nah, diva. You the one. *Y con su sonrisa hermosa.*"

"Ooh, and he speaks Spanish!" Diane the Diva cooed.

"So, Qwess, who is this wit' you? 'Cause I heard from some of my girls on the road that you got an ill team."

Qwess motioned for Flame to step up closer to the mic. "I'll let them introduce themselves to you."

"Yeah, yeah, New York, this ya boy Flame repping Fayettenam, North Crack, ya heard?"

The Diva covered her mouth in surprise. "Oh, so you the brash youngsta I been hearing about. He's a cutie, too, ladies."

Doe saw an opportunity and seized the moment. He stepped to a mic and issued a challenge. "Yeah. I heard NY got those top shottas tuning into this station. I got a G that say nobody fucking wit—oops I mean—messing with my man Flame on the mic."

"Wait, wait, now who are you? Tell the people who you are."

"Oh, my bad. This ya boy Doe repping A.B.P. VP of all operations. And New York, I got a G to any young or old spitter who can take my man Flame out on the mic."

Diane the Diva, loving controversy, amped things up. "Okay, so you telling me you'll give a G to any rapper who can beat your rapper in a battle right now?"

"Yep."

"Wait, you do realize this is New York, home of hip-hop?"

"Yep."

"You can't be serious."

For an answer, Doe pulled out a wad of hundred-dollar bills.

The Diva issued the challenge. "All right, New York. He's serious. All you rappers needing that money call in now. 917-555-1031 or 1-888-555-1031."

In less than an hour, all hell broke loose as a gang of New York rappers was in the lobby attempting to bust in the studio. They all wanted that money. Fuck calling in! They wanted to get their cash firsthand. Diane the Diva had seen rappers come to the studio to battle other rappers before, but never in numbers of this magnitude. She believed it was because the mere thought that a Southern rapper calling out New York rappers was a smack in the face! After all, everyone knew New York started this rap shit!

Security was trying to gain control of the situation, but it only calmed down when some of New York's finest stormed the building, putting an end to all of the ruckus.

"Damn, and I really wanted to tear into these niggas, too," Flame declared over the airwaves, obviously disappointed.

Diane the Diva was impressed. "You Carolina niggas are wild," she said. "I can't believe y'all didn't think New York was goin' to represent. You know it's still real in the field!"

Qwess was pleased with the publicity and assured her, "It's real everywhere."

Doe cosigned that. "No doubt. I'm telling you, my man Flame would've roasted those cats."

Diane the Diva noticed she was outnumbered and was eager to get back on track. They returned from a commercial, and Diane explained to the listeners what had transpired and why no one came in the studio. Then, taking everyone by surprise, she asked Flame to spit an on-air freestyle. She smirked at Doe and shot him a wink, as if to say, "I got ya."

Doe returned the smirk and passed the mic along to Flame. Flame took his place before the mic and commandeered the airwaves. "New York, get your decks ready. It's on!"

Flame had just finished setting the New York airwaves on fire, and everyone was in the lobby preparing to leave when a man accosted Flame and passed him a card. "If you ever get tired of your situation, holla at me. I can get you to the next level," the man offered.

"Nah, that's okay. I'm straight," Flame replied, curving him.

From the side, Qwess observed the whole exchange silently. Watching Flame display his loyalty, he gained a newfound respect for the young rapper.

Later that night, they all attended an industry party. AMG executives had arranged to get the whole crew VIP passes so they could be among the movers and shakers.

While at the party, Doe used some of his old contacts in New York to get next to the number one mix tape DJ in the city. Doe arranged for Flame and Qwess to drop some exclusive freestyles on his next mix tape. The DJ was more than happy to do so because that would give him an edge on his other competitors in the Southern market. He wasn't a fool. He was the number one DJ for a reason.

The South was on the rise. He recognized opportunity and took advantage of it.

Flame and 8-Ball were getting pissy drunk in the VIP section, but they were handling themselves well. Some industry groupies found out that Flame was a rapper and started sweating him relentlessly. Before long, Flame was standing in a dark corner getting head with a huge smile on his face.

While the rest of A.B.P. were languishing in the come-up, the head of the label was off in a corner by himself lost in space. He was having one of those moments.

Ever since Shauntay's murder, Qwess would drift off into deep thought in the most awkward places. It's not that he loved Shauntay tremendously, it was the fact that she didn't deserve to go out like that. He partly blamed himself. He hadn't been calling home much while on the road, and he knew that Reece was taking care of everything. He just didn't know if killing Shauntay's killers would alleviate his frustrations and quell his demons.

Only time would tell.

While A.B.P. was taking New York by storm, Scar was waiting on the Blood Team to arrive. He paced back and forth inside his secluded parking garage looking at his Rolex. He was completely alone, because the Blood Team didn't like dealing with outsiders. They knew about D, but D was the reason they were having this meeting.

It had been more than a month since the Crescent Crew had kidnapped his partner, and Scar was finally ready to get it over with.

It was simple to meet their demand of setting up a meeting with the Blood Team because the Blood Team was still indebted to Scar. Reece was still breathing.

Apparently, everyone had underestimated Reece and

his Crescent Crew. However, Scar swore that wouldn't happen again. Once he got D back, he was going to wage war himself. He didn't care what happened to the Blood Team. Far as he was concerned, if they would've taken care of business properly, then they wouldn't be in this predicament. So fuck 'em. Scar had his vest on his chest, his pistol on his hip, and a getaway car in the back. So, when the heat came, he could go. He didn't know where Reece and his crew were. All he knew is that once Blood Team arrived, they'd be shortly behind. Everything else would be left up to those two parties. Or so he thought. Could it be all so simple?

The 4Runners finally arrived. One entered the garage; the other truck parked out front. The first 4Runner rolled up slowly and came to a stop inches from where Scar stood in his full-length black leather trench.

Murda jumped from the driver's side of the big truck. Scar could make out a silhouette of a passenger in the front, but that person never exited the vehicle.

As Murda walked up to greet Scar, a red dot appeared in the center of his head. Before he could warn him, Murda's head exploded like a melon, spraying Scar with blood and brain matter. A split-second letter, a hole appeared in the windshield on the passenger side of the truck, as the passenger was struck also. He never got a chance to duck before death claimed him.

Inside the other 4Runner out front, T. Gunn watched as Murda's head exploded into a dust of gray and red. He was taken aback and briefly confused, since he never heard the report of a gunshot. However, his confusion only lasted a second. The next second, he was gunning the powerful V-8 engine in reverse. When he spun the truck around, he saw the narrow path leading to the garage was now blocked off by two Range Rovers parked side by side, bumper-to-bumper. Nino, who sat in the passenger seat, immediately stuck his HK assault rifle out the window and began firing while T. Gunn barreled toward the two trucks.

Samson, who was already positioned on the hood of one of the Rovers with a .50-caliber sniper rifle, never flinched when he saw the 4Runner careening toward them. He methodically fired one round into Nino's head, bringing the gunfight to a quick halt. He calmly shifted the barrel to the left and fired one round into T. Gunn's head, ending his existence. The truck skidded to the left, spun out of control, and tumbled toward the Range rapidly. Jersey Ali and Muhammad, who piloted the Rovers, both backed the Rovers up quickly, allowing the flipping 4Runner to flip past them in a heap of twisted metal and smoke.

Back inside the garage, Scar attempted to make a hasty retreat for it, but Seal—he had the name because he used to be a Navy Seal—thwarted his plan. Seal had been posted up on the roof of the garage with his .50-caliber rifle twenty minutes after Scar called Reece to confirm the meeting place. It was he who had orchestrated the wonderful plan, and he was ecstatic to see it playing out to the letter. He had been salivating for the opportunity to prove his worth.

When Scar tried to run to his Corvette parked in back, Seal shot the gas tank. The car exploded in flames. Shrapnel caught Scar in the leg, flooring him, where he lay until the Rovers pulled around back to pick up him and Seal. The hatch of one of the Rovers opened up and Seal tossed Scar in the back. Seal hopped in the back with him, and the trucks sped off into the night onto a rendezvous point to link up with Reece.

* * *

Inside the cabin in the country, Scar and D were tied up sitting across from each other. Surrounding them were Jersey Ali, Born, Muhammad, Seal, and Samson. The crew had orders to bring them there and wait for Reece—no doubt so he could torture them. They didn't have to wait long, as Reece's brand-new green Aston Martin crept up, the wide tires crushing the gravel. Reece hopped out wearing a full-length beige shearling coat. He looked as if he was going out for a night on the town instead of about to commit multiple murders, but that's where he was in life. For Reece, when he was forcing his enemies to pay homage to his strength, that was the equivalent of a night out on the town.

Reece joined the others inside amid admiring stares. "Damn, nigga, where you going?" Samson asked when Reece shed his coat, revealing a green two-piece crocodile suit with matching boots.

"I got a date tonight," Reece whispered back.

"Damn, god. I like those shoes," Samson said, inspecting the intricate details of the Luccheses. "Man, is that a claw I see? Damn, those grooves are deep!" he joked.

Reece chuckled. "Cut it out, let's handle this business."

Before Reece could say anything, D started whining. "Y-yo man. You said you wouldn't kill me if Scar came through for you."

Reece put his index finger to his forehead, then pointed to him. "You know, you're right. I did say that. And . . . I'm a man of my word. Right, fellas?"

His crew shrugged nonchalantly. "I guess."

"So this is what I'm going to do." Reece pulled his .44 Magnum from his waist and emptied all the shells except one. He spun the cylinder. "I'ma let Scar decide. If

you can survive three rounds—huh, no pun intended—
then I won't kill you."

Reece motioned for Samson to untie one of Scar's
hands. He did, and held it steady in a vice grip. Reece put
the pistol in Scar's hand.

"Whaddaya say, Scar. Are you your brother's keeper?"

Scar gripped the pistol and aimed it straight at D's
head with Samson's assistance. With no hesitation he
pulled the trigger.

Click.

Both Scar and D exhaled deeply. Neither one
flinched anymore, because they both understood they'd
never see another sunrise. This was where they would
take their last breaths.

Reece took the gun and spun the cylinder again. He
placed it back in Scar's hand. Scar aimed and pulled the
trigger.

BLAUW!!

"You fuckin shot me!!" D screamed, grabbing his
head.

Reece smacked D upside his head. "Shut the fuck up!
If he was playing right, you would've never known.
Pussy mu'fucka!"

Blood oozed from D's head where the bullet grazed
him.

Reece was fed up. "Fuck it! Just fuck it! Try an' give
niggas a chance . . . fuck it! Yo, Ali, shoot these bas-
tards!"

Reece stood a distance away so as not to get blood on
his three-thousand-dollar outfit. He looked Scar in the
eyes. Before Ali shot him, Reece whispered, "I did this to
you. Me!"

Scar never heard the last word. Ali put his brains in
D's lap. Then he went around and put D's brains in Scar's
lap.

When it was done, Reece congratulated everyone. "This war is now over," he announced. "Now let's reap the harvest of our labor."

Everyone present was relieved. They had been through a war and only sustained one injury when Nino squeezed off his lucky shot into Power's chest earlier that night. Power would live, though, while their enemies were now fertilizer.

"I want everyone to meet up tomorrow at the god hour. Samson, you know what to do with the bodies, right?"

"Of course."

"All right. I got a date. Peace!"

Reece returned to his Aston Martin and slipped off into the night a happy man. While some crime bosses used murder as a last resort, Reece was a fan of using it as a first resort. In his world, murder represented the ultimate balance. If it was done correctly the first time, he wouldn't have to do it again. He hoped that all the blood he had shed in the past few months could be put behind him now. He had remained true to his word and killed two birds with one bullet. He had avenged Shauntay's death, while solidifying his position in the streets.

With Black Vic and his whole crew dismembered, there was no one standing in the way of the Crescent Crew's ascent to the top of the underworld. It was time for expansion.

As Reece put his foot into the raucous V-12 engine, he felt stronger, wiser, and richer than he had ever been. For the first time in life he truly felt like a king. From now on, everyone would address him as such.

Chapter 14

Atlanta, Georgia, was known as the strip club capital of the world, the mecca of the South, and possibly Ghetto, USA, depending on whom you asked. One thing that couldn't be disputed about Atlanta was its women. Atlanta had arguably the most beautiful women in the world. Hands down. A-T-L, as it was called by its residents, boasted more dimes than a piggy bank. And as was customary in a capitalist society, for the right price, you could see anything and maybe experience everything.

Since the ATL was known worldwide for its women, it would come as no surprise that one of its main attractions was its numerous strip clubs. On any given night, you could feast your eyes on some of God's most beautiful creations, from the bottom of the barrel to the top of the crop.

When the A.B.P. posse rolled through Atlanta on its end-of-tour bash, they only wanted the best. So it was only fitting that they invaded Blue Flame. And boy, did they ever!

Since Atlanta was "where the playas played," everyone knew they had to represent lovely. Money attracted money. Therefore you couldn't go into a money spot looking shabby. Even though Qwess was realizing success with his album, Atlantic Beach Productions was still a fairly new and unestablished record label. So, if they wanted to get to that next level, and attract new business with the production arm of the label, they had to court attention at all cost. What better way to say "I'm about business" than your wardrobe. That's why when Qwess, Hulk, Doe, Flame, and 8-Ball fell up in Magic City, they were suited and booted.

Qwess, a Crescent Crew member 'til the death, represented that cream-and-green to the fullest with a hunter-green sharkskin suit with matching boots. From his neck swung the massive diamond chain with the diamond-encrusted A.B.P. charm. His ears glowed like stars were in them from the square-cut diamonds that filled his lobes.

Doe, who had finally come out of his shell, wore a peach-colored linen suit. He capped his ensemble with peach ostrich boots and gold Cartier frames. With his hair in a ponytail, he resembled a Dominican drug kingpin.

Even Flame and 8-Ball represented with matching Versace shirts and slacks. Flame's was red, 8-Ball's blue. Taking a cue from Qwess, they wore gators.

Tomorrow, they were returning to North Carolina to shoot a video. Tonight they celebrated a job well done. They were in a festive mood.

Word had traveled that Qwess and his crew were in the house, since Qwess was well known in these parts. The bartender sent him drinks, for which Qwess thanked him. The dancers wanted to come over and get their grind on, but felt discouraged by the 330-pound hulk in his green Armani suit guarding Qwess. After a moment, Qwess realized the deterrent and ordered Hulk to go have some fun. When he did, the floodgates opened, and Qwess found himself surrounded by dimes.

Flame and 8-Ball were having a ball from the moment they pimped through the door. They had both been to strip clubs in North Carolina, but the women weren't so beautiful, or so . . . naked. I'm talking about butterball, birthday-suit naked! Not a stretch mark, gunshot wound, or honeybun in sight. It was mesmerizing. Women so beautiful, strictly for your enjoyment, with only one rule: You couldn't touch. They had already witnessed one fool get toted out the club by a burly bunch of bouncers.

"Damn, nigga, the hoes clocking these bitches harder than the niggas," stated 8-Ball, observing the large number of women inside the club who weren't dancing.

"Hell, yeah. These dyke bitches are something serious," Flame agreed when he saw a woman giving another woman a lap dance.

"Look at the fucking stage. It's more bitches around that muthafucka than hard heads. I should make one of them hoes raise up out me a seat."

Flame chuckled. "You mean more like two seats, yo big ass," he added, playfully tapping 8-Ball.

"Fuck you."

Doe came up behind them, wrapping his arms around both of them. "You see anything you like?" he asked.

"Hell, yeah!" they responded in unison.

"Well, go for what you know. Ain't no sense just looking at the pussy."

"But I thought we couldn't touch them?" 8-Ball asked, obviously intimidated by women so fine.

Doe shot him a look like what he said was absurd. "Man, we been schoolin' y'all asses for three months now, and you still don't get it. These broads in here to get money, so give them money, and you can get whateva you want."

8-Ball still wasn't convinced, so Doe drove his point home. "Nigga, you think these hoes on the road was fuckin' you cause of your looks?" he asked. "Negro, please! I mean you cool, but a Denzel you're not."

Flame burst out into raucous laughter.

"Fuck you," swore 8-Ball.

Doe punched him in the arm before calling over a thick, bow-legged redbone. She sauntered over on her six-inch stiletto heels.

"What's up, suga?" she asked.

Doe whispered in her ear explaining the situation. Not all of the women inside fucked for cash, but a lot of them did. It was just a matter of finding out which ones did, because money wasn't a thing. The whole crew had cash for days.

On the other side of the club, Qwess had pulled a bad broad with smooth chocolate skin. Everyone had been sweating her all night, for she was easily the baddest chick in the club, depending on your taste. Her hair was cut short, as was she, standing about five-two without her heels. Her skin was so smooth, she didn't wear much makeup, and her eyes were a piercing steel-gray.

She and Qwess had been conversing for a short while before he came straight out and asked her. "So, how much I gotta pay for your time?"

She blew up. "Hold up! I ain't no hoe!"

Qwess had to calm her down. "Hold on, love. Wait. Be easy now. I didn't say you was a hoe."

"Well, you playing me like a hoe. I ain't no trick. I just do this to pay for school!"

Oh, lord, thought Qwess. *Not another hooker with a heart of gold.* However, he said, "Oh, yeah?"

"Yeah," she snapped.

"What school?" he challenged

"Emory."

"Oh. Okay."

It wasn't that Qwess didn't believe her, it was just

hard to take her seriously with her titties hanging out and a G-string crammed in her ass. Yet he liked what he saw.

He told her, "Listen, I wasn't implying that you were a hoe or nothing. I just like what I see, but I also see all these other brothers in here checking for you, too."

She had her hand on her hip. "And?"

"And, I'm short on time and even shorter on patience. I don't want to waste the night tricking bank, competing with these dudes to gain your affection. I wanted you to know if it's about money, I got you."

She sized Qwess up carefully. "Well, it's not about money."

"No?"

"No."

"Okay. Fair enough." Qwess extended his hand. "By the way, they call me Qwess."

"I'm Innocence." They shook hands.

Pouring on the charm, Qwess asked, "So, your mama named you Innocence?"

"Nope. Just like I'm sure your mama ain't name you Qwess."

"Oh, you got jokes?"

Innocence smiled sweetly.

She and Qwess continued to talk for a while. However, when it started getting late, Qwess sprung his line. He hadn't been partaking in the freakfests while on tour because he was still in mourning, and by now he was horny as hell.

He asked her, "Look, I only got one night in town. In the morning, I'll be gone. So you tryna kick it or what tonight?"

Innocence didn't flip this time, though she still felt he was playing her like a hoe.

"Yeah, we can kick it," she calmly replied. "You ain't

getting no ass from me, though. If you want that, you can holla at one of these other broads. I won't have no love lost. I'm sure they'd love to say they slept with a rapper."

"Not even on my mind, we just met," Qwess replied. "It ain't even like that."

Innocence placed her hand on his lips. "Be real, Qwess. If that's what you want, go ahead."

"Nah, ma. Word, it ain't like that. I'm trying to get some of your time. Get to know you."

"Yeah?" she asked unbelievingly.

"Yeah."

"Okay, we'll see."

For the rest of the night, if Innocence wasn't dancing, she was talking to Qwess. When she was dancing, she was looking at Qwess. And when she was in the dressing room, she sent Qwess drinks.

At the end of the night when they all retired to their plush rooms at the Four Seasons, 8-Ball and Flame had two women apiece, Doe had the bow-legged redbone, Hulk had three women, and Qwess had Innocence.

However, while there was an all-out freakfest in the other rooms, Qwess spent the whole morning talking to Innocence. And it felt good. For the first time in a long time, he didn't zone out thinking about Shauntay.

Reece put the finishing touches on the meal just as he heard Samson's music announce his arrival. He looked at his monitor on the wall and could see Destiny being helped out of the massive Hummer truck.

Reece and Destiny were having dinner at Reece's place, and since Reece wasn't too keen on having someone know how to get to his house, he had had Samson pick Destiny up and bring her there. He and Destiny had been kicking it since early spring, and he still hadn't hit, and it was the middle of summer. She had opted not to return to school, citing family problems. It was also her reason for not maintaining a job that didn't matter because she was "daddy's little girl" and daddy "held her down." And even though Reece tried to give her things, she refused them because she didn't want to lead him on. In fact, the reason they were having dinner at his place tonight was because she didn't want him spending any more money on fancy restaurants.

During their considerable time spent together, Reece had all but confessed he was involved in "questionable" activities, though he substantially minimized his involvement. At first she was appalled, but later she warmed up to his truths as she warmed up to him.

Reece put his concoction in the oven and went to get the door. He was preparing a meal he had learned to make during one of his brief stints in the county jail. It was called a "set-up" inside the joint. It consisted of ramen noodles, rice, meat (fish in this case), and an assortment of extras like mushrooms, oysters, and cheese. It was fairly easy to make and only took twenty minutes to prepare. However, Destiny would've never guessed it by the flour liberally sprinkled on his face and apron. Reece wanted to make this moment seem like some special shit.

He opened the door for Destiny wearing nothing but an apron and socks. He ushered her in out of the cool air, dapped up Samson, and excused himself to put on something more appropriate—like clothes. When he turned to walk away, Destiny noticed his nakedness and couldn't resist.

"Hold up. Reece, when you said dress down, I was thinking you meant more like sweats." She modeled her Baby Phat sweat suit, illustrating her point. "I didn't think you meant dress that far down!" She pointed at his nakedness.

"What's the matter? You getting hot and bothered?" Reece queried, spinning around like a fashion model.

"Nah, I was more concerned about the draft in here."

"Ah, cut it out. Listen, I'm going to freshen up. The food will be ready soon. You can sit in my study until I get back."

He led her to the study, and when he left the room, Destiny did her womanly thing: snoop.

The first thing she checked out was his book collection, which took up the entire back wall. It was said that you could tell a lot about a person by what they read. So Destiny ventured to find out more about the intriguing Reece.

Destiny was surprisingly impressed by his collection. Among the prerequisites for all aspiring street generals like *The Art of War* by Sun Tzu and *The 48 Laws of Power* by Robert Greene, she also found a lot of culturally based books. A lot she didn't even know about until she went to college. Books like *The African Origin of Civilization* by Cheikh Anta Diop, *The Destruction of Black Civilization* by Chancellor Williams, and *The Isis Papers* by Dr. Frances Cress Welsing. She even noticed he had a lot of books about Hitler.

The more she learned about Reece, the more intrigued she became. She had first pegged him as a typical drug dealer: ostentatious, egomaniacal, and ignorant. Yet she was quickly learning he was anything but ignorant.

Reece returned wearing a green satin pajama set. They ate dinner by candlelight. She complimented Reece on his culinary skills, but didn't believe him when he told her the true origin of the meal.

After dinner they went into the den to have drinks. Destiny noticed that in every room, there were a huge number of packing boxes, so after a third straight glass of merlot, she asked, "Is someone moving in?"

"Actually, I'm moving out," Reece shared.

"Really? This is a nice house," Destiny admitted, referring to the four-bedroom duplex Reece currently occupied.

"Oh, I'm not getting rid of it. I'm just moving into a larger house further in the country."

"Reece, like you really need more room!"

"Well, since I'm dabbling in real estate now, I might as well take advantage of it," he reasoned. He took a large swig of merlot.

Destiny took advantage of a lull in the conversation to ask about his book collection. "Reece, I noticed you have a lot of black history books. You ever been to college or something?"

He stood up from the sofa, walked to the rack stereo, and turned it on. "Yeah."

Destiny was shocked. "Really? You never told me that. Where?"

"The School of Hard Knocks in Anyblock, USA."

"Uhh, you!" She threw a pillow at him. "I was being serious. The average brother isn't up on stuff like that, except the ones in the joint."

Reece raised his eyebrows. "Actually, when Qwess was inside, he's the one that recommended them to me."

Destiny was eager to explore Reece and Qwess's union. "Oh, yeah? You and Qwess tight, huh?"

"Hell, yeah! That's my brother right there. I'd kill for that nigga." He paused a moment contemplating the many murders he'd committed for Qwess this year alone. "I'd die for him, too."

Destiny could sense his sincerity and had to ask why. "How'd you two become so close?"

Reece was now drinking the merlot from the bottle and was past tipsy. "It's like this," he told her. "Qwess and I are kindred spirits, ya know? Last of a dying breed."

"Last of a dying breed?"

"Yep."

"What breed is that?"

Reece emitted a soft chuckle, glad she asked. "A breed of thoroughbreds that are preyed upon by haters, punk police, diabolical women, and the so-called criminal justice system." Making his point, he downed the rest of the drink in one powerful swig.

Still feeling him out, Destiny decided to question him during his inebriated state, knowing a drunk mind speaks a sober mouth. "Well, let me ask you something."

"Shoot."

"You're culturally inclined, and surely know what is behind the demise of our people. The oppressors, right?"

"No doubt."

"Yet, you aid and abet the oppressor by pumping that shit into the streets. So what's the use of learning about the history of our people if you ain't going to do shit to help 'em?"

Reece couldn't believe this chick was coming at him like this. He reflectively looked at the bottle he held in his hand, debating how far he wanted to take the conversation. Never one to bite his tongue, he decided to give it to her raw.

"I study to gain knowledge of self. To master me. The only way to find out who you are is to find out where you've been, and how you got into the situation you're in. Then and only then can you do something worthwhile about it."

"So all you care about is you?" Destiny challenged. "You don't want to help our people with your knowledge?"

She walked to him, and stood up right in his face, so close he could smell her breath. He looked her right in her hazel eyes unflinchingly and answered.

"Look I useta want to save the world, but then I found out the world didn't want to save itself. The older I got, the more I realized the majority of the population was lost—blind, deaf, and dumb."

Destiny didn't want Reece to stop talking. She loved his mind! His speech. The way words effortlessly oozed from his lips. The merlot, Sade, and Reece's smooth voice provided a lethal aphrodisiac. Destiny was getting turned on by the minute.

"Go on," she told him. "Finish."

"'Specially black people," Reece continued. "We always singing and shit instead of swinging our shit. We always screamin' peace. Make peace with the enemy. Hell, we the only ones talkin' that shit. Our enemy still got his boot on our neck. Power concedes nothing without demand. The white man wanted this country, they didn't ask the Indians for it. They took this shit. By force! Murder, extortion, robbery, you name it. All the stuff they lock a brotha up for today. Ya feel me?"

Despite herself, she did feel him, so she nodded. Reece continued.

"Hell, we were kings in Africa! We fought lions and shit. Now we bow down like we being knighted or something."

Destiny sucked her teeth. "Save me your righteous indignation. I feel you on one aspect, but be honest, too. You like the money."

Reece leveled with her. "Yeah, I like the money, but it's more than that. I just can't see me working a regular job for peanuts. People caught up in the rat race work all day and night and still can't afford to buy a Benz. Or," he added, cupping Destiny's face, "can't even afford to get their loved ones special things they want."

He kissed her. She didn't resist. In fact, she reciprocated, kissing him long and hard. Her body had been wanting this all night, though her mind knew she didn't need it. Despite herself, Destiny was feeling Reece in a big way. Yes, she had issues with his occupation, but oddly enough, she could see why he did what he did. It turned her on to see such a strong man stand firm on his principles. And even though that wasn't her objective, she found herself falling for him.

Before long, their kisses led to caresses, and before either of them knew what had happened, Destiny was on her back on the bearskin rug in front of the fireplace getting her juices sucked out of her.

"Oh, pleeease don't stop!" she begged, panting, raking her long nails through Reece's dreadlocks. "Oooh, yes, yes, yes!" she hissed as he eased two fingers into her tight, warm center. She couldn't take it anymore. "Please make love to me, Reece. Please!"

Reece broke a record removing his clothes. He slid his body between her legs and entered her . . . raw dog. Destiny cried out in pleasure as Reece filled up her insides with his thick member, and before he managed to stroke her ten good times, Destiny's entire body shook with powerful orgasms. Her inner muscles contracted, prompting Reece to follow her over the cliff of climax. He released a powerful eruption inside of her. Destiny wrapped her thick legs around Reece's back. He palmed her soft ass, and they shook together for what seemed like an eternity. Then they repeated their cycle over and over again.

That night something took place that Destiny never intended. She never intended to sleep with Reece. She knew sleeping with him could only complicate things.

Only make situations worse. She knew that falling in love with him was tantamount to treason. Yet, late that night while Reece slept, she traced his jawline with her fingers as she lay on his chest and couldn't help but feel all warm and fuzzy inside. She was truly in a dilemma, and the Sade playing over the Bose speakers summed it up best.

"This is no ordinary love . . ."

Chapter 15

The video for "Street Life" was presumably going to be shot in Charlotte. Presumably, because unbeknownst to John Meyers and the execs at AMG records, the video for "Street Life" was being shot the entire time the crew was touring.

Doe had taken the liberty of ordering the driver to drive through the hood in every city they came through. As they drove through these hoods, Doe videotaped the dope boys in the trap. Some were actually making sales. Others were just standing on the block holding their nuts. Doe taped it all. Then, later, he went back over the tapes and digitally blurred out the faces so as not to incriminate anyone. So, now all the video director had to do was put the shots into a sequence, and it would fit the theme for the song perfectly.

John Meyers wasn't happy when he found out about the revelation because he had spent numerous dollars, time, and energy coordinating the would-be video set. He had all of the top beauties of the South as eye candy, as he was sure this was going to be a video full of excess—albeit meaningless to the subject of the song—since it was typical of the videos in today's rotations. However Qwess reserved creative control, and John Meyers had to fall back when Qwess reminded him. So, in the end, Qwess ended up lip-synching in the cold on South Tryon Street.

There was another artist that AMG was looking to promote on their label named Niya. Looking to kill two birds with one stone, AMG made sure Niya made a guest appearance in Qwess's video to generate hype. She was in the process of releasing her debut album, so John Meyers thought it would be wise to include her in the rest of the tour Qwess was presently on, which was how she ended up on the tour bus when Doe and Qwess arrived in Charlotte. They had driven up in Doe's BMW 760 since they had other business in the city once the video shoot was completed.

Doe went onto the bus to retrieve some forgotten goods, where he saw the most beautiful ass known to man hiked up in the air. Apparently, the young lady was digging between the seats for something she dropped, and was so busy searching for it that she didn't realize she was being watched. When she came up for air, she saw the handsome man looking at her and was instantly embarrassed. Though she thought him cute, it wasn't exactly the way she would like to have made a first impression.

Doe assured her she had no reason to be embarrassed and introduced himself. She told him her name, and in the brief silence that ensued, Doe checked her out. He already could tell she was from upstate by the way she dressed. Blond chukkas and tight denim shirt. She had long black hair pulled straight back into a ponytail and looked like she was of mixed race. Doe casually asked her where she was from, and Niya confirmed his suspicions.

She was from B-more, Maryland, and mixed. Half Italian, half black. When she revealed to Doe that she was going on tour overseas with them, he cracked a big smile. Got her. He definitely liked what he saw, and he definitely planned to get to know her on tour.

Qwess was eager to get the shoot over with, so the bevy of buxom beauties ambitiously vying for his time never even registered on his radar. He was on autopilot the entire time.

For his part, he had reason to be zoned out. He had a million things to do before they left for Europe in two days. There was the state-of-the-art recording studio being renovated and set up right beside his sister's salon. Then there was the compound being built that he had to check on to make sure everything was coming correct. And topping things off was Hope.

Hope had persistently left messages at every conceivable location he could've been while he was on tour. The broad was getting on his nerves! If she had been this persistent when he was in the bing, they'd probably still be together, but pigs don't fly and shit does stink. It was what it was.

Adding to Qwess's to-do list was Reece. Reece was requesting—no, demanding—Qwess get up with him ASAP. Qwess already knew what it was about. It was all the talk of the entire East Coast.

The whole East Coast was buzzing with talk of gangland murders, bodies being found in trunks with either headless corpses or corpses with huge holes in the heads. The icing on the cake was when a police officer walked outside of his precinct to discover a Lexus with two dead bodies and two kilos of cocaine stuffed inside. The cause of death? Obviously the golf-ball size holes in the back of the heads. The police didn't need to see any ID to know what souls once occupied the bodies, as they had been trying to get these two culprits for a long time. They were believed to be responsible for 75 percent of the drugs in North Carolina. The police knew that whoever did these murders had done it to make a point.

The point was not missed by the attorney general for the state of North Carolina, who was holding press conferences daily vowing to bring the people responsible for the recent rise in the murder rate to justice. He even linked these murders to the bombing downtown, and to Qwess's worriment, he also mentioned the Crescent Crew by name. In Qwess's music, he name-dropped the Crescent Crew.

Qwess was going to make sure to mention this detail when he met with Reece later.

The video shoot was almost over, and there was no sign of Flame. He had specifically instructed Flame to meet him there on set so he could get Flame's face on camera. Qwess understood how important it was to get Flame's face seen on TV. The buying public absolutely had to have a face to associate with a name. Plus, he was thinking about marketing Flame as a ladies' man, since he obviously had a way with the ladies.

Speaking of ladies, the eye candy invited to appear in the video by John Meyers were heated because Qwess didn't use them. So, to placate them, to show his appreciation, Qwess made sure they all got paid, all fifteen of them. Top-notch pay. To show their appreciation they all offered to do stuff so freaky, it would make a pimp blush. It took a lot for Qwess to resist, because the women were country fine. The type with hips twice as big as their waists, not to mention that he was hornier than a virgin in a whorehouse. However, in the end, business won out.

Qwess finished his parts and gathered Doe to leave. They were on Highway 74 almost home when Qwess's phone and two-way pager went off simultaneously. As did Doe's. When they called back, it was 8-Ball talking hysterically. Apparently, Flame had gotten himself locked up for illegal possession of a firearm. According to 8-Ball, the rollerz had seen two young black men in a BMW and pulled them over. After roughing them up a little, they searched the car and found a loaded .45-caliber pistol.

Doe made a detour to I-95 and headed to Fayetteville to get the li'l homie out.

Qwess was on his way to see Reece at his funeral home. The day had been hectic. After he and Doe had posted bail for Flame, chastised him, and dropped him off at his new house, Qwess had come back home to check on his family's new compound. It was almost dark when he got there, but from what he could tell all was going well. From there, he went to check on the progress of the studio and see his sister. The studio was near completion. The salon was hectic as usual, but his sister was glad to see him. He also ran into Hope. After a brief convo, he agreed to keep in touch with her while he was finishing out his tour. Hope just didn't get it that they were through. He just couldn't put any faith in her. Without that, a relationship couldn't survive. Qwess didn't plan on crossing the same bridge twice. One thing his father instilled in him was to leave the past in the past. Don't go back to it for validation, justification, or nothing. Leave it where it lay.

Surprisingly, Innocence, the stripper from Atlanta, had called. She and Qwess had been politicking all day. She seemed pretty interested and interesting. Now there was something he wanted to explore. Maybe in due time.

Qwess arrived at Eternally Yours at two in the morning. The only person present was the mortician on third shift, Yusef, who informed Qwess that Reece was on his way.

Qwess was standing outside when a shiny black Porsche Cayenne pulled up. It was rolling on twenty-inch black chrome rims. Qwess knew it could only be one person. The tinted window rolled down and proved him to be correct.

Reece grinned like a Cheshire cat. "Hop in."

When Qwess jumped in the back seat of the sporty truck, the first thing he noticed was that Destiny was driving, and Samson was absent. He thought this strange, because previously Samson never left Reece's side, and Reece never—ever—let a broad drive him anywhere.

Qwess questioned Reece with his eyes.

Reece explained. "Samson with his brother, catching up, no doubt. Don't worry 'bout dat, though, dawg. I got something to holla at you about."

They turned onto Raeford Road, and Destiny floored the big truck. Qwess was surprised at the way it handled.

"Yo, remember that shit them niggas pulled on ya' girl?" Reece asked. "Well, I took care of that shit just like you wanted."

"Yo, what the fuck!" Qwess barked. Reece was going too far. They *never* discussed crew business. He blatantly disrespected Destiny to solidify his point.

"Nah, she cool," said Reece. "She wit' me, yo."

Qwess wasn't convinced. "Nah, dawg. That's not how we do shit."

Destiny cut in. "You don't trust me, Qwess?"

"I don't trust no fucking body!"

"Why not?"

Qwess said nothing. He just shot Reece a scathing look. The tense moment was only interrupted when Qwess's song came on the radio.

"Yo, man, they playing your shit all day!" Reece informed him, excited. "The whole crew is happy for you.

Samson running shit now. I'm on hiatus." He continued to discuss crew business in front of an outsider, oblivious to Qwess's warnings.

Qwess also noticed Reece kept touching his nose and sniffing. He knew what those symptoms meant, but thought better of it. Reece was too smart to get high on his own supply.

Trying to quell the mood, Qwess changed the subject. "So, Destiny, when do you go back to school?"

"I'm sitting this semester out. Family problems."

"Awww," replied Qwess sympathetically.

"No biggie. I needed the break."

"Okay, I see. By the way, where are we going?"

"It's a surprise," Reece answered cryptically.

They drove for what seemed like hours, until they came up to an apartment building off to itself. The writing on the sign said *King's Court*. It was then that Qwess knew what this was: Reece's deluxe apartment building that he had been hearing about.

Reece spread his arms expansively. "Ta-da! You like?"

"Hellll, yeah, it's tight." Qwess inspected the building, admiring the beige stucco exterior and the avant-garde décor.

"Good. I got five more being remodeled all over the city. It's my new vice."

Qwess mumbled. "Seems like it's not the only one."

They all exited the Porsche and followed Reece to the elevator. They got off on the third floor. Reece pulled out a key, and they went inside.

The opulence they were met with caught them off guard. No one would think this type of extravagance existed in a building like this. The building wasn't shabby, but this type of luxury was out of place. The off-white wall-to-wall carpeting was every bit of four inches thick. There was a gold sofa with overstuffed pillows on the back wall. Directly above the chair was a huge aquarium running the entire length of the wall. In it swam a school of piranhas. On the left wall was a huge high-back chair with red-velvet cushions and fourteen-carat-gold embroidery. The chair could only be described as a throne.

Reece told Destiny to sit down while he took Qwess on a tour. They walked through the kitchen where Reece showed off the green Italian marble tile. From the kitchen, the ventured to the rooms. In the first room they passed, Qwess swore he saw a lion cub rambling about.

"What the fuck is that?" he had to ask. He just *knew* his mind was playing tricks on him.

Reece waved his hand dismissively. "That's Divine. He watches the place while I'm gone."

Qwess shook his head. It seemed that Reece had gotten richer this year, though Qwess was the one with the multimillion-dollar deal.

What Qwess couldn't possibly have known was just how strong Reece's hand had gotten in the last three months, but he would soon find out.

Reece led Qwess into the room and closed the door. Reece asked him something, but Qwess was busy marveling at the circular waterbed and other accouterments, so he didn't hear him at first.

"What's on your brain, black man?" Reece repeated, snapping Qwess out of it.

Wasting no time, Qwess told him, "You need to slow down, man. Be careful."

"Why you say that?" Asked Reece.

"Because this, for one." He gestured at the apartment. "More importantly, though, that broad. You telling her too much."

"Come on, Qwess. I got this covered."

"Stop thinking wit' your dick!" Qwess snapped. "Think with your big head. We don't let bitches in our biz, yo. Never have. Don't tell me you pussy whipped."

That was an insult. "Hell, no!"

"Good, 'cause it's unbecoming of you. Now you need to take a fucking break. Rollerz on shit, hard. I'm seeing what's happening here all the way on the news in Florida!"

"Word?"

"Word. They mentioning Crescent Crew and shit."

Reece seemed proud of that fact. "I told you niggas was gon' talk about this shit for years to come," he said, getting excited.

"Calm the fuck down, man!" Qwess hissed, getting extremely serious. "This shit is serious now. Now I know you took care of those niggas, and I'm grateful, although I don't agree with how you disposed of some of the bodies."

It seemed Qwess was insulting Reece, and Reece didn't like it. He went to war, killing shit because of Qwess's girl being killed, and here was Qwess chastising him.

"Yo, why you dissing me?" asked Reece. "I handled shit, defending your honor, taking the Crescent Crew to new heights. Our Crescent Crew. Shit we started. Or are you not repping the crew no more?"

Qwess exhaled loudly. "You know I'm crew to the death. All I'm saying is don't destroy what we built by getting big-headed. Remember pride comes before the fall. Now they are mentioning the Crescent Crew in the fucking media. One of my biggest records has the words 'the Crescent Crew' all through it. Now what you think is going to happen if they put two and two together?"

Reece knew Qwess spoke the truth, but the absolute power he was experiencing was corrupting him absolutely. Yet, he recognized truth, so outwardly he humbled himself.

"Yeah, I feel you," he said.

"Cool. You know I know you handling shit, but be a li'l more cautious. Take a vacation until shit cool down. Samson can handle things. You groomed him for this. We trying to grow old, get chubby, and move to Miami and shit. Not die by a pig's bullet. You know if they murk you, I'm coming back to the street wit' a vengeance. You my muthafuckin' brotha, nigga."

He grabbed Reece in a tight embrace. "Let me stack some of these square's paper first. Don't make me have to come back to the streets behind some bullshit. 'Cause if I do, I'm coming full throttle." He shook Reece a little bit. "Calm your wild ass down. Make money, not mayhem."

As much as Reece felt him and inwardly swore to do right, the forces of nature were already working. Sometimes one has to reach the tip-top in order to be affected by the fall that is inevitable. Such was the case with Reece. He was on an inevitable climb to the top running parallel with the course of his destiny.

For success doesn't lie in never falling, but in always getting up when you do.

Chapter 16

When the Crescent Crew went to war and subsequently eliminated their rivals, they left a void in the drug trade wider than the Grand Canyon. Possessing foresight, King Reece had predicted this and planned accordingly. He had Crescent Crew members come from all over for a meeting. In that meeting he assigned crews and set up a hierarchy consisting of captains and soldiers. Then, he assigned certain towns to certain crews.

He gave Jersey Ali and his crew Fayettenam, Born and his crew Wilmington. Black Phil and his crew Columbia, South Carolina, Muhammad and his crew Greenville, South Carolina.

He divided every little town in the Carolinas up among his crew. When he was met with resistance by the local hustlers from the towns they occupied, he set a stern example. He didn't apply the "get down or lay down" tactic. It brought about too much heat. Instead, he caused a drought. The Crescent Crew had 95 percent control over all drugs coming into both Carolinas. Heroin, cocaine, marijuana, pills, everything. If a two-dollar crumb was sold to a junkie on a back street, there was a 95 percent chance the product was courtesy of the Crescent Crew. Therefore, the local hustlers had to mob down, or they didn't eat.

Before long the Crescent Crew had monopolized the Carolinas and started foraging into Virginia, Georgia, and Tennessee.

Reece, at the helm of the Crescent Crew, went from making sixty thousand a week to clearing over a million a week when the new year rolled in.

His humble used car dealership turned into a five-star automobile dealership offering high-end luxury cars. He started a real estate development company specializing in fixing up urban neighborhoods. He purchased a strip club before the bank foreclosed on the lease.

With all of this "legal" revenue coming in, he built a twenty-bedroom mansion in Raeford, a country town next to Fayettenam. He spared no expense on his mansion. It boasted an indoor/outdoor pool, basketball court, theater, wine cellar, playroom and six-car garage, which still wasn't enough room for his new fleet, which included a Bentley Arnage and Ferrari 360 Spyder.

King Reece's deluxe apartment building, King's Court, was completed and, shocking everyone, Reece leased the apartments through Section 8. So single welfare mothers got a chance to see how the other half lived, free of charge, because Reece wouldn't take any money. As a result of this, he became like a mythic figure in the ghetto. The women adored him, and the men feared him, since it was common knowledge on the streets that if you fucked with King Reece's reign, you would end up found dead or never at all. A lot of people took their last ride to Reece's crematorium.

Meanwhile, as the weeks turned into months, Reece and Destiny became extremely close. With Samson in charge of the Crescent Crew, Reece and Destiny traveled more than flight attendants. They went gambling in Vegas, shopping in New York, sightseeing in L.A., parasailing in Hawaii. They even flew to Paris to see Qwess perform live. Reece was in a state of bliss. He had never found a woman he could love. Both his mother and father had died when he was fifteen in a freak car accident. He had lived with his cousin Doe's family for a year. The following year, he started making moves with Qwess and was soon on his own. Therefore, he could never love anyone out of fear of abandonment. This was what made him such a lethal killer. He thrived on other people's pain. He felt life had dealt with him unjustly, so it simply made his dick hard to be able to cause others pain.

With Destiny, his pain subsided, replaced with the love she gave him. His only complaint was how she felt she had to consult with her uncle Lou all the time. Reece felt she was his woman. He took care of all of her needs, so she shouldn't have to check in with any man but him. It pissed him off to think of another nigga riding shotgun in the CL Benz he bought for her. Family or not. Reece was territorial like that. He was overzealous about Destiny. He felt she was perfect for him. Cultured, classy, and a freak behind closed doors. Plus, she had a way of dealing with police. Every time they were stopped for DWB (Driving While Black), Destiny was able to pour on the charm and slink out of harm's way. In fact, Reece noticed that since the winter rolled in, the police had called off their witch hunt and the AG stopped going on TV every day talking mumbo.

Everything was going so well, Reece couldn't possibly see this was the calm before the storm. One bad thing about being at the top is you can look down to see everyone and everything, but it's impossible to see the most important thing.

Yourself.

* * *

Doe felt someone kissing him on the cheek and awoke to find Niya showering kisses all over him. He readjusted himself in the plush, spacious seat in the first-class cabin of the jumbo jet to allow Niya room. She had totally invaded Doe's space and now shared the seat with him. Doe heard snickering and looked over to see a very amused 8-Ball crowded between a sleeping Qwess and Flame and a very alert Hulk.

The nubile twenty-one-year-old nestled herself underneath Doe and basked in the comfortable silence. This union hadn't started off so sweet.

When the tour first hit Europe, they landed in Frankfurt, Germany. The A.B.P. posse was all pumped up. Conversely, Niya and her entourage were unsure and hesitant.

The first show was in Amsterdam, the Netherlands, and the first thing Doe noticed was how huge hip-hop was in Europe. The real hip-hop packed with similes and metaphors. Europeans loved it. All over town were posters of Wu-Tang Clan. They were like the Beatles over there.

Qwess, Flame, and now 8-Ball—who had taken to removing his shirt and reveling in chunky glory—performed before a packed house. The audience knew every word that passed from Qwess's lips and were just as smitten with Flame. After the show they went to a weed shop, which resembled a coffeehouse, to wind down. That was the first time everyone saw Qwess's video playing on a television behind the counter. Inside the shop, they also ran into an established New Jersey rapper with an affinity for red. He congratulated Qwess, telling him he had been a fan for quite some time.

At that same show, Niya was booed, and when she came backstage broken up, it was Doe who consoled her.

From Amsterdam, they crossed back into Germany to do a show in a town called Würzburg. Initially, Doe thought they were on the wrong side of town, judging by the huge number of pale bald heads. However, this turned out to be one of the best shows. They were performing at an indoor pool party, so everyone dressed accordingly. When the *fraulein* saw Qwess's chiseled body as he performed in nothing but swimming trunks and jewelry, they literally tried to rape him on stage. Doe had heard that German women adored black men, but this was damn near idolatry! Hulk had had to intervene and stop a busty blond from giving Qwess fellatio right on stage.

Niya performed that night in her two-piece bikini and had every man lusting after her. That was the night she gained the much-needed confidence necessary to give a stunning performance. That was also the night Doe hit it for the first time on the balcony of the hotel in the falling snow.

When they performed in Paris, France, they were met with a pleasant surprise. At the end of the show a smiling Reece was waiting on them with a blushing Destiny on his arm. They all retreated to the hotel, changed clothes, and brought the morning in gambling in Paris's numerous casinos. That was the night Niya and Doe had their really bad first argument. Seems Niya was upset when she found out a pretty Parisienne was stroking Doe's manhood at the blackjack table the entire time they were playing. However, the sun rose on Doe and Niya having fabulous make-up sex.

In Italy, they visited the Ferrari plant and the Lamborghini manufacturers, where Qwess ordered a purple Diablo Roadster, with nineteen-inch gold OZ racing rims. It was to be delivered in the States by the time the tour was over.

Ironically, it seemed that Qwess was biggest in the places he least expected. They tore the house down in Italy so hard that Qwess was invited by Giorgio Brutini himself to go shopping for alligator shoes the following day.

In London, England, Qwess was mobbed. He was absolutely huge in London! Londoners had always had an anti-government stance, so they ate up Qwess's politically charged rhymes and drank them with their famous tea. It was in London that Qwess truly realized how large he had become, and they all begrudgingly had to give props to John Meyers and AMG. If not for their injected capital and resources, it probably would have taken them five years to get to this point.

Now, they were on their way home. It felt good to be successful and finally on that next level, but it felt better to be coming home. AMG had extended the tour, so they had been on the road in Europe for a total of four months. It was now early October, and the seasons were changing into Doe's favorite time of year. Last year this time, he had been working a job for someone else for menial pay. This year he was calling shots as the VP of one of the fastest-rising record labels in the industry. He was knocking off the baddest up-and-coming R&B artist, and able to buy himself any muthafuckin' thang he wanted.

Boy, what a difference a year made!

Part 3

The Start of the Ending

Chapter 17

The jumbo jet landed at Charlotte Douglas international airport at ten p.m. on a Sunday night. The air was thick and humid as the A.B.P. Crew deplaned. Once they grabbed their bags, they headed to the parking lot. Someone from the crew was supposed to be picking them up.

Once they reached the curb of the airport and stood for a few seconds, they spotted a white stretch Escalade limo slowly creeping up. It stopped right in front of them. The window slowly descended, revealing a smiling Samson.

"Someone called for a cab?" he joked. Hulk, ecstatic at seeing his brother, almost snatched the door off the hinges getting it open. Samson was snatched out the back of the car by the bigger Hulk, and the two hugged on the pavement as if they hadn't seen each other in years. Passengers gawked at the sight of the two identical giants. One woman even stopped to take a picture. When the greetings were done, they all climbed into the limo.

Once inside the limo, the surprises continued. There were bottles of Cristal on every seat.

"What's the occasion?" Qwess asked.

"Yo, y'all are superstars now, so everything is first-class. No more second-rate," Samson replied. "Reece has all types of surprises for you." Qwess could tell by Samson's speech, demeanor, and dress code that Samson was playing on the next level. He deferred credit to Reece because Samson understood Law Number One of the Forty-eight Laws of Power: Never outshine the master. It was obvious to see that Samson was that nigga! A part of Qwess swelled with pride, knowing he had turned the country boy into a boss.

"What kind of shit y'all up to?" Doe inquired, realizing something was amok.

"Don't worry. You'll see." Samson was barely able to conceal his humor.

The rest of the three-hour drive home, everyone got toasty with the champagne and smoked blunt after blunt of hydro weed. The tour had been a success. Record sales were up, and everyone was healthy. If there ever was a time for celebration, this was it.

When they arrived at Reece's mansion, mouths dropped. The mansion wasn't completed yet, but the most vital parts were. From what they could see, it was huge! No one knew Reece was doing it like this.

The limo let them out at the center of the circular driveway, and a butler collected their bags, taking them inside. The group went inside also.

The first thing that they saw when entering the mansion were the huge pillars of granite on either side of the door. As they walked through into the foyer, they were met by circular staircases on each side that went up to form a balcony that framed the entrance. A huge Crescent Crew logo shined in the center of the green marble floor. As they walked under the balcony following Samson, Reece emerged out of a side room.

"My niggas!" Reece's voice echoed from the marble floor to the cathedral ceiling. He was wearing green trunks and was naked up top, save for a huge platinum chain with a crown the size of a saucer dangling from it. On a leash walking step by step beside him was his lion cub, Divine, who wasn't so small anymore. "Welcome home! Follow me. Now we can get this party started!"

They followed Reece through the rest of the house, noting a basketball court encased in glass to the left. As they got closer to the back, faint sounds of bass could be felt thumping underneath their feet. Soon they realized the source of the music when they got out back. There was a pool party in full swing. DJ Technique was spinning records, and all the men in the house were Crescent Crew. All family. Providing the entertainment were some of the finest woman south of the Mason-Dixon line. Some were scantily clad, most were topless, if not completely naked. There were enough women that each man could have two or three to himself. All shades were represented, too: caramel, chocolate, vanilla, Chinese, Spanish; whatever your sweet tooth, it was sure to be filled.

"Welcome to my castle!" Reece exclaimed, expanding his arms as if conjuring up a spell. When the women noticed Qwess had fell up in the place, all eyes were on him. It was known that he was single now, and every woman wanted her turn.

With Reece's blessing, the crowd dispersed. Flame bolted to the poolhouse with Doe and Hulk close on his heels. 8-Ball went to the grill, where Born was cooking up T-bone steaks.

Before Qwess could disappear into the decadence, Reece grabbed him and whispered in his ear. "Don't get too wild. Jersey Ali still got a surprise coming for you."

* * *

Jersey Ali looked at his Movado again, confirming the time. He paddle-shifted his Maserati into another gear and floored it. He was already thirty minutes behind schedule and still had to drop Bone, who rode shotgun, off in the trap.

"Yo, dawg, slow down. Last thing we need is the rollerz. You know I'm dirty."

Jersey Ali grimaced. "I know, Ock, but if I don't pick this broad up from the airport and get her to that party, Reece gonna shit!"

Jersey Ali was already regretting his decision to handle business before he left to go to the party, but Bone had needed his work. Thus far he had been a loyal and prosperous worker, so Jersey Ali couldn't deny the kilo he had requested. His dilemma was caused by waiting until the last minute to go to the stash spot.

He turned onto Bragg Boulevard and gunned the Bimmer. At this time of night traffic was scarce so he breezed through lanes with no problem at all. He heard "Street Life" come across the radio, and he bumped the Bang & Olufson speakers up to ignorant levels.

"You know this my nigga here, right?" Jersey Ali yelled over the music to Bone.

"Word?"

"Hell, yeah! He helped start the Crescent Crew. He's a good nigga, too. I'll let you meet him one day. That's whose party I'm going to."

Bone wasn't born and raised in Fayettenam and wasn't a part of the Crescent Crew when Qwess was at the reins. He was from Columbia, South Carolina. Jersey Ali had reunited with Bone fresh out of prison. They met at Jumu'ah one Friday. Bone had expressed his dismay at the way the system had given him its ass to kiss because of his criminal record. Jersey Ali sympathized and, wanting for his brother what he wanted for himself, put him on.

Since then, Bone had been a heavy earner, lining Jersey Ali's pockets with tens of thousands of dollars.

Jersey Ali finally made it to Murchison Road, also known as "The Murk," which is what happened to those who slipped on this strip. He was just blocks away from the trap when he saw the bubble gum flashing in his rearview.

"Ah shit! Not now. Not now!" Jersey Ali prayed aloud.

"Oh, hell, the rollerz!" Bone exclaimed, petrified. "Shit, nigga, don't stop. I already got two strikes! I ain't going back to no cage."

Jersey Ali was in a bind. He wasn't "dirty," but he did have his pistol under the seat. He knew the rollerz weren't trying to hear that shit. Two black men in a hundred-thousand-dollar car with guns and dope? Shit, they'd never see the sun as free men. Yet he did want a chance to live the lavish life. He was just starting to see real money. He knew that he could outrun them in the Masi, and he knew he was down for whatever, but he wasn't sure about Bone.

"Yo, what you wanna do, Ock?" Jersey Ali asked Bone.

"Yo, I'll hold court in the street if need be," Bone replied, cuffing his pistol for emphasis. Jersey Ali liked that. A man after his own heart.

"A'ight, check it. This what we'll do. I'ma pull over up here by Fayetteville State. When I stop, you jump out. You got the work, right?"

"Yeah."

"A'ight. You jump out with the work and get light. I'ma pull off. Make them chase me a li'l bit, then pull over. By then, you should be long gone. When I get to safety, I'll hit you on the hip. A'ight?"

"Yeah," Bone answered, ready to make his move.

Jersey Ali put on his signal to pull over and slowed a

bit. Next, he pulled over into the parking lot of a gas station and stopped. However, to his surprise, the rollerz were rolling two deep. And when he pulled over, the cop on the passenger side of the police car was already positioned on his open door with his gun drawn.

"Driver, step out of the car with your hands up!" the officer commanded.

Bone opened his door slowly. He put both feet out of the vehicle onto the pavement and . . . came out dumping!

The heavy Desert Eagle bucked in his hands as he squeezed round after round at the cruiser. The first shot sent the police officer heading for cover. Right back inside the vehicle. The other shots provided just enough cushion for Bone to get light—and boy, did he ever!

At the same instant Bone fled, Jersey Ali sped off into the night with all cylinders of the Ferrari-derived engine pumping at maximum capacity. The rollerz gave chase just as Jersey Ali anticipated, and a high-speed chase ensued.

The Chevy Caprices were no match for the powerful Italian engine. Jersey Ali quickly put distance between himself and his pursuers. He busted a left onto Pamalee Drive and continued to gun his whip. He ran into a little traffic on the road that caused him to slow down a bit. The rollerz got close on his bumper, and he stuck his arm out the window and let a few shots rip for sport.

That was his first mistake.

The rollerz slowed a little, allowing the distance to increase, if only for a moment. They continued to pursue just enough to keep Jersey Ali in sight.

Jersey Ali, caught up in the fun, pulled up the emergency brake and whipped the whole car around into a one-eighty, where it came to a complete stop.

Everything inside him told him to stop there. The

mission was accomplished. Bone was free with the work, and at best he was only facing a few charges that his lawyer could fight, nothing serious enough to box him in forever. That's what his mind was telling him, but the adrenaline coursing through his veins had him disconnected from reason. He was having too much fun!

Jersey Ali turned the stereo up to full blast and peeled off in the direction whence he came.

That was his second mistake.

Jersey Ali was on a high as the Maserati engine roared and the B & O system pumped "Street Life" through the car. He rapped along with the words as he barreled toward the rollerz.

> To the trigger-happy cops destiny has tran-
> spired
> Retaliation for unwarranted cop-fire
> 'Cause we aspire, to what destiny ordained
> Kings of the world and our thrones we came
> to claim . . .

Jersey Ali was having the time of his life! He was higher than a mountain, so the experience was heightened. He flew past all twelve of the rollerz now in on the chase and cracked up when he saw their surprise. He was having so much fun until . . . he saw the ghetto-bird. A big, black helicopter flew right over his head with a rifle-man hanging out the door. At the same time he saw the helicopter, he spotted the roadblock at the intersection of Pamalee Drive and Murchison Road.

"Oh, shit!" he muttered, noticing for the first time how deep he was in it. Seeing the roadblock blew his high. Now sober, he came back to his senses. He had no intention of dying tonight. Bone was long gone, along with the threat of any major jail time.

Then he remembered Reece. Damn! *That nigga was
gonna be livid,* he thought. He figured the best way to get
out of this jam with Reece was to get bailed out of jail.
Then he'd have to understand his dilemma. That was his
thinking as he stopped in front of the roadblock.

That would be his third and final mistake.

In no time his car was surrounded. When he lifted his
hands to surrender, Fayettenam's finest set his hundred-
thousand-dollar car on fire like napalm with round after
round of heavy gunfire. When the smoke cleared, there
wasn't a closed chamber on the whole scene.

Luckily for Jersey Ali, he didn't feel fifty-two of the
fifty-three shots that hit him because the first shot from a
twelve-gauge killed him on impact.

Back at the party, everything was in full swing. DJ
Technique had taken the party down bottom, playing all
the hits from the godfather of Miami bass. There wasn't a
sober party goer to be found, which was evident by their
actions. The poolside resembled a nude beach, as the
strippers from Reece's club exhibited their best behavior.

Reece sat in his lounge chair stroking his lion's smooth
coat, taking it all in, when Qwess approached him.

"Yo, where is your girl, Destiny?" Qwess asked. Reece
sat up, giving Qwess his full attention. Even after all
these years, Reece still looked up to Qwess in his own
way, for it was Qwess who had originally got the connect
to get the Crescent Crew started.

"She wit' her punk-ass uncle Lou," Reece replied dis-
gustingly. "I swear, man, that's the only nigga other than
me she feels obligated to. I hate that shit. If I didn't think
it would kill her, I'd kill him."

It seemed like Reece was joking, but Qwess knew he

was serious. A part of Qwess hated the way Reece used murder as a remedy for everything, but another part of him empathized. He used to be the same way.

He noticed Reece kept looking at his watch, so he asked him, "Yo, you expecting someone?"

"Yeah, man. Jersey Ali was supposed to be here an hour ago with your surprise. It's not like him to be late. Hold up. Aye, Vee!" Reece yelled across the compound.

Vanilla came teetering over on her stilettos. Reece had installed her as general manager of his strip club, Flesh, since it was she who tipped him about the club in financial trouble. That, coupled with the fact of her experience, made her an obvious choice. He kept the original staff on hand but made Vanilla GM so she could keep an eye on things. Vanilla was deathly scared of him, therefore fiercely loyal. To keep her happy, Reece gave her an apartment in King's Court and employed her as his concubine from time to time, because though Destiny had a good shot on her, there was nothing like having your own personal freak!

"What's up, *mi rey*?" Vanilla asked, affectionately calling him king in Spanish.

"Yo, go call Jersey Ali on his phone and see what the fuck is taking so long. He got my brother waiting here with a hard dick."

Eager to please, she replied, "That's no problem. I can get any of the girls to take care of that, with pleasure I'm sure."

Reece dismissed her. "Yeah, yeah, just do what I told you to!"

Not needing a second command, Vanilla peeled out. Minutes later, she came running back about to fall.

"King Reece, King Reece, you better come look at this!!"

"Now what?! Gotdamn, it's always something," Reece swore as he got up from his lounge chair and followed Vanilla inside, with Qwess right behind him.

Once inside, he followed her to his bank of televisions located in one of his dens, where all of the TVs were broadcasting the same thing. Reece almost lost it when he realized what he was seeing.

There was a special report on television about a high-speed chase and subsequent shooting. Reporters were on the scene live. In the background Reece could make out Jersey Ali's Maserati, which resembled a cheese grater. The reporter was saying that the police attempted to pull the car over in a "high-crime" area when the car stopped to simulate a traffic stop. Then the driver got out firing a high-caliber pistol at the officers. A chase ensued, and when police set up a roadblock, the subject attempted to run through it. The officers had no choice but to open fire.

When the reporter finished her spiel, an officer in charge on the scene came up next. He indicated that another suspect was still being sought. Then he offered all types of rewards to induce lesser men to snitch. However, as Reece looked at the tube, he knew he didn't have to worry about snitches. Everyone around knew Jersey Ali was Crescent Crew, and when you crossed the crew, the crew crossed you out.

It took a moment for Qwess and Reece to gain their composure. Jersey Ali was a lieutenant from the first regime, therefore close to Qwess as well as Reece. Vanilla sensed they wanted to be alone, but before she exited she made sure King Reece didn't want anything. He didn't, so she quietly excused herself.

Once they were alone, Qwess asked, "What's on your mind, brother?" Reece didn't say anything. "Do you want me to end the party, so you can handle things?"

Reece looked offended when he answered. "No, man. This is your welcome home party. Ain't nothing gon' stop you from having fun. Hell, that's where Ali was supposed to be going."

Qwess didn't understand. "What you talking 'bout?"

"The broad. Ya know the broad from Atlanta, Innocence."

"Innocence?" Qwess replied, shocked that he knew.

"Yeah, nigga!"

"How you know about her?"

Reece shot Qwess a look insinuating he really didn't understand how much pull he possessed. "Come on, man. I own a strip club. Hello? Anyway, we had some bitches from Atlanta up here on some feature shit. She came up. Asked Vee about you. Vee told her about your party. She wanted to surprise you."

Qwess didn't hear anything after strip club. "Strip club? Nigga, when you started owning a strip club?"

"Oh, ya didn't know? I see we got a lot to get caught up on," Reece told him. "For now let's get back to the party."

"The party?"

"Yeah, the party."

"What about Ali?"

Reece responded, the embodiment of control. "We'll send the troops to check on that in the morning. It's too hot now, and ain't shit we can do about it with the fuckin' rollerz everywhere."

"Yo, man, you don't seem like you care much."

"Oh, I care," Reece clarified. "But ain't shit we can do about it right now. We can't get that back. We all know the consequences of our acts. We can't get yesterday back. Just like we can't get tonight back, so let's go party. I guess ole girl ain't coming, so go ahead and do you."

This was said with such finality that Qwess knew an argument was futile. The king had spoken. The subjects had to obey.

When Qwess and Reece rejoined the festivities, it was hard to tell tragedy had visited their doorstep. Flame and 8-Ball, acknowledging they were partying with sure 'nuff shot-callers, enjoyed every moment. 8-Ball was posted up by the grill getting his eat on, while cracking jokes with some ladies. Flame was talking to a chick probably old enough to be his mother. The way he was spitting in her ear, you'd think it was his inauguration speech.

Hulk and Samson were taking turns throwing naked women into the main pool with the crown embossed "R" on its floor. While Born frolicked in the smaller pool, Chocolate massaged his shoulders. Muhammad sat in the Jacuzzi getting fed grapes by a bevy of beautiful women.

Qwess didn't want to interrupt the mood. His young guns were having so much fun. They had definitely earned it after the strenuous tour. In addition, he also wanted Flame to be in the presence of real gangstas so he would know the penny-ante shit he was into wasn't worth it. He wanted him to be in the presence of some real soldiers dedicated to a life of crime. When a person is around a more dominant person, you can feel their aura, their presence. It's on the most primal level of all things living and breathing. Qwess knew Flame undoubtedly felt it, for Qwess felt it every time he was in the presence of his father.

Reece didn't want to interrupt things because his crew, his family was reaping the benefits of "their life." It felt good to see brothers he personally helped reach the next level have fun. Especially before a life was snatched before their eyes, like Jersey Ali's. He was a good soldier. He would be missed.

Reece walked beside Qwess and sensed he was deep in thought as well. Reece could always tell when Qwess's mind was heavy. After all, they were kindred spirits. So he offered Qwess an escape, to which he agreed, and they deftly exited the party heading for Reece's theater.

Reece's theater wasn't the size of an actual movie theater. It only seated about thirty people. However, the screen was big enough to rival any theater's in the world. As did the surround sound. The movie room was intended to be an escape. It served its purpose in spades.

Reece settled Qwess into a comfortable seat and exited to the control room. Moments later, the opening credits to *Heat* appeared on the massive screen. Reece returned with snacks, drinks, and his lion Divine in tow. He sat down next to Qwess with his lion's head in his lap and a joint of hydro in his mouth. He now wore a robe covering his enormous jewels, which glistened under the lights when they peeked from under the robe.

"Aw, man! So much shit has happened since you've been gone . . ." Reece began, and with that he proceeded to fill Qwess in on the latest news.

An hour later, Doe joined in as Vanilla led him into the movie room.

"Vee, don't let no one else in. This a family reunion of sorts." Reece passed Doe a joint and continued where he left off. "Yeah, so after Ali blew the nigga brains out . . ."

Qwess was loving it and hating it at the same time. He loved the action. He loved the fact that his niggas were so thorough. He hated the fact that he couldn't have been present. He hated the fact that other brothers had to die. Unlike Reece, prior to Shauntay, he had never had anyone close to him get murdered. Ever since that night, a part of him felt different about murder. Despite the fact that he had murdered on several occasions. Maybe he had accepted the record deal at the right time, because you can't be in the streets straddling the fence. Also, music was his outlet for all the transgressions of the past built up inside of him. When he was controlling a crowd, nothing else mattered. It gave him a sense of power that nothing else could.

"Anyway, I'm glad that y'all back, man," continued Reece. "Now we can all ball out as a family. I mean the crew is family, but y'all are fam-lay."

A phone rang, interrupting the flow of conversation. Reece reached into his robe pocket, pulling out a phone. "Yeah? Yeah, I saw it on the news already." Pause "No, I'm not going. Seriously." Pause "A'ight. I'll keep the phone with me." Pause. "A'ight. Bye."

Reece slipped the phone back into his pocket.

"Who was that?" Qwess and Doe asked in unison.

"Destiny."

"Where she at?" Doe asked.

"Wit' her punk-ass uncle. They in Virginia at a conference."

"What she talking 'bout? Ali?" Qwess asked.

"Yeah."

"How she know about that if she in VA?" Qwess wondered, confused.

Reece shrugged. "The TV, I guess."

"What y'all talking 'bout? What about Ali? Hell, which Ali?" Doe asked.

For an answer, Reece hit a button on a remote, and the screen no longer showed the movie. Instead a live feed of the news replaced it. Reporters were still on the scene, and Jersey Ali's bullet-riddled whip was still in the background.

"Gotdamn!" Doe exclaimed. "What the fuck happened?"

The news reporter answered for him.

. . . Once again, the driver who has been confirmed dead is believed to be part of a drug ring called the Crescent Crew. Authorities say they've been after him for a while. It's believed the suspect was responsible for a huge influx of drugs in the area—

Reece shut the news off and returned to the movie. No one said anything for a long time. Doe didn't know what to say. He knew Jersey Ali, but not to the extent Qwess did, because Doe had never been in the street like that. Therefore it didn't hit him as hard.

Finally, Reece spoke, as much as to himself as anyone else. "Yeah we'll go down tomorrow. See what happened. If any foul shit went down, we gon' flush it. My man not gon' get buried with any debts left unpaid." Reece pulled deeply on the blunt before continuing. "That includes cops, too."

On the screen, bank robbers were shooting it out with the police and winning. Reece turned the volume on the surround sound up to maximum power. The powerful speakers made the room echo every time one of the bank robbers on screen released a volley of rounds from an automatic rifle. A cop went down with a shot to the face, blood squirting from the wound.

Fuming, looking at the screen, Reece formed an idea in his mind. Slowly but surely his scowl turned into a smile. He started chuckling. Then laughing. Doe and Qwess both looked at Reece, dumbfounded.

Reece kept cackling, while stroking his lion's fur.

True to his word, the next morning Reece informed a hungover Crescent Crew about the previous night's events.

Then he dispatched a fact-finding squad to gather details. He wanted to know who was riding with Jersey Ali, the name of the officer who initially initiated the traffic stop, and how heavy the police presence was at this moment. King Reece was on edge until his results came back. He knew it would be no problem finding out who was riding with Ali. It had to be a Crescent Crew member or affiliate. Crew members didn't ride around with off brands.

While waiting on his crew to get back, Reece contacted Jersey Ali's parents in New Jersey. They no doubt wanted him buried in New Jersey. Reece had to make arrangements through his funeral home as well as the airport. Oh, yeah! He was definitely going to the funeral. Plus he had to make sure Ali's people were straight. All crew members made a vow coming in that if just one of them was rich, then none of them would be broke. Each one would be the other's crutches. Being that all members should at least be hood rich by now, and Reece was NBA rich, Ali's people should want for nothing. The Crescent Crew was playing with digits like toll-free numbers.

The fact-finding squad returned to the mansion at a little after two with everything Reece wanted to know. Reece had a lot of plans and a little time, so he wasted none. He mounted up a convoy and headed to Fayette-nam.

Murchison Road was packed for a Monday, but all action ceased when the convoy that contained two black Range Rovers with a white Bentley sandwiched between them crept up. King Reece was solo in the back seat of the Bentley, but no one knew that, since the heavily tinted windows were airtight.

When the convoy stopped in front of a popular pool hall, word quickly spread that King Reece was in town. Everyone knew of him. No one knew him. However, everyone knew who he was here for, so in a matter of minutes Bone appeared.

King Reece rolled the window down just enough for his sinewy arm to stick out. It seemed everyone on the block saw his slender finger beckon Bone to enter the car. Of course Bone did so. He was duly impressed, too. He had never been inside of a Bentley before. The British car was something to behold.

The convoy pulled off, and for a while Reece said *nada*. He used the silence to intimidate Bone. He already looked menacing with his long locks hanging in his face, not to mention the mere presence of his three-hundred-pound chauffeur. Coupled with his reputation, the most thorough dude would be a little unnerved. However, Bone kept his cool.

When King Reece finally spoke, it was so low Bone had to strain to hear, even inside the tomblike confines of the Bentley.

"So you were with Jersey Ali last night, huh?" Questioned Reece.

"Yeah." Real strong. Real firm.

"So, what happened?"

Bone related the story piece by piece, leaving nothing out. Then he added, "The rollerz murdered him, though."

Reece had already surmised as much, so he was glad to hear this. It played right in with his plan. So he prodded Bone on. "How you figure?"

"'Cause I saw when the car came back to the intersection. Dude had stopped the car. They ain't even give him a chance to get out. They just shot the car up."

King Reece took it all in. "How you feel about it?"

"Shit. I feel fucked up!"

"Good. 'Cause you should. That was your fuckin' brother! Our fucking brother. You smoke?" Reece asked pulling out a joint.

"Yeah."

Reece passed him the joint. Then he started putting his plan in motion.

"Yo, Jersey Ali told me about the work you been putting in. Said you was a real good soldier. Loyal, too." Bone nodded his head. Reece continued. "So, what you was working with? Don't answer that," he quickly corrected. "You owe anything out? Answer that."

"Yeah, I owe . . ."

"Don't tell me how much. I just wanted to know if you owe. Obviously you do." Reece paused for effect. He cracked the window to let the smoke out. Then he pulled his locks out of his face so Bone could see his eyes clearly.

"Listen up. Jersey Ali was a soldier. He can't be replaced. But his death left a void that needs to be filled. Now I've heard only good things about you. You know the area, but more importantly the area knows you. I want you to fill this spot. It's a no-brainer, really. However, you got to have heart to be a Crescent Crew captain. You got heart?"

Bone couldn't believe his luck! He hadn't been out of the bing a year, and here he was 'bout to get blessed by the man himself. "Hell yeah, I got heart!" Bone exploded, almost too anxiously.

King Reece eyed him suspiciously. "Oh, yeah?" he asked.

"Most definitely."

"All right, we gon' see." Reece nodded. "I got a job for you. Sort of a 'paying your dues' type thing. You do this and you get Ali's spot. You get hit with what he was getting hit with. This job will show you can handle what it takes to be a captain. Hell, you'll be rich in no time."

Bone was loving what King Reece was spitting. Shit, he didn't care if he had to kill the president to get the spot. He wanted the type of paper Ali was folding. And wasn't nothing going to stop him.

Bone picked his time and asked, "So, what's the job? Whatever it is, it was done yesterday."

King Reese liked that. Ambitious and ruthless. So he leaned over and whispered in Bone's ear exactly what he wanted done. When, how, where, and who.

Bone couldn't believe that was all he wanted done. Hell, he would've done that on the strength, but he wasn't about to tell Reece that. He just nodded acceptance instead.

That being that with that, King Reece two-wayed the lead truck in the convoy a message instructing him to return to the pool hall.

When they arrived at the pool hall, Reece told Bone, "By the way, whatever you owed, keep it. It's yours. Consider it a prelude of things to come."

With that, Bone exited the Bentley a new man. His step was unusually light. He had heard King Reece was just as generous as he was ruthless, but he always thought niggas was just blowing the nigga horn. Now he knew firsthand.

As the sun parted the clouds, Bone took it as an omen. It was definitely going to be a good winter.

Jersey Ali was buried on a Friday morning in Trenton, New Jersey. Various members of the Crescent Crew attended, including Qwess and Reece, with Destiny right by his side. East State Street was backed up with traffic as mourners braved the chilly air to pay last respects to a fallen comrade. Every car seemed to be playing the song "Thug Holiday" by Trick Daddy as it left the *masjid* en route to the burial ground. Only close family was permitted at the grave site to control the crowd.

As Jersey Ali was lowered in the ground, Reece sent a message on his two-way pager and waited for a response . . .

Back in Carolina, Bone tailed the recently promoted Sergeant Attucks in a nondescript car. Sergeant Attucks was in his POV. When Bone received the page on his two-way, he acted.

First, he passed Sergeant Attucks. Then he settled in front of him, slowing down gradually. He checked his rearview to see how many people were following on the two-lane highway. Not any close, which was good. Coming near a stop sign, he pulled his mask down over his face. He stopped at the stop sign and lingered long enough for Sergeant Attucks to draw right up to his bumper. Bone had been tailing him all morning, and it came down to this moment in time.

Bone grabbed his loaded AK-47 from the passenger seat and sprung out the door all in one fluid motion. When Sergeant Attucks noticed the man in black fatigues walking to his car, it was too late. Bone was firing from the moment his feet hit the pavement. He unloaded the full fifty-round clip into the car. Then he pulled his Glock from his waist, walked to the open window, and shot Sergeant Attucks three times in the head. Point-blank range. Bone didn't even flinch as the blood sprayed his fatigues.

After the job was done, he calmly strolled back to the stolen bucket and drove off slowly. The car hadn't hit second gear good before Bone two-wayed his new boss.

When Reece received the page on his two-way, he stood up and walked to where Ali's body lay in the ground partially covered with dirt. He reached down, scooped up two handfuls of dirt, and threw them on the body.

Ali was having a proper Muslim burial, so his body lay open in the ground for now. The dirt smacked him in the face, and Reece silently whispered, "All debts paid." Then he returned to his seat. All other Crescent Crew members followed suit in the ritual, including Qwess. When they were done, Ali's immediate family followed suit.

Reece and the crew left before the conclusion of the service, but before he did, he gave Jersey Ali's mother a bag containing $100,000. He told her if that wasn't enough, let him know. If she needed anything, let him know. From now till eternity. After all, Jersey Ali was family. And that's just how family do.

Chapter 18

I'm from the block with the red beams
The cops and the narc teams
The block where the fed scheme
Get robbed if your neck gleam
I done seen hollows follow dudes to their
*   doorsteps*
Get shot by their mom's foot
Robbed for their Gore-Tex.
At the bar they hate on me
So I'm forced to keep four pounds of extra
*   weight on me*
These niggas ain't no good
They want to wet Flame up for his goods
And leave him somewhere slumped in a
*   coffin for good.*

The studio was packed as Flame laid down his verses in the booth. Qwess sat behind the boards manipulating the equipment to get the best sound out of it. Doe was sitting with Niya preparing her to go into the vocal booth to sing the hook. There were a few women present from Fatima's hair salon next door as well.

It was the middle of May, and everyone was getting prepared to go to bike week in Myrtle Beach during the week of Memorial Day. Qwess and his artist Flame were already slated to perform at the House of Blues in North Myrtle Beach during that weekend. It was a huge event, since everyone came from all over the world to attend. That being the case, Qwess threw a favor Niya's way and let her perform on Flame's single, which he was going to debut at that show. Qwess was ecstatic, because he was going to be returning home to a hero's welcome. The event might have been billed Myrtle Beach's bike fest, but the action happened on Atlantic Beach, Qwess's hood, and he looked forward to attending.

"All right, Flame, come on out. The vocals are laid," spoke Qwess into the headphones.

Flame emerged from the booth feeling himself. "Hell, yeah! That shit is hot, right? Niggas can't see me, dawg," Flame said, dapping 8-Ball up. 8-Ball agreed with him, of course. Qwess gestured for Niya to go into the booth. When she stood and 8-Ball saw her stretch pants palming her tight ass, he couldn't help himself.

"Damn! Now that's what I call an ass!" He whistled.

Doe threw an empty soda bottle at him. "All right. Don't get your thick ass tossed up," he threatened.

8-Ball copped pleas. "Damn, nigga. I'm just playing."

Doe was just joking, but he had been spending a lot of time with Niya since they returned from the tour. He was really feeling her, too. Normally, he wouldn't go for the young chicks, but Niya was very mature and a lot of fun to be around. To Doe, it was refreshing to have someone to kick it with. He had recently moved into a bigger house, and he and Niya had made love in all thirteen rooms. She wasn't real freaky, but she did have a bomb shot.

Niya stepped into the booth and laid her vocals.

> *If you don't know 'bout my side of town*
> *I'm gonna show you how thugs get down*
> *We 'bout that paper and hold big heat*
> *So come here stuntin' you'll get left in the*
>   *street . . .*

As Niya cooed the chorus to the song, Qwess had mixed feelings. He had to admit the song was somewhat formulaic. He personally believed that music just shouldn't be about what would sell. He felt it was about artistic expression. However, he was a CEO of a record label and thus recognized the need for a marketable artist, equipped with said formulaic song. In business, if it doesn't make dollars, it doesn't make sense. And what was Qwess, if not a businessman?

On the bright side, at least Niya could sing, unlike so many other female vocalists. Additionally, Flame definitely had skills. In reality, Qwess could mold Flame to be whatever he wanted him to be. Qwess's album *Janus* was selling like crack in the ghetto since it had been released worldwide. Therefore, the label wasn't hurting for money, and thus it wouldn't need to intentionally go mainstream.

Qwess's two-way pager vibrated incessantly. He looked at the message, shocked by its sender. He had just known it was Hope. They had been corresponding a lot since he went overseas. This message wasn't sent by Hope, though. It was Meka, Shauntay's best friend. Qwess was surprised she paged him because of what had gone down last time they saw each other.

It had happened when Qwess was home during the tour intermission. Meka had called saying she needed to see him. Qwess knew she was taking things hard, so he went to see how he could help her. He was not prepared for what greeted him upon arrival at Meka's house. First of all, she opened the door wearing a nightgown just a little too short and a little too sheer for a friendly visit. Yet Qwess gave her the benefit of the doubt and sat down anyway. It was only when Meka returned with a drink for Qwess, and bent over right in front of him to place it on the coffee table, that Qwess really knew what was up. Meka wasn't wearing any panties, and when she bent over Qwess could see her hairy snatch busting out from under the gown. Upon closer inspection, he realized she must have been playing with herself, because pussy juice oozed out and was starting to trickle down her leg. Qwess's joint got rock hard, but he wasn't grimy enough to hit his dead girl's best friend. That was a little too close for comfort. In the end, Meka apologized, blaming it on her loneliness.

She hadn't contacted Qwess since, and now here she was hitting him up. It had to be important because her pride had been damaged after that ordeal. Qwess decided to holla at her when he finished in the studio.

Niya exited the booth excited as well. Qwess was pleased, but still not satisfied. He wanted more oomph. Something he could feel. Something not so much an ego trip.

"Yo, Flame, you finished that hook you was working on?" Qwess asked.

"No doubt," replied Flame.

"Well, go in the booth so we can track it. You been worrying me about it since we got back," Qwess said. Flame jumped up from his spot where he was rolling a blunt and fled into the vocal booth. When Qwess cued the beat, Flame went into a hook he had been contemplating since he came back from tour.

> *I've been all around the world and back to*
>   *Cackalack*
> *Philly got redbones, Atlanta got 'em stacked*
> *Japan got 'em real thin, 'n' Sweden they fat*
> *big up to Cali ladies they got the best snatch.*

Flame repeated the chorus over and then started freestyling about all the different chicks he smashed while on tour. Qwess had coached him on how to take life experiences and apply them to his songs. Until now, Qwess hadn't thought he was listening. However, hearing what came through the speakers, it was evident that he was. Flame was exhibiting proper syntax, flow, inflection, and he was on beat the entire time. Before Flame even finished spitting, Qwess knew he had a hit record on his hands. He could just see the video in his head. It was going to be crushing.

When Flame came out of the booth, the mood was surreal—the type of feeling when you know you've just been a part of something real big. It was unexplainable, but it was felt throughout the room. Even Flame didn't emerge from the booth with his normal swagger. Instead he was introverted. 8-Ball went to pass Flame the newly rolled blunt, but Flame declined. He wanted to experience this moment with complete clarity and sobriety.

Qwess demanded everyone break for something to eat and then sent one of the broads from the hair salon to get the food. While she was gone, Qwess stepped outside to get some fresh air.

As soon as he stepped outside, he spotted the detectives' car parked across the street and waved. Qwess was

used to them following him now. Ever since they returned from Jersey after Ali's funeral, Qwess had ac-
quired a second shadow. He didn't know why they
followed him, though, because he was clean. Qwess was
aware that the police officer who had pulled Jersey Ali
over had been gunned down in his car. However, Qwess
was sure Reece wasn't responsible, because Reece had
been with him in Jersey at the time it happened. Plus,
Reece never mentioned it. Qwess assumed the police
were tailing him to get to Reece, since Reece had been
holed up in his mansion with Destiny for the past few
weeks. Nonetheless, it didn't matter. He could lose them
at will, just as he did when they tried to follow him on his
motorcycle.

Qwess really felt for Reece because the heat was
coming in all directions now. Feds were busting his dope
spots left and right. The AG was back on TV daily prom-
ising results. His hardest plights were trying to get someone to roll on the Crescent Crew and capturing one of its
members alive. Too many times to count, the rollerz had
got behind one of the crew members in attempts to arrest
him. Too many times the crew members held court in the
streets, often ending up with a dead officer, or dead crew
member. Qwess was starting to think Reece taught that at
the meetings. Be your own judge and juror.

Qwess walked next door to his sister's salon to see
what was going on. He could hear the gossiping before he
even opened the door. Walking in, Qwess noticed how
much his sister's clientele had changed since he put his studio next door. Fatima used to have classy, upscale clients,
but ever since he put his studio next door, it seemed she attracted all the hood supastars.

Nicole, Fat Cat's girl, was present.

Jasmine, Big Man's mistress, was there.

Venus, Big Boss's girl, was in the house as well.

Hell, thought Qwess. *The rollerz might be scoping these broads out.*

The females were wearing so much jewelry Nefertiti would envy them, and shorts so short they bordered on being lingerie. Qwess couldn't help but look between their legs. Shit, Venus looked like her cat was alive, the way it was pulsed! When he caught her eye, he realized she was teasing him by making it jump. She smiled a sexy smile, insinuating he could get it if he wanted it. This scene wasn't new to Qwess. Every time he came in his sister's salon it was the same way. Even before he got his deal with AMG. At first, it was flattering. Then, it became annoying and disheartening. It tripped Qwess out how the women, who were involved with some of the most infamous dudes in town, still would fuck on a dime if he showed interest.

Fortunately for Qwess, he wasn't hard-up anymore. He had been breaking Innocence's back for the past six months now, either when she came to Carolina or when he was in Atlanta. It was purely sexual. No strings attached. Just the way he wanted things from the beginning. She was cool peoples, but Qwess wasn't trying to get in anything serious. It was bad enough he had started back talking to Hope on a consistent basis.

Hope wanted more than he did. He just enjoyed her insightful opinions and felt he could talk to her because of their close friendship. Hope wanted a relationship, which Qwess wasn't trying to feel.

"What's up, li'l bro?" Fatima greeted.

"Heeey, Qwess!" the other ladies chimed.

"What's up, ladies?" Qwess spoke. "'Tima, where my little mans an 'em?" he asked, alluding to his infant nephews.

"Mom got 'em. You know ever since she moved in

the other house, she don't like being alone. Oh, by the way, Dad said he need to talk to you about something important."

Qwess inwardly kicked himself. He had completely forgot about going to see the old man. He had been so busy with preparing for Bike Week, he hadn't had time. So he made a mental note to square things up later.

He walked to the phone. "Get off the phone, Monique. You ain't talking 'bout jack," Qwess joked. Monique shot him a contemptuous look and mumbled something. While Qwess was waiting for the phone, he could hear the women behind him talking shamelessly.

"Yes, girl. That nigga is fine! He can get it right now," one of them said.

"Um-hmm, what you talking bout. I been coming to this spot for weeks now trying to see him. The nigga act like he don't like pussy or something. I know my shit is the bomb!" another one said.

"Ladies, ladies, not so graphic. This is a place of business," pleaded Fatima. She was really more concerned with the assault on her brother's sexuality. Though she knew the assumption was preposterous, she was still overprotective of her brother.

Qwess paid it no mind. He wanted nothing to do with the uncouth chicks, so he couldn't care less about their thoughts. As far as he was concerned, Monique passed him the phone in the nick of time. He couldn't hold his peace much longer.

He dialed Meka's number. She answered on the first ring. "What's up, yo?" Qwess asked, straight to the point.

Meka was somewhat hesitant. "I need to see you about something, Qwess."

"Meka, I hope you ain't playing them games."

"No, Qwess! This is on the up-and-up," she interrupted. "You may thank me later."

"Well, look, I'm in the studio now. I don't know when I'll be able to get over there," Qwess stated.

"We'll see, just come when you can, all right?"

"A'ight."

"Cool. I'll see you then."

Reece slowly crept down the hall of his mansion toward his master bedroom. He could hear the sounds emanating from the other side of the door. Sounds of passion and pain. Loud moaning. He couldn't believe it was still going on. He had already gone downstairs and retrieved his gun, and they were still going at it. Oh, yeah! He was definitely about to fuck something up! As he got closer to the door, the sounds got louder, in constant competition with his drumming heartbeat. He was just outside the door now, and the moans were so loud it was like he was in the room. Moans so familiar. Moans that cried out his name repeatedly, several times a day. Moans that were now calling out another man's name. In his house! Reece gently touched the doorknob. The door was already slightly ajar. No wonder the sounds were so loud! Reece quietly chambered a round in his pistol. Then . . . he slowly pushed the door open.

He could see Destiny riding someone, gone in the throes of passion. She arched her back, threw her head to the sky. Reece could see her biting her lip in that way she did when she was about to climax. She moaned loudly. Each moan was like a dagger to the heart. Reece could see the sweat glistening on her body. He thought he saw hands palming her splendid ass. Reece had the gun raised, but he couldn't pull the trigger. Nor could he move. He wanted to, but he couldn't. Destiny's wet hair swung back and forth as she bucked violently. Then, suddenly, Reece could see her body tense up and begin its rhythmic shake as Destiny climaxed. Her ear-shattering screams echoed throughout the spacious room. Reece couldn't take it anymore. He went to move, but for some reason he couldn't. He attempted to cry out, but the words never escaped his lips. He raised the pistol again, but couldn't pull the trigger. *This isn't happening,* he thought. *She's gotta die. I gotta kill this bitch!*

On the bed, Destiny unstraddled the stranger and dove between his legs headfirst. She started giving him fellatio. It was dark, so Reece couldn't make out the details clearly, but he knew from the way her head bobbed up and down, she was giving him the royal treatment. The more Destiny got into it, the more her ass rose up in the air, until it was on full display. It was almost like she knew someone was watching. Reece was mesmerized. From the moonlight cascading through the glass door leading to the balcony, the room was slightly illuminated. Reece could see Destiny's moist pussy as the moonlight shone on it. As she got deeper into her fellatio, juice just oozed out. Reece had had enough.

He slowly became able to walk. He started his descent to the elevated bed. Destiny and her soon-to-be-dead companion were none the wiser to his presence. He walked right up the two steps leading to the bed unnoticed. He was going to shoot her first, but decided he wanted to see her expression when she saw her nigga's brains get blown out. Destiny was so busy between dude's legs that she didn't even raise her head when Reece stood by the bed. The man had a pillow over his face muffling his screams. Perfect. Reece didn't act. He wanted to see the surprise on Destiny's face when she realized he'd caught her trick ass! However, he couldn't take it anymore. He snatched the pillow off the man's face. Then . . . all hell broke loose!

Armed men burst from the closet pointing red beams

at his head. They threw him on the bed, roughing him up. Funny thing was, Destiny never stopped sucking. Reece had to see who the man was. He just had to! Reece flung two of the men off of him, and looked to identify the man on the bed. Reece saw, but couldn't believe what his eyes told him. He was looking at the headless torso of Hardtime, Black Vic's right hand man. A headless torso was the recipient of Destiny's wonderful blow job. *What the fuck is going on,* Reece thought . . . albeit briefly, because the armed men were right back on him. In the fracas, Reece had dropped his pistol, so now he fought with his bare hands.

"We got you now, you dope-slinging motherfucker! You're under arrest!" the men shouted as Reece continued to resist. Reece finally was able to repossess his pistol, and he wasted no time squeezing the trigger. "Die, cocksuckers!!!" Reece yelled as he slaughtered them one by one. Then, suddenly, out of nowhere he felt himself being grabbed from behind in a powerful hold. Too powerful to break.

"Get off me! Get off me!" he screamed. Then he . . . woke up in a fit of rage. His screams claimed the room as he hit Destiny in the process of waking up from his nightmare.

"Baby! Baby! Wait! It was a dream!" Destiny grabbed Reece, attempting to placate him. Reece finally gained his composure when Destiny grabbed him in a bear hug from behind. "Calm down, baby. It's me. I got you. I got you," she whispered over and over in his ear.

Reece finally calmed down and left the bed. He walked onto the balcony where the cool air massaged his naked body, instantly drying the sweat that had accumulated during the dream. For a long time he just stared out at the grounds trying greatly to gather his thoughts. He took note of Divine prowling the grounds below.

He was lost in thought when Destiny came behind and started stroking his locks, which now extended to the middle of his back.

"You wanna talk about it?" she gently asked. She moved around to his front and started stroking his chest. "Huh, baby. What was the dream about?"

Reece still didn't answer, so Destiny coaxed him on. "You know you can talk to me, baby. I got you. Now what's up?"

Instead of answering, Reece took her angular face into his hands. He stared at her for a moment before speaking.

"Are you cheating on me?" Reece blatantly asked. Destiny's face showed a look of pain and confusion.

"Why would you ask me that?" Destiny frowned.

Reece exhaled. "Because it's a lot of secretive shit going on. When we together, you don't answer your phone. I walk into rooms and you hang up phones and shit. When we first started kicking it, I thought you was getting rid of a Billy or something."

"A what?"

"A Billy. Ya know, old boyfriend. Anyway, it's almost a year later and you still doing the same shit." Reece gripped Destiny's face a little tighter. "So I need to know, is there someone else? You can be honest. I'll be a man about the situation."

Reece was lying through his teeth! He knew that if there was someone else, and he found out, he'd bury both Destiny and the dude together, Destiny for treason, the guy for playing in his shit!

"Reece, baby, please! You know I ain't creeping on you. You all I need. You treat me so good." Destiny attempted to kiss him. Instead Reece just held her head in his hands and stared at her intensely like he was looking for something in her eyes.

Destiny felt uncomfortable. When she gazed into his eyes lately, it was like looking into a black hole. "All of this because of a dream?" she asked.

"Yep. I learned that there's a little truth to every dream."

Destiny contemplated what he said for a moment. Then she responded, "You're probably just stressed with everything going on. You drawing conclusions to stuff that's not there."

She continued to stroke his chest. Then she moved her face just inches from Reece's face and whispered, "You don't have to worry about me, my king. I got your back. If I can't help you, I still won't hurt you." Then she kissed him. At first, Reece didn't return the kiss. Then, being caught up in the feelings he had for her, he began to kiss her slowly, then more forcefully. As the passion intensified, Reece suddenly pulled back. He fiercely gripped Destiny's face. They were both out of breath.

"Listen real good, Destiny. I love you, but if you cross me, I will kill you. Understand?"

Reece released his grip, and she nodded in the affirmative. Then she kissed him passionately on his neck and descended down his naked torso. She lingered at his belly button for a moment. Then she took him into her mouth with all the intensity she could muster. Reece cried out in ecstasy. His eyes were slits as he looked out over the grounds, while receiving his oral favors. Soon, he ejaculated into Destiny's mouth. She swallowed and commenced to sucking harder.

Reece loved Destiny, but he meant what he said. If she ever crossed him, he would kill her, with no hesitation. He had let her into the most intimate moments of his life. More important, among all the expensive things he had given her, he had also given her something priceless.

His heart.

* * *

Qwess sat back in the chair in deep thought. He couldn't believe what Meka had just told him. He had to ask again.

"You telling me a dude is willingly cooperating with the police?"

"Um-hm."

"All because he salty over his man getting killed?"

"Um-hm."

"I thought they were supposed to be gangsta?" Meka shrugged her shoulders. "I don't get it, Meka. Who is this cat to you?" Qwess asked.

"Just some fuck nigga I used to mess with."

"Okay, so why is he puttin' his man on front street?"

"They fell out. Somethin' to do wit' some money. Plus, he really didn't put him on front street, because he didn't tell me who it was."

Qwess thought about this. Meka was effectively telling him that an outsider had infiltrated the Crescent Crew working for the police, all because he was mad about the Crescent Crew killing his man. Therefore, he was a confidential informant trying to take down the Crescent Crew. The sticker was that the guy didn't tell Meka who the CI was. So why even tell her anything if he wasn't going to tell her everything?

"What kind of bullshit is this?" asked Qwess. "How he gon' tell you half the story? Where he at anyway?"

"I don't know where he at now. And I think the only reason why he ain't tell me everything is because he had a change of heart."

"A change of heart!" Qwess exploded. He stood to leave, but thought about something. "Why are you telling me this anyway?" he bluffed. "I ain't part of the crew no more."

Meka shot Qwess a sarcastic look.

"What?"

"Come on, Qwess. Everybody know you are Crescent Crew to the death." She accentuated quotation marks. "Besides, I'm telling you so you can let ya boy know what's up."

Qwess decided to test her sincerity. "Ya know my boys play for keeps. If I tell them, your friend might come up missing."

Meka didn't flinch a bit when she said, "It serves him right, too. He ain't shit. It's niggas like him that killed my girl."

Qwess laughed. "Damn, girl, you done got gangsta, ain't you?"

"Nah, I'm just tired of niggas playing games. If he was a man, he would handle it in the street."

Qwess couldn't deny she had a point, but it was unusual to hear Meka talk like this. He always knew her as a hoe. That was about as street as he knew her to be— messing with street niggas.

Not wanting to show his hand much, he kept things short. "All right then, good looking. I'm 'bout to pipe out." When Qwess got to the door, he turned to Meka. "Oh, by the way, thanks for putting some clothes on this time." He was referring to her boy shorts and tank top.

"Fuck you, Qwess!"

"I thought we already went through that." He smiled. Meka threw a pillow at him. He dodged it as he went through the door.

Once inside his Escalade, his thoughts ran wild. He couldn't help but wonder if there was any truth to Meka's story. Reece normally recruited soldiers personally. Yet since they expanded so fast, he had authorized his captains to draw people in.

On one hand, it didn't matter. A mere foot soldier could never get close enough to Reece to damage him.

On the other hand, Qwess knew every big thing started small first. In the end, Qwess was obligated to tell Reece. Even though Qwess was no longer a part of the Crescent Crew's illegal enterprises, he still had helped build it and thus felt indebted to it. Additionally, he had known a lot of those brothers since they were kids. He brought them in himself. He would hate to see them brought down by a lesser man. That was unacceptable! He decided that much immediately.

He had to tell Reece as soon as possible. His only concern was, how would Reece handle it?

Chapter 19

It was once said that the music game was like the dope game. The high flossing whips. Pretty chicks. Stacks of chips. They all were synonymous. Well, during Bike Week in Myrtle Beach, the two definitely merged. Some of the hottest artists in the music industry converged on Myrtle Beach, South Carolina, to frolic in the sun with some of the nation's top ballers, finest females, and prettiest whips. Some of the artists performed during the week. If you were hot enough. Others just came to partake in the festivities. A.B.P. came to do both, and they came to do it well.

There was a convoy off Highway 9 leading to the beach. Qwess and Doe were in Qwess's purple Lamborghini roadster with the top out. Behind them were Reece in his Ferrari 360 Spyder with the top down. Next in the convoy was Samson in his brand-new Viper. Of course, the top was down. His twin brother, Hulk, was riding shotgun. Way behind them in traffic was Flame in his BMW with the top peeled back. He had a crew of trap niggas riding with him. Finally, behind them were the three Rovers with two motorcycles hitched to each one.

Additionally, most of the Crescent Crew were also present driving their numerous luxury vehicles or riding their bikes.

Qwess, Reece, and Samson raced to the beach. However, when they ran into a traffic jam as they neared the beach, they were forced to forfeit. As they crossed the big bridge, they were met with what Bike Week was all about.

They were still in a traffic jam, but they would be entertained down the remainder of the strip, as girls were shaking what their mamas gave 'em. Beautiful women of all shapes and sizes and colors were crammed into tight clothes with thongs on full display. At least the ones who cared to wear them were. Some women just wore high heels, thongs, and bras! Others were topless as they hung out of sunroofs in rimmed-up, high-dollar foreign and domestic cars, mostly souped-up Chevys.

"Damn, the hoes is out this piece this year!" Doe told Qwess as they inched along in traffic. The Lamborghini was so low to the ground, Doe and Qwess had to look up at bikes. As they crept by motorcycle after motorcycle, all they were met with were healthy thighs just inches from their faces.

"No doubt!" Qwess responded. "Shit is gon' be lovely."

Behind them in the Ferrari, Born was telling Reece the same exact thing.

"Hell, yeah, nigga. I got my video camera. I'ma see how many hoes I can fuck this weekend. I'm talking threesomes, foursomes, whateva! Too bad you can't play," he teased Reece.

"Don't get it twisted, nigga!" Reece snapped. "I run shit. I don't get ran. I can do what the fuck I wanna."

"A'ight, we'll see," Born taunted.

As the convoy progressed down the strip, word slowly started to spread that Qwess was in town. Females hung out their windows trying to get a glimpse into the purple Lambo. By the time they made it to their hotel, they had a full following. They pulled into the parking garage where security was deep. Non-guests of the hotel were quickly detoured.

The entire crew checked in, checked their bags, and in a matter of minutes—literally—they were back out on their bikes. All wore similar outfits: Timbos, jean shorts, and wife-beaters or no shirt at all. All flew their flags. The platinum diamond-encrusted Crescent Crew pendants hung from all of their necklaces almost down to their nuts.

They hit Highway 17 and headed straight to Atlantic Beach, the place where the thoroughbreds partied, where everything was legal. In years past, a heavy police presence attempted to thwart the heavy influx of traffic that amounted to most of the black-owned businesses' yearly revenue. However, since they elected a new mayor, the youngest mayor in the history of South Carolina, things were different. Things were returned to the days past with Mayor Waajid participating in the festivities himself. As a result of this, all of the young and old who wanted to have a good time ventured to Atlantic Beach. Oh, there was still a police presence, but they only policed violence. Everything else was fair game.

Thus when the Crescent Crew/A.B.P. turned onto 30th Avenue, burnt rubber assaulted their lungs. Naked flesh assaulted their eyes. Nothing but boomin' bass soothed their ears accompanied by high-revving motorcycle engines. Who said there wasn't heaven for the ghetto?

As they neared the bottom of the street, they could vaguely see the ocean. The bottom of the street also served as the burn-out pit. GSX-Rs, Ninjas, Mustangs, Vettes. They all left their marks on the pavement to the raucous cheers of the crowd.

When Reece reached the bottom on his Ducati, he set his tires ablaze. Then in unison, all of their entourage stopped on a dime and smoked their tires, much to the amusement of the crowd. Smoke lit up the street like a forest fire. They had all day to ball out and have fun since Qwess wasn't scheduled to perform until the next day.

All the way on the other end of the strip in Myrtle Beach, Flame was behind the wheel of his Bimmer. He had been to Bike Week plenty of times before, but never on this level. He had more dough than he had ever seen, one of the hottest whips he'd seen so far, and he was a rapper on the rise. The boy was in heaven.

"Damn, look at that white bitch right there, dawg!" 8-Ball pointed to a thick sister walking the strip. "She got an ass like an African."

"Damn!" J.D. said from the back. "Yo! Woo-wee!! Pink-toe!" he called out. The young lady looked back to see who was calling her. Upon seeing the rims spinning on the Bimmer, even though it was stopped, she scurried over.

It didn't take long for J.D. to get her in the truck. A few choice words spit through his gold teeth and she was game. Five minutes later, she was in the back of the BMW getting all of her holes explored as J.D., Fat Black, and Lil J put their fingers all inside of her. Five minutes after that, she was going down the line blowing each of them. All the while, 8-Ball had the camcorder taping the whole thing. Flame had to drive, so he couldn't participate.

Thirty minutes later, they kicked her out and picked up two more broads with tans so deep they looked black. Instead of getting hit up in the car, they decided to take these two to the room. The women were obviously bisexual, judging by the way they kissed each other. The fellas wanted to see a freak show.

That was their intention when they returned to the hotel.

Doe, Reece, Qwess and some top captains of the Crescent Crew were enjoying a pool party with some of the industry's top entertainers and models when the call came through.

Qwess was throwing the "Eye Candy of the Year" in the pool when his cell phone rang from a lounge chair. At first, he didn't want to answer it, but he knew when it rang relentlessly that it might be something important.

"Salaam alayka," Qwess answered.

"Uh, Qwess, it's me," a voice said.

"Flame?" wondered Qwess.

"Uh, yeah."

"Man, what's wrong with you? Where you at? What's all that noise in the background?" Qwess fired away, already fearing the answer. The eye candy had collected herself from the bottom of the pool and was now throwing water at Qwess. He waved her off.

"Yo, I'm in jail, man," Flame whimpered.

"What?! For what?" Qwess couldn't believe this shit.

"It's a long story, dawg. I need you to come get me out."

"No shit!" Qwess spat. "Where you at?" Flame told him. "A'ight, I'll be there in a few, hold tight."

Qwess hung up and dropped the phone. He called out to Doe, who came running over.

"What's up?" he asked.

"We gotta go. Somethin' came up."

Doe already knew what time it was. "Flame?" Qwess nodded. "Damn."

They left the pool party and headed to Myrtle Beach. Qwess was on the phone the entire time. By the time they arrived at the Myrtle Beach police station, Flame was already out and waiting on them. Qwess went in to sign some papers and returned shortly. He jumped in the back seat of the Rover with Flame.

"All right, what happened?" Qwess demanded.

"A'ight, check it. We in the tellie wit' two gray broads. They freakin' each other out eating ass and shit, the whole nine. Right? Niggas sticking fingers all in the puss, everything. The hoes loving it! Okay, we blowing pine getting right. All of a sudden, it's a knock at the door. 8-Ball open it, it's one-time, the rollerz. They come in, see the two gray broads on the bed naked wit' pipe in they mouth and start freaking out."

"Why 8-Ball open the door in the first place?" Qwess wondered.

"I don't know what the nigga was thinking, but he got light soon as the rollerz came in the room.

"So anyway, po-po start asking for IDs. Niggas pull 'em out, give 'em to 'em. Then the broads didn't want to give up their IDs, so po-po said nobody could leave the room until the broads show their ID. Okay, niggas start panicking, knowing somethin' ain't right. Po-po see this and start searching the room. Look right under the bed and find an ounce of dro."

"Word?"

"Yeeah! So check it. They ask who it belong to. Nobody say nothing, so they took all of us in."

"What about the broads?" asked Qwess.

"Shit, they locked up, too!"

"A'ight, where's 8-Ball?" Doe wanted to know.

"Man, your guess is as good as mine. He got light when they first came in."

"So, let me ask you this," Qwess said. "Whose weed was it?"

Flame hesitated before answering. "It was J.D.'s."

"And he didn't own up to it? Even though he knew you had a show to do this weekend?"

"I guess so," Flame managed, shrugging his shoulders.

"So where he at now?" Qwess inquired.

"He still in there. Everybody still locked up! Hell, I don't even know how I got out, 'cause they was like ain't nobody going nowhere 'til they find out who the li'l gray broads are. All I know is a CO came and told me to roll, so I dipped."

"Man, how many times I told you, you gotta watch the company you keep?" Qwess admonished.

"Yo, I was. I ain't even fuck them broads, yo!" Flame pleaded. "When we get J.D. and them out, you'll see."

"Say what?" Qwess frowned.

"I said when we get J.D. and them out, you'll see," Flame repeated.

Qwess asked, "Who said we getting J.D. and them out? Them niggas don't give a fuck about you, so why should you give a fuck about them?"

Flame looked surprised. Everybody know you gotta stay real with your hood. "'Cause they my homies," Flame answered, stating the obvious.

"Your homies?"

"Yeah."

"Your homies get you locked up over a fuckin' ounce of weed. Weed?! What the fuck is a li'l weed charge? Here you are about to be a fuckin' superstar, and your homies get you locked up because they don't want to take they own weed charge. What kind of fuckin' homies are those?"

Qwess shook his head. Flame got offended that Qwess

was throwing salt on his homeboy until Qwess broke it down.

"Hulk, turn the music down," Qwess ordered. They were stuck in traffic on Highway 501. Qwess took the time to explain a few things to the young buck, Flame.

"Let me tell you something, more times than not niggas want to see you do bad more than good. Even your homies, matter of fact, mostly your homies! You think niggas want to see you riding in big whips and shit while they stuck on the block grinding? All because you got a gift with your mouth. Hell naw! I know niggas that would kill—literally—to have the talent you got, and you 'bout to fuck it up over your so-called homies. You remember this: Your homies are the brothas who got your best interest at heart. Far as I can see, these niggas don't." Qwess stabbed at the air to make his point. "I got niggas that would murder shit just to see me do good in the game. That's real homies! Like I told you before, you got to separate yourself from certain crowds, certain environments, to stay successful. It's not a matter of staying real. It's a matter of staying smart. Ya understand?"

Flame nodded. He had never seen things that way before. All he cared about was keeping it real. But the lecture wasn't over.

"See, Flame, you got to study history, man! If you don't study history, you'll become a part of it. Like take MC Hammer for example. The brotha went broke by trying to take care of his homies, probably niggas he ain't seen since the baby crib, but he still felt obligated to keep it real. Now he's real broke and them niggas real gone. Ya think them niggas asking Hammer if he need anything? Hell, naw! Niggas will do you the same way if you let 'em. That's why you gotta be smart." Qwess leaned back in the seat to calm down. He had gotten worked up schooling the youngster. Qwess knew firsthand about disassociation. He only dealt with certain people while he was doing his thing, and the Crescent Crew was way more thorough than J.D. and them. He really liked Flame because he was smart and hungry.

"Plus, you got to think about the money lost over stupidity," piped Doe from the front seat. "You 'bout to be filthy rich. I'm telling you. If you just play your part, this time next year you'll be a superstar."

Flame understood what they were saying, but damn, enough was enough.

"So what we gon' do about J.D. and them?" he asked.

Qwess scoffed. Obviously, Flame didn't get it. "Nothing," Qwess stated plainly. Then added, "This is going to be your first lesson: how to worry about Flame. Them niggas said, 'fuck you,' so fuck them."

That was that with that. As far as Qwess was concerned, that conversation was over.

For the rest of the night, Flame remained with Qwess. They returned to the pool party, which was really over considering everyone had broken up into couples for the remainder of the night. When they arrived back at the hotel, 8-Ball awaited them. He was standing on the balcony, smoking a blunt, looking at the ocean.

"You fat muthafucka! Where you been?" yelled Flame.

"Right here."

"Right here?"

"Yeah. When po-po came, I dipped downstairs. I came back when I saw y'all leave. I tried to get wit' Qwess, but the dude Reece said was already gone to get you. So I came back."

Qwess opened the door to leave. "Flame, I'm all in for the night. Don't go nowhere. You wit' me for the rest of the weekend," he said icily then slammed the door.

"Damn, what happened?" giggled 8-Ball.

"Aww, man." Flame flopped on the bed. "You won't believe it. Check it . . ." He proceeded to retell the night's events.

The following morning Reece awoke to the sounds of more booming bass and more loud pipes. During Bike Week, the beach was like New York in that it never slept. You were likely to find just as many people out and about at four a.m. as you would at four p.m.

Reece looked at the night stand clock: 11:40. Reece stretched out over the bed. This was the first night in ages that he'd slept alone. It felt real unfamiliar. He walked onto the balcony nude and looked onto the already packed oceanfront.

Pressing on his mind was what Qwess had relayed to him a week ago. Reece absolutely despised rats! After meeting privately with his top captains about the dilemma, he had come to a conclusion. Someone had to be eliminated. Even if it wasn't the right person, it would stir the waters up, and eventually the rat would tell on himself. Reece hated to take out one of his own, but treason was unacceptable. After taking a consensus with his captains on who it would be, as always, the last hired would be the first fired.

Reece thought about Bone, who just missed the cut by one last member. It would've been a shame to take out such a good soldier. Bone possessed what was necessary to succeed inside the Crescent Crew: ambition, discipline, and reckless disregard for police. And Reece liked it! Last hired was always first fired, so today would be the day. Bishop would be accidentally struck by a truck while riding his motorcycle. Reece didn't like it, but it was essential.

Reece picked up the phone and called home. Destiny answered on the third ring.

"Hey, love," Reece greeted. "What are you doing home on a Saturday?"

Destiny sucked her teeth. "Don't play games. You know I can't leave. You turned on the alarms and locked the house down. I can't open any of the doors or windows."

"What! Really?" Reece mocked, playing dumb.

"Yes. Really, Reece! You know what you did. You know what? This is getting silly," Destiny concluded. "So you don't trust me now?"

"Trust you? Yeah, I trust you. I just don't trust me."

"What's that supposed to mean?" snapped Destiny, pissed.

"It means I don't know what I would do if I was to come home and you're not there. You're my boo, and I need you available for me at all times," Reece said.

Destiny was getting fed up. "Reece, this is juvenile! We're supposed to be in a trusting relationship."

"Look, trust isn't one of my strengths. So I learn as I go along, a'ight."

Destiny, sensing the conversation was going nowhere, asked, "So when do I post bail?"

"What?"

"When are you coming home?" Dripping with attitude.

"In the morning. Qwess performing tonight. We leave in the morning."

"All right," Destiny conceded. "And Reece?"

"Yeah?"

"Make sure you take your phone."

"Don't I always have my phone when you're not with me?"

"Yeah."

"A'ight then."

They said their last words, and Reece replaced the phone in its cradle. He felt a tinge of guilt for locking Destiny inside the house, but hey, he was new at the love thing. He didn't know it couldn't be controlled. He was used to acting to make things work in his favor. After all, that's what shot callers did. They called shots. Reece had no idea that by its very nature, love couldn't be contained. That was a lesson he would learn the hard way.

Because of the performance scheduled that night, everyone was taking it easy. They were spending the day on the oceanfront, frolicking in the water. Doe had yet to see Niya until he spotted her preparing to get in the water in her hot-pink bikini. He snuck up behind her and whispered in her ear.

"How ya doing, beautiful?" he said.

"I'm doing fine, but flattery will get you nowhere."

"That's good, because I'm right where I want to be."

"Oh, yeah. Where is that?" Niya teased.

"Right here with you." Doe kissed her, then scooped her in his arms and ran to the water. He dived right into a wave with her headfirst. That was the first of many to come as they spent the entire day together. When night fell, everyone prepared for the show.

In one room Doe helped Niya into her knee-high stiletto boots. In another, Flame rehearsed his verses in the mirror. Next door to him, Qwess did the same.

In yet another room, Reece talked on the phone, feigning surprise that Bishop had been hit by a truck on his motorcycle. Reece only relaxed when it was confirmed he was dead.

* * *

The House of Blues, located just between Atlantic Beach and Myrtle Beach, was packed. Because of its location, its patrons consisted of the best of both worlds. Hippie, yuppie whites, and thugged-out blacks. On this night, the thugs heavily outweighed everyone else. See, not only were Qwess and his protégé performing, but the hottest rapper worldwide was performing also. This rapper had gained the reputation for being a thug's thug. He had even been shot multiple times which added credence to his image. So, as much as Qwess wanted to be the headliner, he knew that this rapper was the main draw. Ever the optimist, Qwess reasoned that if the crowd was this huge and diverse, he was going to make sure they remembered A.B.P.

It was an hour before Qwess was scheduled to perform. Qwess stood at the railing over the dance floor looking into the crowd. It was still early, yet the House of Blues was packed like a prison. Flame stood on the left of Qwess, Doe on his right. Qwess was nervous, and Doe could sense it. He patted Qwess on the back in an attempt to ease his anxiety.

Qwess was nervous about this performance because it was personal. He knew most of the locals and they knew him. It was nothing to perform. That was easy. Qwess desired to turn the joint out! He wanted to represent for his hood. It wouldn't be right to let an outsider come to the beach and outshine its prodigal son, no matter the sales or the stature of the artist. Qwess had already spotted mad hustlers from his block, some new and some old. He knew they would expect him to represent to the fullest.

A tap on his shoulder caused Qwess to turn around. He looked into the face of Mayor Waajid, the head man on Atlantic Beach. He and Qwess had grown up together.

In fact, Mayor Waajid was only two months older than Qwess.

"Is this the li'l problem child?" Mayor Waajid asked, pointing to Flame.

"Yeah, this him," Qwess answered. He had to scream to be heard over the music. He tapped Flame on the shoulder. "Say thank you to the man who got your ass snatched out the clink," Qwess instructed. It was Mayor Waajid who had made the call to spring Flame from the slammer so quickly.

"Thank you," offered Flame.

Before Mayor Waajid left, he pulled Qwess to the side and screamed in his ear. "I thought you might want to know, you don't have to worry about seeing those other guys out here tonight. They're still in jail. They've been transferred to J. Reuben Long Detention Center."

"What for?" a surprised Qwess asked.

"Well, it turns out these young ladies were underage. The guys were charged with statutory rape. They won't receive a hearing until Tuesday at the earliest."

"Damn."

"Yep. Thought you might want to know." Before the mayor walked off, Qwess told him he owed him.

"No, you don't. Just seeing you do good is payment for me. Now turn this shit tonight!"

An hour later, with the mayor's blessing, Qwess did just that. The highlight of the show was when he dived into the crowd. They caught him and passed him around on his back, all the while chanting "A.B.P.! A.B.P.! A.B.P.!"

Flame took the stage after Qwess. He performed his new song, "Worldwide Ladies," and got the audience crunk. He took them to the brink and brought them back. Flame was a natural. Just when the crowd thought he was done, he brought Niya out. She looked stunning in her boots, football tights, and halter jersey. Her long hair was pulled into a ponytail. She wasn't mentioned in the billing. She was a special guest. Thus when the people who knew her recognized her, they gave up props. Niya's star was starting to rise in certain markets, so the love was genuine.

Niya sang her chorus with the poise of a veteran. She hit the high notes on key, and even finessed things with a little vibrato. Hustlers in the crowd threw money on the stage in appreciation. Niya took that as disrespect; however, she took it in stride. She was just glad the crowd appreciated her. She performed her last song solo and left the stage.

When Niya and Flame along with Qwess came back onstage to take a bow, the crowd demanded an encore.

Later when the headline artist took the stage, he was met with mediocre responses from the crowd. It was definitely a prelude of things to come if he wasn't careful, because everyone affiliated with Atlantic Beach Productions has all intentions of putting the game in a chokehold.

The following morning, Reece and the majority of the Crescent Crew returned to North Carolina. Qwess, Hulk, and the rest of the A.B.P. family stayed behind, as did Niya. There was a huge bash going on at the Myrtle Beach drag strip that included a bikini contest, car show, and of course motorcycle racing. Qwess was tapped to be one of the celebrity judges in the bikini contest, so he was excited.

The Myrtle Beach drag strip used to be an air force base, but due to military budget cuts, it was forced to close its gates for good. Looking to capitalize on the huge event Bike Week grew to be, the city of Myrtle Beach opened up its gates to cater to special events.

From the time the drag strip opened up, it was crammed with people. If you looked at the array of cars entering the gates, you'd think the entire crowd was coming to compete in the car show. There was more candy than in a bag of Jolly Ranchers, with chrome so bright it was like stars had fallen from the sky.

Qwess pulled his Lamborghini on the strip, with Doe riding shotgun, at a little after noon. Hulk was behind him in Samson's Viper. A nervous Flame sat beside him. As Qwess made his way through the crowd, people pushed pieces of paper in his face requesting his autograph. It seemed like the deeper he drove into the crowd, the more people knew him. Where the crowd got thick, the women were pulling their breasts out flashing him, or trying to jump in the car with him. It was a nice eighty-five-degree day, so the top was out, to take advantage of the uncharacteristic low humidity. By the time Qwess parked and took his seat at the judge's table, he was exhausted. He felt like he was on the verge of being a prisoner to his newfound fame.

There were three judges in all. Qwess and an R & B singer were already seated, but the middle chair remained unoccupied awaiting the third and final judge. After a brief wait, the final judge appeared. It was the infamous New York rapper who had been the headliner for the previous night's show, Maserati.

"Yo, what's up, beautiful," he greeted the R & B singer. He didn't even acknowledge Qwess, which didn't faze Qwess. He knew Maserati had a penchant for starting beefs on wax in order to sell records. After he was shown up by Qwess at the show, everyone knew it was only a matter of time before he tried to redeem himself.

"Hey, sexy." She smiled back.

The emcee grabbed the mic and got the show on the road. There were nine girls competing in all. They had to walk out on the platform, model their bikini, then come back and stand with the group. There would be three rounds, with three eliminations per round. Contestant number one walked out first.

She was petite and tall with four-inch heels on her feet, which made her appear taller. Her hair was cut short and blond, which blended well with her caramel skin. She wore a bikini that was "this" big. Triangle patches just covered her nipples, and her thong seeped in her cheeks as she sashayed down the platform. At the end of the platform, she turned with her face facing the judges and her shapely behind to the crowd. Then she touched her toes, mooning the crowd, who went berserk.

When the smoke cleared, only contestant number one stood with a buxom beauty dipped in the smoothest chocolate Mother Nature could muster. Her name was Innocence.

Innocence had been trying to get with Qwess all weekend, but he was always one step ahead of her. When she found out he was judging the bikini contest, she made earnest in joining it. She wanted to show Qwess firsthand just what he was missing. He hadn't hit her in weeks.

The emcee told the contestants they had to do something extra special to win the contest. The prize was a date with one of the celebrity judges and a handsome cash purse. He instructed the judges to bring their chairs from behind the desk, front and center, to get a good look for judging purposes.

The DJ started the music and contestant number one started rump-shaking. The contest had long gone from a bikini showing to an amateur strip-off. Contestant number one, not knowing what her competitor had planned, decided to set the bar high from the jump-off. She lay on her back and rolled her legs over her head. At first, it seemed she was just lying in that position. Then, upon further observation, one could see her bikini being sucked in and out of her hole deeply. It almost looked like something—or someone—was inside of her pulling the fabric in by a string. Umm, talk about Kegel exercises! The bar was set.

Innocence was up next. She knew she couldn't lose in front of Qwess to another bitch, which is why she had a trick up her sleeve the entire time. Before Innocence started dancing, she pulled Qwess's chair up by itself. Then she started dancing in front of him. She went through the regular routines, making each butt cheek jump together, then separately, getting low and all. For the finale, she walked toward Qwess facing him. She got right in his face and did a handstand, throwing her legs across his shoulders. Qwess's head dipped briefly; when it came back up, he was sucking on a lollipop. The crowd erupted!

The female judge grudgingly announced Innocence as the winner. As did Maserati, but with hate, because he wasn't the one sucking on the lollipop.

Innocence collected her prize money and walked over to Qwess. "Thank you," she said, slipping the money into his pocket.

"What's this for?" asked Qwess, referring to the money she had slipped in his pocket.

"For you. I know time is money. I'm willing to pay for your time. You're worth it."

Qwess kissed her on the cheek. He saw Maserati about to join his bulletproof-vest entourage. Qwess ran over to him and stopped him.

"Yo, main man." Maserati looked at him with obvious contempt.

"Yeah?"

Qwess stuck his hand out. "See you at the top." Maserati didn't shake it. Instead, he scowled and walked off. Qwess laughed and left to join his crew, but he etched the moment in his memory forever.

Chapter 20

Reece had never been in love. He had never paid attention to the way his father treated his mother, or vice versa. Therefore, he didn't know how to reciprocate love, either. The only thing Reece knew about was controlling things. He had come from nothing to a big something by sheer cunning and calculation. After all, didn't destiny bend to an indomitable will? And what was Reece's will if not indomitable. He was the king of the Crescent Crew. He was used to people obeying him, no questions asked. He was used to crushing enemies underneath his designer footwear.

Unfortunately, King Reece had never done battle with love. The love that empowers a woman, yet weakens a man. The love that is questionably the most powerful emotion known to mankind. So, when King Reece moved Destiny into his mansion and bought her a brand-new Mercedes, he did it for love. When King Reece started bringing Destiny along on his business trips with him, yep, that was for love, too. And when King Reece decided to take Destiny along with him to Mexico for the remainder of the year, of course, it was for love.

Things were finally getting too hot for Reece. The police were closing in. They had been relentlessly pursuing him ever since the police sergeant was assassinated in his car. They couldn't put him at the scene, but they knew he was responsible. The number of times the sergeant was shot indicated the hit was retaliation for Jersey Ali.

When the autopsy was performed on Jersey Ali, the first thing the medical examiner had noted was the huge Crescent Crew tattoo sprawled across his shoulder blades. Upon further investigation, the police realized that the Crescent Crew tattoo signified Jersey Ali belonged to a gang that had expanded throughout the entire Carolinas. The gang was responsible for multiple homicides and tons of drugs in the last few years. The state bureau of investigations launched an all-out offensive with federal help. The feds later revealed that they had been after this particular crew for a while. Now, this "group of thugs" had agreed to work in a concerted effort to bring them down.

King Reece had found out about the plan almost as soon as it left the chief's mouth, which is why he was on the low lately. However, Reece could still feel them closing in.

Never one to sit back and let life take its course, Reece devised a plan. His connect Manuelito had been trying to get Reece to come to Mexico for the longest. He offered to put Reece up in his own home and show him property that he would invest in for an eventual move to Mexico for when situations get rough. Mexico had a non-extradition clause, so as long as Reece was in Mexico, the feds couldn't touch him. Manuelito had already heard stories of how treacherous Reece could be, so he had no doubt that Reece could handle himself well in Mexico.

Sensing things had gotten bad, Reece decided to finally take Manuelito up on his offer. Not that he was running; Reece just realized that a vacation of sorts was necessary. He had made a shitload of money so far, and Samson proved more capable of taking care of the family for six months. Just six months. That presumably was all that was needed. He planned to start the New Year off on a good foot.

Destiny was running late, which was usual. She had known about the trip for at least two weeks, and here she was still late packing. "A little more of this, a little more of that," she said. Reece could only pace and look at his watch.

Manuelito was sending his private jet from Mexico to retrieve Reece and Destiny. The jet was already waiting for them in a private hangar just outside the city. Samson was on his way to scoop them up and deliver them to the hangar. Destiny insisted on knowing where the hangar was located, like she didn't trust him or something. "Ooh, the nerve!" She had been on the phone with her uncle all morning. Reece was really getting tired of the fucker.

Reece checked and double-checked everything when he saw Samson's truck at the front gate. He had everything he needed. He only wished he could see Qwess before he departed for Mexico. That wasn't possible because Qwess was spending the day in the Virginia hills visiting his father in the federal penitentiary. Oh, well, Qwess was getting money now. Maybe when Reece copped him a nice villa in Mexico, he could invite him down to spend a few weeks.

Destiny was finally ready to go, just as Samson rang the doorbell. Reece answered the door, and Samson greeted him with a bear hug.

"You ready, God?" Samson said.

"Yeah. Soon as Des come down. Yo, baby, let's go!" Reece yelled. Destiny trotted down the stairs, bags in tow. Samson grabbed them and took them out to the truck.

"Damn, girl. You got a body in here or something?" he joked. Destiny didn't respond. She had seemed rather distant all morning. Reece chalked it up to the argument they had had last night.

Right when they went to bed to prepare for the day's journey ahead, Destiny decided to discuss Reece's "business." She even called him a murderer when he told her he didn't want to talk about it. In the end, Reece conceded and they spent the entire night talking. Destiny said something Reece had never heard her say, and she kept repeatedly stressing that she loved him, no matter what. They went to sleep a little less confused, but Destiny was still visibly upset when they awoke. Reece reasoned that once she saw the splendid Mexican sun, she'd lighten up.

They all loaded into the vehicle and began the journey to the hangar. During the ride, Reece took the time to cross all the T's and dot the I's. Samson nodded his agreement. He seemed to have everything under control.

When they arrived at the hangar, the gate was locked. The black Gulfstream jet idled on the tarmac resembling a giant bird. The steps were down awaiting its passengers. Other than the jet, the tarmac was empty.

They waited impatiently for the gate to open. After a short time, a man appeared wearing a dark windbreaker. He slowly slid the gate open, talking into his walkie-talkie.

Just as the truck rolled through the gates, sirens barked in the distance.

"What the fuck?!" Reece frowned. He peeped back and spotted red and blue lights flashing profusely, headed straight in their direction at full speed. He looked to the plane and saw the pilot and crew members crowd the doorway of the plane. They waved for Reece to come on.

Right away, Reece knew the plane was safe. If he could make it to the plane, he was home free. He knew Manuelito's men would not be apprehended at any cost. The plane's engine roared to life.

"Samson, you strapped?" Reece asked.

"Ya know it." He pulled out two Dessert Eagle pistols, passing Reece one.

"Get the bags on the plane. I'll lock the gate!" Reece commanded. Samson gathered the bags in one swoop and exited the vehicle.

When Samson exited the truck, the man who had opened the gate pointed a pistol at him. His windbreaker had FBI tags sticking out everywhere. Samson froze. The bags tied up both his hands, so he was defenseless.

"Drop the bags and put your hands up!" the agent ordered. In that split second, Reece acted. He popped out the passenger door with gun in hand.

"Noooo!!!" Destiny screamed, but it was too late. Reece fired two shots straight to the head. It exploded like a melon. Reece ran around and locked the gate, while Samson shot toward the plane with the bags.

Destiny sat in the back seat shivering.

"Come on, baby! We gotta roll!" Reece screamed. The feds were less than a hundred yards away. "Come on, baby! Come on!"

Destiny did not move.

Samson came back and grabbed Reece's arm. "Come on, God! We can't wait. We gotta move now. The plane is ready. She'll be all right."

Reece tried one last time to get Destiny to move, but she wouldn't move. Reece bolted in the direction of the plane. He was halfway there when Destiny screamed his name.

"Reece!"

Reece turned to look, and Destiny was standing in the middle of the tarmac with a Glock aimed right at him. "What the fuck you doing, girl?! Now ain't the time for games. We gotta go!"

"Reeeece," Destiny chanted. "You are under arrest!"

"What? Quit fucking playing. We gotta go." The feds had finally made it to the gate. "Fuck it, I'm gone!!"

Reece ran toward the plane, where Samson was waiting in the doorway waving him in. Reece had never run so fast in his life. He could feel his legs pumping like pistons. He was ten feet from the plane when he felt his left leg go numb. Simultaneously, he looked down and saw blood burst from the front of his thigh. Someone had shot him. He fell to the pavement in agony.

"Arrgh!!" he cried out. He knew instantly he wasn't going to make it to the plane, so he waved it off. The pilot wasted no time taxiing down the short runway, and took off.

Reece rolled over on his stomach in the direction from which the shots had come. His pistol was aimed right where he looked. Right into the eyes of Destiny, where she was crouched into a shooting position, gun still smoking. For an instant, everything else was blocked out. The cops entering the gate. The excruciating pain in his leg. Even the bitter taste of betrayal.

All that remained was a stare-off between Destiny and Reece. He looked into her beautiful hazel eyes. All he had to do was pull the trigger, and her life would be extinguished. All he had to do was pull the trigger, and retribution would be exacted for the ultimate betrayal. A cop! A fuckin' cop!!?

Destiny looked into Reece's opaque eyes. All she had to do was pull the trigger, and she would put an end to the killing, the drug dealing. How could one person be so full of love, yet so cruel like Reece? All she had to do was pull the trigger and exact justice for so many mothers. She had been with him for over a year, she knew first-hand the evil that lurked behind those dead eyes. All she had to do was pull the trigger . . .

But she couldn't.

She really loved him.

As Reece did her.

Therefore, there were no more eruptions of gunfire. When the police ran past Destiny to apprehend Reece, he gave up without a fight. They kicked him a little bit, but he was oblivious to that. The whole time they cuffed him and Mirandized him, his eyes never left Destiny, who had yet to move from her crouching stance.

When they escorted him out the gate past Destiny after receiving medical attention, a wheezing sound was emitted from his throat like a wounded animal. They carried Reece to a tinted Suburban and waited on a Lieutenant Harris.

Reece sat in the back of the truck foaming at the mouth. All of a sudden, the door was snatched open and Reece was face-to-face with a man he knew well. The tag on his chest read "Lieutenant Harris," but Reece knew him as Uncle Lou.

The plot thickened.

Chapter 21

Reece was on his way to the courthouse. He was glad to be out on bail, albeit on the day trial was to start. That was okay, though. At least he got to eat a decent meal, and feel the comfort of a big bed. He actually couldn't see himself willingly coming to court to face so-called justice. He knew they were going to railroad him if he gave them a chance, especially with his charges. He was charged with murdering a federal officer, operating a continual criminal enterprise, *and* they had hit him with the RICO act: Racketeering Influenced Corrupt Organization. A New York case in fucking Carolina! That was proof in itself that they were going to try to hang him out to dry.

Try, because Reece had plans of his own. He was already out on a million-dollar bail, which was unheard of for these types of charges. It was proof that the system was able to be manipulated. Hell, if they knew the type of paper Reece had, the judge would've asked for a two-million-dollar kickback, rather than one million for granting him bail. Reece would've willingly paid it, for he had to be out to execute his plan.

Kidnapping the juror's daughter was easy. As soon as

the jury was selected, Reece scoped them out to see which one was vulnerable. He had someone research their files, gathering all the information possible. Then, he put his plan in motion.

Reece knew that from the moment he set foot out of jail, feds were going to be trailing him. They wanted him to run so they could kill him. They had been trying to provoke him the entire time he was in custody. Sending lesser men to eavesdrop, or trick information out of him. Picture that! Reece was a soldier, and soldiers hold strong . . . to the end.

By them trailing him, it created the perfect decoy. He would keep the feds occupied while some members of the crew kidnapped the little girl.

Oh, the crew was still intact. Reece was still de facto boss, and Samson was still in charge. Only thing was, Samson was exiled in Mexico. He had not returned to the States since the day he had fled on the plane when Reece was shot. No one was stupid. They knew if Samson touched U.S. soil, he would be put in a box. Either a wooden one, or a cement one. That would be detrimental to the crew. So he remained in Mexico running the Crescent Crew with an iron fist.

In the States, Born's word was law. He would send an emissary to the county jail to speak to Reece to figure out his plans. At first, Reece told them to stand down. It was too much heat. He knew the feds were looking to bust one or more of the members so they could roll them and make them testify against him. Then, when he realized the demand for product, he gave the order to continue business with one additional rule: Death Before Dishonor, which was needless to say.

During Reece's first two weeks in captivity, the feds tried desperately to debrief him. They wanted contacts, sources, the whole shebang, in exchange for thirty years.

Reece just ice-grilled them the entire time. His mind was on Destiny.

Turned out Destiny was an FBI agent sent specifically to bring down Reece. The feds were on to Reece when he was a $60,000-a-week peon. They targeted him because he had a penchant for violence. They wanted him off the streets quickly. However, he was always too smart. Always one step ahead of them. They could never catch him with anything or find anyone willing to cooperate. They knew from investigating him, he had a weak dick. He was a sucker for a new piece of pussy. So they brought an agent from out of state to set him up. He took the bait. Hook, line, and sinker.

That day at the restaurant, Destiny had been watching Reece, waiting for the right time. Reece made it easy when he ran into her, causing her to drop her purse. When he stared in her eyes, as he assisted her in picking up the spilled contents, she knew she had him.

Reece hadn't seen her since the day she shot him. If he had known she was going to disappear, he would've shot her. He had all of his people combing the streets looking for her. There wasn't a sign of her anywhere. Even in his motion of discovery, she wasn't scheduled to testify. She was only identified as agent 0919. That was okay with Reece. After he beat these charges, he was going to hunt her down, cut her heart out, and feed it to her.

Hulk pulled into the courthouse on Hattesburg Road in Raleigh, North Carolina. According to his watch, they were running a little late. Reece kept prompting him to speed up from the back seat, but the numerous news crews camped out in front of the courthouse prevented him from going any faster. Reece's lawyer, Malik Shabazz, had called three times already in the past hour.

Malik Shabazz was a tall, light-skinned brother who

had been preaching law for twenty years as a criminal attorney. He was known coast to coast for being *the* go-to man when your back was against the wall and big bank bulged from your pockets. He had never lost a drug case, and despite the odds stacked against him, he didn't plan on losing this one, either.

After realizing the truck couldn't get them any closer to the courthouse quicker, Reece jumped out with Born, Muhammad, and Power on his heels. He headed up the steps of the courthouse and was met with a barrage of flashes.

"Mr. Kirkson, Mr. Kirkson! Is it true you executed a federal officer in broad daylight . . ."

"Mr. Kirkson! What do you say of the allegations that you headed a criminal enterprise . . ."

The reporters had questions for days. Reece's entourage just pushed on past. They were headed to the main courtroom upstairs. When they exited the elevator, Qwess and Doe awaited them. They already knew Qwess and Doe were there because they had seen Qwess's Lambo parked outside.

Qwess had gone through a lot to be present. He was in the studio working on Flame's album and tweaking his own new album. The trial was tentatively expected to last weeks. Qwess made an oath to be there as much as possible.

They all linked up and entered the courtroom. They were met by more cameras and noted a gallery full of spectators. Everyone took a seat when the judge banged his gavel, except Reece, who went to greet his lawyer.

"Boy, you had me worried for a second," Mr. Shabazz told Reece. Reece cracked a retort and smiled. He and his lawyer were dressed similarly in tailor-made Italian suits, except where Mr. Shabazz accented his dark suit with a maroon tie, Reece wore a bright burnt orange.

Instead of black Stacy Adams, Reece wore ostrich-skinned boots the color of his suit.

Reece took his seat at the defense table. The judge banged his gavel again, opening up court. Prosecutor Long stepped up to deliver his opening argument.

"Ladies and gentlemen of the jury. I come to you today for justice . . ."

While Long filibustered, Reece casually sized up the jury. His eyes lingered on juror number six, who sweated profusely. Juror number six pulled at his collar. It was getting hot. Juror number six discreetly locked eyes with Reece briefly, and nodded his head.

That was all Reece needed to see. He was cooperating. For the remainder of Long's diatribe, Reece sat confidently. When it was time for Mr. Shabazz to address the court, Reece perked up.

Mr. Shabazz stood, shot his cuffs again, and sauntered to the center of the jury. He was fairly attractive with a shock of red hair neatly cut low and groomed to perfection. He had no facial hair, which made it easy for him to belie his fifty years of age. A lot of his cases were won on sheer skill, but it was his looks that got him over the hump, for if you couldn't endear a jury to you from jump, your case was already lost. Malik Shabazz came off as cool, but not arrogant. Classy, but not bourgeois.

"Ladies and gentlemen of the jury, I'm sure you just heard of the elaborate crime syndicate Mr. Long alleges that my client operated. The vast criminal enterprise that spans the entire Carolinas. The brutal atrocities committed in the name of the almighty dollar. Ladies and gentlemen of the jury, I'm sure you heard the stories painted by Mr. Picasso"—an audible gasp could be heard—"yes, Picasso, because only an artist of extraordinary talent could paint a picture so vivid. So far-fetched! However, even Picasso needed a prop. An example. A proof, if you will, to paint his magnificent masterpieces. So I ask you, ladies and gentlemen of the jury, where is the proof ? The proof, I say! I'm sure when this is over, you'll see Federal Prosecutor Long's case is as flimsy as wet tissue!

"My client is a self-respecting businessman . . ." By the time Malik Shabazz finished speaking, even Reece thought of himself as a self-respecting businessman, as he sat cross-legged in his seat looking dignified. It seemed the whole courtroom was convinced. Everyone except juror number six. He knew firsthand the prosecutor's depiction of the defendant was closer to the truth.

Day one of the trial was spent largely covering motions. The parties were excused for the day at four-thirty.

Day two started promptly at ten a.m. with the government calling its first witness. Reece casually looked around hoping to get a glimpse of Destiny somewhere, to no avail, because Destiny wasn't in the courtroom. Instead, her "Uncle Lou" strutted to the stand.

He took the stand and was sworn in.

"Could you state your name for the record, please?"

"Victor Harris."

"And what do you do, Mr. Harris?"

He cleared his throat. "I'm a lieutenant with the Federal Bureau of Investigation."

Mr. Long coached him on. "Were you in charge of the detail responsible for investigating the defendant?"

"I was."

"Could you tell the court the first time you had the displeasure—"

"Objection!"

"Withdrawn. Excuse me, the pleasure of meeting the defendant."

Lieutenant Harris went on to explain how he was introduced to Reece at the party and a few other occasions—which Reece didn't recall. He made mention of

Destiny several times, but referred to her as Agent Hill. Each time he did so, Reece saw red. It was the only time he allowed himself to be fazed by what went on in the courtroom. The rest of the time he doodled on the pad or twisted his long locks reflectively.

The majority of day two was spent with Lieutenant Harris on the stand. It grew redundant until he introduced into evidence Reece's cell phone. It was really a listening device, and was responsible for hours of evidence. With no way to get the cell phone suppressed as evidence, it would seem like Reece was a dead man, for a conviction would automatically result in no less than life imprisonment. Yet, Reece still sat unfazed. He had a ringer in the jury. A sure thing, too, because fear and love did battle as the strongest emotions known to man. Both fear and love were present in juror number six, so Reece was straight. Love of his family and fear of death for them. This would undoubtedly keep juror number six smart.

Days three, four, and five were spent with a bunch of police testifying. Judge Epps had to admonish Reece for laughing out loud in court when one of the officers explained a gruesome murder scene in detail.

"I apologize, your honor, but he's lying," Reece told the judge. Reece had held court many times with himself acting as the judge. He knew disrespect for the court was unforgivable, so he deferred to the judge every chance he got. Reece understood that just as in his court, an angry judge made for a screwed defendant.

On day six, the prosecutor tried to pull a coup. He called an Officer Cureton to the stand. Officer Cureton arrived to the stand via a Hoveround. His legs were amputated from mid-thigh, which looked awkward in his uniform. Apparently, the prosecutor was going for shock and awe.

Officer Cureton took the stand and was sworn in. Mr. Long got the particulars out of the way and dug in.

"Officer Cureton, I'm sure everyone is dying to know how you're connected to this case. Could you please tell the court?"

"Well, I've experienced the brutality of Mr. Kirkson firsthand. He cost me my legs." Mr. Long feigned surprise by covering his agape mouth. The rest of the courtroom's surprise was authentic. No one's surprise was more genuine than Reece's. He had never seen this man in his life! What kind of bullshit was this?

Officer Cureton recounted the events that cost him his legs, and Reece remembered. It was when they blew up Black Vic. Reese chuckled at the thought.

"I'll never forget those dreadlocks for as long as I live," Cureton was finishing on the stand.

Shabazz couldn't wait to cross-examine Cureton. When his time came, he jumped from the table, shedding his coat, revealing biceps that threatened to burst through his shirt and a barrel chest that stretched his vest to its limits.

"Mr. Cureton, you say you saw my client clearly. Tell me what was his facial expression when you allegedly saw him toss a hand grenade into an open car?"

"Uh, I don't recall."

"Um-hmm. You say he was on a motorcycle, correct?"

"Yes, I remember that vividly."

"Good, do you also remember that North Carolina law requires its motorcycle riders to wear helmets? No matter how fast they're going—especially downtown."

"Um, well, actually I didn't see his face."

"Oh, really?" Shabazz smiled. "Well, what did you see?"

"I saw his dreadlocks flapping in the wind as he fled the crime scene."

Shabazz mockingly flailed his arms in the air. At the prosecutor's table, Mr. Long planted his face in his hands. He knew exactly where this was going.

"You saw his dreadlocks! Is that all? So tell me," Shabazz said, strolling over by the jury box. Long knew what was coming because he had tried to excuse juror number four during voir dire. "For all you know, this gentleman here could've done it!"

Juror number four wore dreadlocks. Shabazz had kept him on the jury because he knew someone would bring Reece's hairstyle into play sometime, especially from the prosecution. The plan worked splendidly.

The courtroom erupted into laughter. Even Judge Epps had to stifle his giggles before regaining order.

That testimony signified a dramatic shift in momentum for the defense. For the rest of the day, Shabazz ate witnesses up like he was breaking a fast. The week ended on a positive note for the defense. The judge dismissed court for the weekend, but before he allowed Reece to leave, he made him wear a monitor.

The weekend was uneventful, and court resumed on Monday with more suppression motions. Shabazz desperately tried to get the phone and its results suppressed. Judge Epps wasn't hearing it. He may have paid a million dollars to grant Reece bail, but favors stopped there. Another million was required to show favoritism during trial.

After motions were handled, the government called its next witness, which was a taped deposition. It seemed the witness was scared to show his new face in court. The government had put the witness in its protection program in exchange for testimony. They even supplied him with plastic surgery, which went well with the surgery Reece had already performed on him. The witness was Tyrone Beaman, the man whose finger Reece had confiscated as collateral in a back alley.

Shabazz had objected to the deposition, arguing that it showed his client in a negative light. Judge Epps overruled him, and the tape began.

Tyrone—whose face was blacked out—began to explain how everyone feared "King" Reece. And how his Crescent Crew had the lowest drug prices in the Southeast. In the end, the testimony wasn't too damaging, and Shabazz started feeling he could actually beat the case . . . until Day ten.

Day ten was the day the prosecutor started arguing count two in the indictment: murdering a federal agent. So many police were present in the courtroom that day, it looked like an FBI convention. Judge Epps ordered extra security around Reece, since death threats were being issued. In addition to the judge's security, the Crescent Crew came out deep as well, although most of the members were from out of state to ensure no one was snatched up on outstanding warrants. The courtroom was so packed, they didn't stick out anyway. HLN network was now covering the case, so the trial became a spectacle.

Prosecutor Long called the first agent to the stand who was present the day Reece blew the cop's brains out. By the time Long finished, it was three days and fifteen agents later. Long was preparing to wrap up his case, but he had one more crucial witness. Being that it was late, Judge Epps adjourned court until Monday.

Reece still was free on bond, but he still had to wear the monitor, so his actions were limited over the weekend.

Bright and early that Monday morning all parties involved in *The United States of America v. Maurice Kirkson* returned to Raleigh. Reece was feeling pretty good.

He had slept and eaten well all weekend, and this thing was almost over. He even wore a new suit.

Everyone filed in and was seated. The government called its next and final witness. Katrina D. Hill. At first, Reece didn't catch the name, so he continued to give himself a manicure. Then it dawned on him, and he looked up just in time to see Destiny hobble to the stand. Reece was halfway to the witness stand when Destiny turned around, forcing him to freeze of his own volition—way before the bailiffs tackled him to the ground.

Reece peered through the sea of bodies that covered him to get another look at Destiny. To prove his first glance correct. He was barely able to see, but he saw enough.

Destiny was pregnant.

She had to be at least seven months, which would make the baby . . . his! The realization hit Reece before all hell broke loose.

The Crescent Crew had jumped the rails and fought the bailiffs that held Reece down. The FBI agents joined in the fracas as well, and out of nowhere a brawl ensued.

Reece was led into the courtroom in chains. He was seated at the table, and the jury was brought in. Reece looked back to the empty gallery, noticing he was alone. Because of the previous day's brawl, Judge Epps closed the courtroom to everyone who wasn't participating in the trial—reporters included. Even the FBI agents were barred. The courtroom was so empty, voices echoed throughout the walls.

Judge Epps gave a curative instruction telling the jury to disregard the defendant's restraints. Yeah, right! Judge Epps meant well. It was all he could do not to call a mistrial and have to go through another grueling three weeks of trial.

When things were settled, Destiny was called to the stand again. Reece observed how she hobbled, and surmised she might be eight months pregnant. He was going through so many emotions, he couldn't stick to one. Hate. Pain. Jealousy. Rage. Betrayal . . . Love.

Despite everything he still loved her, especially with her carrying his seed.

Destiny was sworn in, and Prosecutor Long did away with the particulars. Destiny started explaining how she first met Reece. The whole time she avoided eye contact with him. Reece, on the other hand, stared at her, willing her to look his way.

"Agent Hill, did you ever see the defendant murder anyone other than Agent Darius at the hangar?" Long asked.

"Objection! Speculation."

"Sustained." Judge Epps.

"Excuse me. Did you ever see the defendant murder anyone while you were undercover with him?"

Undercover! The thought of him being played made Reece fume. He was practically foaming at the mouth, unable to keep his cool any longer.

"No," Destiny replied.

"Well, Agent Hill, weren't you responsible for placing the bug in the cell phone that resulted in hours of evidence?"

Destiny was visibly shaken. Her eyes were bloodshot, and she kept wiping her forehead. Still she answered.

"Yes," she croaked more than spoke. Then she finally looked in Reece's direction. It set him off.

"You backstabbing BITCH!! I loved you!" Reece exploded, standing up. The restraints prevented him from moving.

"I loved you, too!" Destiny cried out, before she could control herself. Then she broke down in tears on the stand and grabbed her stomach. The bailiff immediately ran to her, gathered her up, and carried her into an anteroom. Judge Epps heatedly called for a recess.

When court resumed an hour later, Judge Epps was about to call a mistrial, but after much prodding from the prosecution and the defense, he decided to continue on.

Agent Hill was in no shape to testify, and Judge Epps refused to grant a continuance, so the government grudgingly rested its case. The defense began to present its case the following morning.

Malik Shabazz didn't have much evidence to refute the allegations wielded against his client, so he had to resort to character witnesses and entertainment.

He chartered a bus to Raleigh with all of the single welfare mothers Reece had helped on it. There were at least a hundred ready and willing to testify in his cause. Malik Shabazz had furnished them with modest business suits to look the part.

At ten a.m., Taquisha Pineta started what would turn out to be a long line of women, testifying roughly the same thing. "Reece was generous. He would never do those things." "All he ever did was help me." "Drugs? Heavens no!" "Uh-uh, wasn't him." "Why the white man always try to bring down good black men?"

After two days of the same thing, Judge Epps had decided he'd heard enough of the shenanigans, and ordered the defense to prepare for its closing. Reece never took the stand, so the government would close first, Shabazz last.

* * *

On the last day of trial, a full month and three days from its start, federal prosecutor Long stood before the jury in a steel-gray suit and delivered a powerful closing. He hit on all the points, especially Agent Darius's blatant execution. He even used the lack of witnesses willing to testify to his advantage. The witnesses were more scared of "street justice" than the judicial system. He even used Agent Hill's breakdown as proof of intimidation. Four hours after he began his closing, Prosecutor Long had all but put Reece in a box.

Judge Epps ordered a recess before the defense was to begin its closing. Reece's bail was revoked, so he sat in the courtroom alone waiting on his attorney to return.

Despite the crushing closing delivered by the government, Reece still felt optimistic. He hadn't heard any backlash about the juror's daughter being kidnapped thus far. Each day he had allowed the little girl's mother to speak with her so she'd know she was safe. As long as her father did as he was told, the little girl would be returned safely. Reece even set it up so the family would be compensated handsomely for the "inconvenience."

Only Reece and the bailiff were in the courtroom when Destiny appeared, accompanied by a bailiff. She hesitated a second when she saw Reece, but then began walking in his direction like she was on a mission.

Destiny sized Reece up as he sat in the chair shackled like some animal. She noticed he had put on a few pounds of muscle. He looked good. Destiny hated that it had come to this.

In the beginning, she had been genuinely impressed by him. In fact, the day they met in the restaurant parking lot, she doubled back to let him off the hook. She didn't feel she could adequately do her job, because she was immensely attracted to him. Yet he was so insistent on proving himself, she gave him the chance to do so. Hey, after all, she was a woman. Initially, she dismissed him as just a regular dope-boy, just like his profile suggested. Then, the more she got to know him, the more enraptured she became. His mind was potent. His drive determined. He walked with the surety so many black males lacked.

She was only supposed to be inside long enough to gather pertinent information to arrest him on. In the beginning, Reece was like a nutshell, hard to crack. After he began trusting her, she could easily extract information. She probably could've completed the investigation. Truth was, she enjoyed spending time with him. She enjoyed going first class everywhere. She enjoyed being treated like a queen. She enjoyed the respect granted when they were together. It was easy to be with Reece, because he wasn't ignorant like most big-time drug dealers. To her, he seemed more like a businessman, or a scholar with the vast knowledge he possessed.

Sleeping with him definitely complemented things. That was one thing she didn't do for the bureau. That was done for Katrina Destiny Hill. She wanted to feel Reece with every inch of her being. And he didn't disappoint. She wasn't a virgin by any standards, but the things Reece did to her would make a whore blush. Needless to say, she was hooked from the first time his penis entered her. Now, she was eight months pregnant with his baby.

She honestly didn't want to see him hurt, which was why she didn't continue with her testimony. She thought she would've been able to go through with it, but she wasn't so strong. She recognized the pain in his eyes. The discomfort in his posture. To the spectators, he may have seemed in control, but she knew better. She had crushed him more than any conviction could, and all she wanted to do was ease his pain. Even as she looked at him shackled to a chair, she wanted to stroke his locks and tell him everything was going to be okay. But she didn't, because that was one promise she couldn't make.

"Reece, may I have a word with you?" Destiny asked. The bailiff escorting her formed a wall between them. Reece sucked his teeth and turned his back to her.

Destiny understood what that meant. "Look, I just want you to know, I never wanted to hurt you." Reece said nothing. "I know you hear me, Reece. Please say something!"

Reece swiveled around in his chair, looked Destiny directly in the eye real cold like. "Girl or boy?"

"What?"

Reece pointed at her stomach and repeated the question.

"Boy," Destiny whispered.

Reece chuckled and leaned back in his chair with his hands steepled. "Don't worry about this here. I'll be home no sooner than this is over," he said. "Maybe I'll get at you in traffic. Heh, heh, heh."

Destiny started to respond, but the bailiff cut the conversation short when people started filing back into the room.

Malik Shabazz returned to the table and went over a few points for his closing. The jury filed into their box, and court was back in session.

Malik Shabazz coolly strutted to the center of the courtroom and shot the jury an infectious smile to begin his closing.

During the closing he focused on proof, or lack thereof. He called the government's escapades a witch hunt and referred to the numerous women who ventured two hours to Raleigh just to see that justice was done for a man who always helped them. His client was a "saint" and should be applauded instead of harassed with aspersions. Malik Shabazz's word play was so eloquent that even Destiny, who lingered in the back of the courtroom, was almost convinced.

Almost—she knew better, as did juror number six.

In the end it was a toss-up. The facts of the government, or the charisma of the defense.

After an hour of instructions from Judge Epps, the jury finally retired to the deliberation room.

Outside, single mothers picketed with signs reading "Free King Reece" in front of the courthouse.

None expected to receive a verdict within the day, so it was to the shock to everyone when after only an hour, the jury sent word that it was hopelessly hung. It seemed everyone thought Reece guilty of at least one count in the verdict, if not all. Everyone except juror number six, who wasn't convinced.

Judge Epps recalled the jury and issued an Allen charge, encouraging them to end their deliberation. Thirty minutes later, the jury returned the same note.

When Federal Prosecutor Long observed the cool look on Reece's face, his suspicions were confirmed. He dialed a number and waited. When his phone rang with confirmation, he requested to see the defendant alone in an anteroom. Reece agreed, but only if they removed the shackles.

Moments later, Reece was led into a room. Inside the room was a huge conference table, a microwave, coffeepot, and a television situated in the corner.

Prosecutor Long stood on the other side of the table with his right foot in a chair, elbow on his thigh. Reece pushed the door close and elected to stand beside it.

Long began talking with his hand by his mouth. "You know, I couldn't figure out why you were so confident during trial. I mean, I know you people have a lot of pride, but you were just too cool. So about midway through trial, I figured it out. You put the fix in. You spread some of your dirty money around. I knew you would do it, and you proved me correct, although I figured you would bribe the judge. That being so, I prepared a little contingency plan. You didn't know I was a Gulf War veteran, huh? Oh, yeah, I was. One thing we always emphasized was a contingency plan."

Long took his foot down off the chair and stood straight up.

"See, you're smart. I'll give you that, but you have a weakness. Every man has a weakness."

Reece sensed Long was stalling for some reason. When Long's cell phone rang, Reece found out why.

After Long put up his phone, he turned on the television. What showed on the screen made Reece gasp.

Long laughed at Reece. "Behold your weakness, you prick!"

On the screen, Qwess and Doe were being led out of their studio in handcuffs. Across the bottom of the screen the ticker read, *Street Rap CE. Arrested on Federal Racketeering Charges*. The word *LIVE* flashed, indicating things were happening in real time.

Long had made his point. "Here's what's going to happen," he said. "Somebody's going to jail for a long time. Either you or them. You decide." Long paused to let the words sink in. "Now Qwess, he could probably handle it. This isn't his first rodeo. I've been on his black ass for a while, but could never get him. Now thanks to you, I can! Ha!"

Long taunted Reece, trying to get him to break.

"Rolando? He'll crack, sure as shit. It's not in him. Inside the joint he'd definitely be someone's bitch. You know it as well as I do. After all, he is your cousin. Judging from the audio we collected from the wire Agent Hill provided you with, I could easily get both of 'em for accessory to murder, conspiracy, et cetera. And Qwess, I could probably do some backtracking and surely pin a murder on that sneaky bastard! Either way, their lives would be ruined. I can guaran-fuckin'-tee you that. Those pricks would never see another piece of ass, except a hairy one."

There it was. Long had played his final card.

"It's on you, King Reece. Some-fuckin'-body's going to jail! It's up to you who goes."

Reece stared at the television. Qwess and Doe were being put into the back of a tinted Suburban by FBI agents. A million thoughts crossed his mind.

"So, what's it going to be, King Reece? We haven't got all gotdamn day! Make your choice."

Epilogue

Nine months later

The annual hip-hop Source Awards were being held in Miami, Florida. The entire weekend was being made into an event culminating into the awards show itself. Everybody who was anybody was in town. Collins Avenue was littered with tricked-out Bentleys, Lambos, Ferraris, and Benzes. Hip-hop was in town. There were other awards shows, but the Source Awards were hip-hop's own baby. They catered specifically to the urban experience. Therefore, when you received a Source Award, it meant something. It wasn't a token award given out during an otherwise lily-white ceremony. A Source Award was an award for the people, by the people.

All weekend the buzz was about the best album nominees and best new artist nominees respectively. Everyone was anticipating the artist Maserati to do a repeat sweep again. The previous year he had taken home the honors for Best Album, Best New Artist, Best Video, Best Single, and Hip-Hop Quotable of the Year. This year he wasn't eligible for the Best New Artist, but he had formed a colossal group of rappers who were.

Their main competition was a solo artist who had taken the rap world by storm. At just twenty years old he had heads worldwide singing his new-age ode to area codes. Maserati's main competition was the young artist's label mate and CEO.

The night the award show took place, everyone crowded into Miami arena, which was transformed into an elegant ballroom. The show kicked off with an electric performance from R & B sensation Niya. She licked her lips and wiggled her hips, getting the crowd excited. Immediately after her, another rap nominee performed. The show was kicked off in style.

The master of ceremonies, a veteran comedian, took the stage to crack a few jokes on the audience, then got down to business.

"All right, y'all. We gon' get to the main awards right now, because from past experience, this show is liable to be interrupted at any time." The audience laughed as they remembered the show two years prior. "Y'all know what I'm talking 'bout. Niggas—oops, I ain't supposed to say that, but I did. Ha ha! Niggas be mad 'cause they ain't win. Stop saying your man rhymes, and you might win somethin."

The crowd barely giggled.

"All right, all right. I know y'all saying, 'get on with it.' So here goes." He whipped out the envelope. "The nominees for Best New Artist are: The Gangstas for "I be killing ish"; Flame for "Worldwide Ladies"; Lady Treacherous for "My p is the bomb"; and Saigon for "Queen Spittah." Damn, the ladies representin'! Fellas you better step your game up. And the winner is . . ."

He opened the envelope up, then screamed, "My man, FLAME, repping that A.B.P.!"

Applause!

Flame sauntered on the stage solo in a white linen suit with the heavy A.B.P. pendant swinging from his neck. He accepted the award and gave a brief speech.

"I'd just like to thank God, my hood family. Fayette-nam, stand up!! My managers. And a special shout out to my mans an' 'em J.D., Fat Black, and Lil J in the bing. Hold ya head high. Tough times don't last, tough people do. Thank you."

More applause.

The MC introduced a hot new actress to present the next award. She slinked onstage in a see-through top that showed her red nipples clear as day.

"Um, I'm here to present the next award, which is Album of the Year. So, without further ado, here are the nominees: Maserati for "Pearl Tongue"; Qwess for "Long Live a King"; and J Rize for "New Jeru Souljah.""

The actress opened the envelope.

"Ooh. I just found out that the winner for Album of the Year is also the winner for Best Video, Best Single, and Hip-hop Quotable of the Year. Ooh, a clean sweep! Well, y'all, that person is . . . Qwess!!"

Thunderous applause! Standing ovation.

Qwess slowly walked to the stage with Doe, Flame, and Hulk in tow. When he stepped to the podium, the actress hugged him, whispering in his ear, "Call me." Then she commandeered the microphone, shocking everyone.

"Um, I'd just like to congratulate Qwess for keeping it real and stepping out to say what needs to be said. In such a fake world, it's refreshing to find a genuine person. Congratulations, handsome."

Qwess thanked her and spoke into the mic.

"First off, *Alhamdulillah*! Without him, nothing's possible. Thanks to the fans for feeling my pain. Doing this album was really cathartic for me. There was a lot going on in my life, and without music, I couldn't cope. So, thanks for sharing my pain. To my fiancée, thanks for hanging in there. And most importantly, to my man King Reece, who this album is titled after and dedicated to . . ."

Qwess held up the platinum- and diamond-encrusted crown around his neck.

"You showed the brothers what true sacrifice is all about! May they learn from your shining example. Hold ya head up. I got you, my nigga. I got you!"

Hundreds of miles away in a federal penitentiary in Lewisburg, Virginia, Reece watched the awards in the dayroom. When Qwess called his name, the other inmates dapped him up heavily. Outside the dayroom, on the tier, brothers started chanting: "King Reece."

Reece was oblivious to it. He eagerly awaited Qwess's performance. He was performing his single, "Ode to the King." Reece was excited for Qwess. Seeing him get an award was like seeing himself get one. After all, he made the sacrifice for Qwess and Doe to stay free. A sacrifice he would make again without a moment's hesitation.

In the end, Reece ended up pleading to conspiracy and getting five years. The federal prosecutor wasn't happy about it, but it was either that or let him go free altogether. So he went along with it. Reece could appeal at any time. All he had to do was reveal he had bribed a juror. Of course, everyone would believe him because only one juror moved out of state, purchased a new house and car, and was never heard from again . . . although Reece knew where to find him. However, five years was nothing for a multimillionaire to do, so he rode with it.

Qwess was finally performing his single when the CO tapped Reece on the shoulder.

"What?!" Reece barked, irritated with the audacity of interrupting him.

"Here's your mail." The CO passed him an envelope. Reece didn't even look at it until the performance was done. When he did, he smiled.

He knew it would only be a matter of time.

The envelope's sender read: Katrina D. Hill.

Prologue

April 9, 2009

The man's naked, chiseled torso dripped with sweat as he pounded out a set of pushups. Headphones covered his ears, blasting raunchy rap music at ignorant levels. The song hadn't been released yet, but the man had an exclusive copy. He jammed the song so much that he knew the lyrics by heart.

He rapped, "When it come to my bars, niggas fear 'em like prison, they start squealing like pigeons, praying to God that I miss 'em! Ooooh!!!"

The last line hyped him up so much he hopped from the floor and threw a few imaginary punches at the air. He was in his zone now, doing his normal routine to break the monotony of his predicament. He lived vicariously through the music. When he bumped his tunes, he drowned out the sounds of prison. With the right song playing, he wasn't confined to a USP; he was a teenager again, roaming the halls of 71st Senior High looking for a classmate to battle. Or he was in the trenches again, putting in the work that would make him a legend in the streets. The right song dictated his mood. With the now-popular trap rap booming in his ears, he reveled in his status as a Trap Lord, and for a brief moment, he wondered what would have become of his life if he had decided to pursue a music career on his terms.

However, when the music stopped, he was forced to deal with the reality of who he was.

King Reece pushed the headphones from his head and allowed them to rest on his neck. He inhaled the stale air inside his cell and focused his attention on the wall in front of him. Taped to his wall were newspaper clippings and photos of the last four years of his life. It was his shrine of sorts, the thing that kept him going. Each portion of the collage served a purpose for him.

On the top left of the wall was the article that started it all. The headline read, "Heavy Is the Head That Wears the Crown." The article spoke of his trial and the mysterious five-year plea agreement. The article made him seem larger than life, mythic even. It detailed some uncorroborated stories of his drug empire—tales of kidnappings, murders, and lynchings. They estimated he and his gang, the Crescent Crew, had amassed more than $50 million in just two short years, and that his personal wealth was somewhere around $30 million. In the article, the writer stressed that the Crescent Crew lived their ethos—Death Before Dishonor—to the letter, in that no one from his organization turned rat in his absence. They were rumored to still be operating in his absence and stronger than ever.

King Reece had placed this article strategically first in his collage. He read the article daily to remind himself who he was and of his purpose. Being in prison was a constant battle of the mind, and even the strongest man felt weak at times. This article reminded King Reece of his stature, of his family who believed in him. This article reminded King Reece of the empire he had built from the ground up and why he couldn't fall victim to the instability of his incarcerated thoughts.

Beside the first article was another clipping. The headline read, "Music Mogul Dodges Prison." This article spoke of Qwess, King Reece's right-hand man, brother, and co-founder of the Crescent Crew. King Reece had taken his plea agreement to save Qwess from any further investigation by the feds. Qwess was on the cusp of superstardom as a rapper, producer, and label head when King Reece was apprehended and set to stand trial. Before his trial began, Reece had one of the Crew abduct one of the juror's children in exchange for a not-guilty verdict. He acted ultra-cocky at trial, and the federal prosecutor knew the fix was in. To insure a conviction, the government arrested Qwess and threatened to pin a charge on him unless Reece took a plea agreement. In the end, Reece sacrificed his life for that of his comrade.

Beside this article were numerous photos of Qwess attending industry events, photos of him on *60 Minutes*, *Forbes* listing photos, and other media clippings.

This section was important to Reece because it bore witness to the strength of their brotherhood and the results of his sacrifice. King Reece would travel out of the galaxy and fight the sun for his brother Qwess to live in peace, and he knew Qwess felt the same way. They lived, breathed, and were willing to die for each other. This was Crew Business.

A Young Jeezy song screamed from the speakers around King Reece's neck, a song about how amazing he was. Reece could relate, so he threw the headphones on, hit the floor, and got some money. After he completed his set of fifty pushups, he stood and studied his mural again.

The next section of his mural was a testament to false love, his only mistake and Achilles heel in an otherwise beautiful tapestry of the right decisions in life. The headlines read, "Disgraced FBI Agent Resigns Amidst Conspiracy Suspicions," "FBI Agent Has Lovechild from Imprisoned Kingpin." There were no fewer than ten articles surrounding a picture of the woman they spoke about: Katrina Destiny Hill.

This section of King Reece's mural was the most important for him. Although it ripped his heart like old stitches every time he looked at his wall, he forced himself to endure the pain just to remind himself to never make that mistake again. She had caught him slipping, warmed up to him, then served him on a cold platter to the federal government. King Reece—the Five Percent God-Body—adjusted his mantra to that of the Jews: never again.

The orthodox Muslims turned toward Mecca and offered their prayers every morning, the Buddhists meditated. For King Reece, this wall was his shrine, the place where he cleansed and replenished his soul every morning. His time inside was nearing its end. He had to prepare himself to reclaim his place in society and right all the wrongs inflicted upon him, beginning with Destiny.

The country had just elected a black man to the Oval Office. Surely, the world was ready for the return of King Reece.

Chapter 1

April 19, 2009

The tinted-out Suburban skated down the gritty North Carolina street en route to its destination. In back, a man clad in all black checked the rounds in a magazine then slammed it in the butt of his AR-15 assault rifle. Next, he readjusted the infrared beam mounted on the weapon's barrel and clicked it to make sure it was working. Satisfied that his weapon was ready, he radioed the two Suburbans trailing him. They reported that they were loaded and ready to go as well.

"We ready," the man said to his driver. The driver gunned the engine, and the heavy SUV rocketed forward.

Moments later, all hell broke loose as three trucks skidded to a halt in front of a duplex. Children across the street watched with mouths agape as man after man exited the trucks in all black carrying big guns. The first two men carried a battering ram, which they slammed into the front door of the duplex without warning, exploding the heavy door off its hinges. As the door crashed into the wall, the men swarmed inside like killer bees with their assault

rifles leading the way. They were met with immediate resistance as the first two men to rush through the door
were tagged in the chest by heavy gunfire. Their bullet-
proof vests prevented death, but the impact blew them
back through the door for a reluctant retreat.

The army of men behind them regrouped and charged
again. This time they were more careful. They rushed
through the door and quickly dispatched the resisters with
two shots to the chest. Then they cleared the rest of the
house in under a minute, pouring into room after room
until they were sure the only people inside were their victims lying on the floor gasping for breath.

The leader of the federal assault team stood over one
of the men and aimed the barrel of the rifle at his melon.
"Just tell us where he's at, and you can go," he said
calmly. Meanwhile, the other men posted up at the windows of the home with their weapons ready.

"You wasting time, man. You gonna bleed out. Come
on, what's it gonna be?" he prodded. "You gonna tell us
or what? We know he was here earlier. Right here in this
very damn house! Now you tell us, or we gonna toss this
muthafuckin' house up while you bleed to death."

The federal agents had invaded this town on a tip.
They had good reason to believe that the number one man
on their Most Wanted list had just been in this very house
moments ago. They had been pursuing him for nearly
half a decade, and they were finally closing in on him.
They refused to let him escape this time.

"What's it gonna be?" the agent asked one last time.

For a response, the man simply held out his left hand.
"Listen good, because these will be the last words you
hear," the man named Muhammad began. "There is nothing you can do to me that would make me feel worse than
betraying *my* leader." He opened his hand to reveal a grenade.

The masked man's eyes fell on the grenade. "Whoa . . . wait a minute. Calm down," he pleaded after seeing the explosive. "Put that thing away now. Close your hand back over it real slow," he instructed, backing away. He removed his mask to reveal a pale face and striking blond hair. "We can work this out, Muhammad. Nobody has to die. All we want is your leader."

Muhammad chuckled and completely opened his left hand, revealing a full view of the grenade. Both safeties were already removed, and when he opened his hand, the spoon popped off. He looked the blond-haired leader of the assault team in his eyes and barked, "Death before dishonor! Crescent Crew to the death!" Then he tossed the grenade into the air.

The men tried to escape, but it was too late. In three seconds flat, the house exploded, taking everyone, including Muhammad, with it.

Down the street, in the woods, a lone man observed the explosion with a demented smile.

DON'T MISS

Blood Ties

by Shaun Sinclair

Trained to be a Special Forces killer, Leader came back from his tours of duty broke—and near broken. So when the streets came calling, he rose from ruthless hood enforcer to a powerful international cartel's most feared "cleaner." And when tragedy hit home, his sensitive son, Justus, turned out to be a natural assassin—and unshakably loyal to his father.

Together they are an unstoppable team who leave no trace behind. . . . until a mysterious woman from nowhere begins working Leader's deep-hidden weaknesses. Slowly, she's exploding all his secrets—and turning Justus's devotion into a weapon. Now with father and son gunning for each other, survival is down to sheer killer instinct, nothing left to lose—and shattering betrayal only family can deliver . . .

Available wherever books are sold.